"Can I be of assistance?"

Antoinette found herself gazing into the concerned gray eyes of a ruggedly handsome man in his early thirties. He went on, "As we crested the hill my driver thought he saw you being set upon by two young rogues."

"They were trying to steal my locket," explained Antoinette, unable to explain to herself why the very sight of this dark gentleman should have started her heart beating so wildly.

"It is dashed unfortunate that we didn't reach you in time!" he declared. "I hope you are not too distressed by the incident?"

"Thank you, no. I am fully recovered," murmured Antoinette.

"Well, since I failed so abysmally to see those blackguards off, the least I can do is offer you the convenience of my carriage," said the stranger. "I assume you are on your way to Harrogate?"

"Indeed, yes," replied Antoinette slowly, "but I feel it would be best if I did not accept your kind offer. You see, you are the third person today to offer me a lift. The first will most likely lose his job because of it, the second robbed me of everything but my locket—which is my most treasured possession. So you see, if I ride with you, I dread to think what will befall me!"

Novels By Caroline Courtney

Duchess in Disguise
A Wager For Love
Love Unmasked
Guardian of the Heart
Dangerous Engagement
Love's Masquerade
Love Triumphant
Heart of Honor
Libertine in Love
The Romantic Rivals
Forbidden Love
Abandoned For Love

Published By
WARNER BOOKS

CAROLINE COURTNEY

Abandoned For Love

WARNER BOOKS

A Warner Communications Company

Abandoned For Love

One

"What a tragedy!"

"Aye, it's real hard on poor Miss Aston. To lose her only two close relatives, one after the other in the space of six months. Such a shame!"

The women at the church gate of St. Michael's stood respectfully aside as the slender girl in the black veil moved toward them. They watched, surprised, as she shook her head at the carriage driver, and murmured, "Thank you, but I think I would prefer to walk home, Hutton."

Perplexed, the driver shook his head. "But 'twill be dark within the hour, Miss Aston. And the frost hasn't melted all day. You'll catch your death if you stay out in this weather!"

Mrs. Burnsall, the baker's wife, abandoned her position by the church gate, and rounded briskly on the protesting Hutton. "Less of your huffing and puffing, man! Have you no sensitivity? Can't you see the poor lass just needs to be on her own for a while, to recover from the ordeal of the funeral?"

The driver stamped his feet and blew on his frozen hands. "I was merely pointing out to the young lady, Mrs. Burnsall, that the weather is inclement—even for February. I'd remind you that my wife is housekeeper to the Aston household, and if Miss Aston catches a chill because I didn't take her straight home in the carriage, then Mrs. Hutton will be severely displeased!"

The women at the church gate glanced at one another with dancing eyes. Poor old Hutton! Was it not common gossip that he was the most henpecked husband in the entire village of Linton-on-Craven?

Mrs. Burnsall stood hands on hips, glaring at the luckless Hutton. "Miss Aston has eyes in her head, man! She can see for herself what the weather is like. You'd do well to mind that she's not one of your nesh society ladies. Miss Aston is a true Yorkshire lass. She'll not fade away with fright at a few degrees of frost, will you Miss Aston—"

But the lady in question had already gone. The group near the church watched her disappear through the trees, taking the path that led by the icy waters of the River Wharfe.

The village women exchanged sympathetic glances. "Best to let her be for a while," they murmured. "She was devoted to her poor aunt and uncle, you know. Devoted . . ."

On the river path, Antoinette Aston glanced quickly around to ensure that she was out of sight of the watching women. Then she tore off her black, veiled bonnet and flung it with all the might of her nineteen years into the gushing waters of the River Wharfe.

"Free!" she exulted, shaking loose her golden hair into a mass of curls that tumbled on to the shoulders of her black pelisse. "Mercy be, I'm free at last!"

Resolutely, she turned away from the river, and set off to walk the mile back to the pretty village of Linton. As she did so, she was struck by a pang of guilt over her impetuous action in throwing her mourning bonnet into the river.

Oh dear, she thought, *whatever would the good hearted village women think of me had they witnessed such a shocking sight! How heartless of the girl, they would cry, wide-eyed with horror. Why, the good Doctor Aston and his wife gave her a comfortable home and everything she could want. And now they are both in their graves, their niece will inherit Beck Lodge and no doubt a tidy sum of money besides. Why then, should Antoinette Aston be in such unseemly haste to discard her mourning clothes?*

Antoinette sighed as she made her way through the stark bare trees. Yes, it is true. My Aunt Edith and Uncle George did their duty by me. After my poor parents were drowned at sea when I was a mere babe, my aunt and uncle took me in, clothed and fed me, and provided a much needed roof over my head.

But what they never gave me was affection. Even as a child, if I fell down and bruised my knee, my Aunt Edith would tell me briskly to get up immediately and not be a cry-baby. Not once, in all our years together, do I recall her putting a tender arm around my shoulders and comforting me. It was not that Aunt Edith was unkind. She, was simply unfeeling.

And Uncle George was always so strict. Why, mused Antoinette, most of my contemporaries are married now, some with children of their own; Mary Burnsall, the baker's daughter, Violet Hebdon, the Rector's daughter . . . Ellen Tate, the milliner . . . Antoinette had stood in the lovely church of St. Michael's and watched them all whisper their marriage vows.

But Uncle George would never allow me to walk out with a young man. If any of the village lads so much as smiled at me, Uncle George would glower at them, march me home and send me to bed without any supper.

But then, acknowledged Antoinette, in the past few years there has been scant opportunity for me to encourage a beau. When I was seventeen, Aunt Edith's health began to fail, and nursing her took up all my time. And after she died, Uncle George displayed little will to live and took at once to his bed. They say that doctors invariably make the worst patients. How true that was of Uncle George! Every day I read to him, helped Mrs. Hutton prepare his food, and in the last dark days I sat with him day and night, doing everything in my power to comfort him.

But in his view, nothing I did was right. My voice was too loud, then too soft. His food was too hot, then too cold. He wished I would not hover over him so . . . yet when I left the house for a breath of fresh air, he immediately summoned me back again, accusing me of callously deserting a dying old man.

Antoinette bit her lip. No, it is wrong, she berated herself, to think ill of the dead in such a manner. Where is your sense of Christian charity, Antoinette? You must remember the good about your uncle. He was after all, an excellent

9

doctor, tireless in his care of the sick of the community, whether they be rich or poor.

And yet, the cold voice of truth persisted, he offered you no soothing ointment for your bruises the day he beat you black and blue when he found you turning the pages of the Aston family Bible.

"But uncle," the young Antoinette had protested tearfully, "I was merely curious to examine the Aston family tree in the front of the Bible. I wanted to look at the names of my dear Mama and Papa . . ."

But the Bible had been wrenched from her grasp and placed under lock and key. Antoinette had been severely punished, forced to promise that she would never touch the Bible again.

"That Bible is extremely valuable," Aunt Edith snapped at the weeping girl. "It has been in the Aston family for generations. No doubt your uncle was worried that in your eagerness, you would tear the pages and spoil them forever."

Antoinette's lustrous blue eyes misted at the memory. How she wished she could remember her parents! But she had in her possession not so much as a single portrait of the tragic couple who had drowned that stormy night somewhere off the French coast.

But I must not be downhearted, Antoinette reminded herself. After all, I have been blessed with a respectable (if joyless) upbringing. And although my aunt and uncle never professed to love me, they will have left me Beck Lodge to live in for the rest of my life. At least I shall not be homeless —or penniless. For although my uncle was by no means a rich man, he was comfortably off. As his nearest surviving relative, I can be sure of inheriting a modest fortune. Providing I continue to live simply, I shall have sufficient income for my needs. And who knows, in time, perhaps I shall marry. Now that my uncle is no longer here to scare away the local beaux, why, anything is possible!

As she approached the village of Linton, Antoinette quickened her steps against the biting wind sweeping down from the Dales. It was growing dark, and already the lamps were being lit in the gray stone cottages bordering the village green. At the far end of the green, Antoinette observed a young maid drawing the curtains in the Fontaine almshouses.

The sight caused the golden-haired girl to count her blessings once more. The almshouses had been founded for the benefit of the poor women of the community.

How lucky I am, thought Antoinette fervently, to be a woman of independent means. How dreadful to be obliged to live in one of the almshouses, supported by charity for the rest of my life!

Antoinette hurried across the clapper bridge which spanned Linton Beck, and there to the right of the stream lay Beck Lodge, Antoinette's home. The front door of the squat, gray stone house was opened by Mrs. Hutton, the house-keeper.

"I was wondering where you'd got to, Miss Aston," declared the iron-haired woman anxiously. "There's a gentle-man here been waiting on you for the past half hour. He's a Mr. Tomkins, and he's come all the way from London!"

Antoinette smiled. "Oh yes. That will be my uncle's lawyer, come to advise me of details of the Will. Would you show him straight into the drawing room, Mrs. Hutton. I'll see him immediately."

Antoinette handed the footman her pelisse and gloves, and was about to enter the drawing room when Mrs. Hutton exclaimed, "Miss Aston! If I may make so bold . . . your hair! Your dress!"

Hastily, Antoinette glanced at her reflection in the hall glass. The walk back from the church had tousled her curls, and lent a sparkle to her eye, a glow to her cheeks.

Oh dear, thought Antoinette, aware of Mrs. Hutton's disapproving face. Indeed, my healthy demeanor is hardly suitable for one returning from a funeral! And I fear the hem of my dress is splashed with mud from my riverside stroll. Yes, I had best run upstairs and change before I meet the lawyer from London.

Antoinette's bed chamber was situated on the west side of the house, overlooking the garden. As she changed into a fresh mourning dress, Antoinette resolved that once she was legally mistress of the house, one of the first things she would do would be to change the decor of her room.

How I loathe these dull browns and sombre dark greens, she thought. In the Spring, I shall have the room painted in pale primrose, with new, gold-colored bedhangings and curtains. Then every day, whatever the weather I shall wake up to sunshine! And after that, I shall turn my attention to the dining room. I have never yet eaten a meal in there without suffering a stiff neck from the draughts. No doubt my aunt and uncle would disapprove, but they always seemed impervious to the cold. Even in the depths of winter they would never allow the fire to be lit in the dining room, for Uncle George maintained that coal smoke destroyed one's digestive juices.

Remembering that her uncle's lawyer awaited her, Antoinette swept up her hair into a severe knot and smoothed a little white powder across her cheeks to effect a suitably wan appearance. But even this harsh treatment could not disguise her breathtaking good looks. The simple black dress set off to perfection her slender figure, long neck and flawless complexion.

Even Mr. Tomkins, accustomed to the sight of London's renowned beauties, found himself suppressing a gasp of admiration as Antoinette entered the drawing room of Beck Lodge. As her cornflower-blue eyes met his, he could not resist the thought that if only he were twenty years younger . . .

But Mr. Tomkins was a lawyer, and legal men are trained to concern themselves with facts, not flights of fancy. Sternly, he pulled himself together, adjusted his spectacles and invited Miss Aston to sit down.

Antoinette demurely subsided onto the sofa, politely refraining from pointing out to the hawk-nosed lawyer that as she was now the mistress of Beck Lodge, it was in fact *her* prerogative to invite *him* to be seated! As he took up a stance by the mantel, Antoinette murmured, "It is indeed most kind of you to travel all this way to read me my uncle's Will, Mr. Tomkins. Before we attend to the business in hand, may I offer you some refreshment?"

Mr. Tomkins nodded. "Ah yes, I do believe that would

be in order, Miss Aston. Some brandy, I think, would be the most beneficial beverage under the circumstances."

Concealing her surprise, Antoinette rang the bell. She had expected Mr. Tomkins to accept, perhaps, a small glass of wine. But that he should boldly request strong spirits! However, reasoned Antoinette, Mr. Tomkins is a London lawyer, after all. Perhaps it is the thing for lawyers in the capital to quaff brandy at four in the afternoon. And the weather is so inclement. No doubt he is feeling the cold.

When the brandy was brought in, Antoinette poured him a generous measure, which he placed untouched on the table near the sofa. Then Mr. Tomkins opened his small leather case, and drew out a sheaf of papers, which Antoinette took to be her uncle's Will.

Abruptly, he began to read:

"*I, George Frederick Aston, being of sound mind, hereby declare this to be my last Will and Testament . . .*"

"Mr. Tomkins," interrupted Antoinette, "pray forgive me. But since this reading of the Will is only really a mere formality, would it not be simpler for you just to outline to me the conditions and bequests?"

As Mr. Tomkins stared at her, Antoinette continued with a smile, "I assume that I am the main beneficiary of the Will, and that there are small bequests to the servants, and the Church of course."

To Antoinette's surprise, the lawyer seemed suddenly reluctant to meet her eyes. He fussed with his papers, adjusted his spectacles, and ran his finger several times around the collar of his shirt.

When at last he spoke, his voice was dry, and grave. "Oh dear. I can see there is no easy way of breaking this to you. I was hoping just to read you the Will and let you hear the truth that way. But I realize now that I should have prepared you . . . damn it, Miss Aston, your uncle should have told you the facts himself!"

Amazed at this outburst, Antoinette sat perfectly still. "What are you trying to tell me, Mr. Tomkins? What facts should my uncle have revealed to me?"

The lawyer took a deep breath. "I am afraid you must

prepare yourself for a shock. You see, the truth is that Dr. and Mrs. Aston were not your aunt and uncle at all. In fact, as far as it is known, you are not related to them in any way whatsoever!"

As Antoinette's lovely face drained of color, the lawyer quickly pressed the glass of brandy into her hand. "Please, drink this, it will do you good."

Obediently, Antoinette sipped the fiery liquid and whispered, "But if I am not the Astons' niece, then . . . then who am I? They told me my parents drowned in a ship wreck . . ."

Mr. Tomkins shook his head. "I am afraid the identity and whereabouts of your parents remains a mystery, Miss Aston. All that is known for sure, is that you were abandoned as a baby, and left on the doorstep here at Beck Lodge, along with a note which read: *Please take care of baby Antoinette.* Out of the kindness of his heart, Dr. Aston took you in, and brought you up as his own niece."

"No!" Antoinette's blue eyes blazed. "Forgive me, Mr. Tomkins, but that does not ring true. My uncle was a conscientious doctor, but he and my aunt had little of the milk of human kindness in their veins. Why should he take me into his household, and claim me as his kin? Why did he not pack me off straight to the local almshouses?"

Mr. Tomkins flushed, and cleared his throat several times. "Ah. Here I regret to say the matter becomes a little . . . delicate. Please believe me, Miss Aston, when I tell you that there are some matters into which it is not wise to probe too deeply. Things which are best left buried by the merciful mists of time, if you understand me."

"I fear I do not comprehend you at all, Mr. Tomkins," replied Antoinette coldly. "Since it is my identity, my future which is at stake here, I should be glad if you would tell me the true facts, however painful they may be."

The lawyer raised his eyes to heaven, and muttered, "Very well. It transpires that twenty years ago Dr. Aston was foolish enough to, er . . . become enamored of one of his patients, a Miss Eleanor LeStrange. The relationship was terminated after a quarrel between the two and Miss Le-

Strange left the neighborhood. But then a year later, you arrived on the Beck Lodge doorstep."

A glimmer of amusement gleamed in Antoinette's blue eyes. "And Dr. Aston believed me to be the fruit of his relationship with Miss LeStrange?" That would explain, she realized, why "Aunt Edith" was always so brusque toward me."

"Yes, Dr. Aston did fear that to be the case," Mr Tomkins went on. "Naturally, he was terrified of a scandal. It was his wife who finally solved their dilemma by suggesting that they should pass you off, as it were, as their niece. It was only when you were fully grown, that Dr. Aston happened upon Miss LeStrange in Harrogate where she was now residing. From their conversation, it transpired that Miss LeStrange had never borne any children to any man. But by that time of course, it was impossible for the Astons to turn around and declare that you were not their niece after all."

Dazed, Antoinette sank back against the sofa cushions. "But Mr. Tomkins," she whispered, "is nothing known at all about my parents? Is there no clue as to who I really am?"

The lawyer said apologetically, "I regret not, Miss Aston. Apart from the note, all that was found with you in the basket on the doorstep was this—"

He drew out of his leather case a round, blue velvet box, and handed it to Antoinette. With trembling fingers, she prised open the velvet lid.

A gasp escaped her lips as she gazed on the exquisite gold locket lying in the box.

"Oh, this is so beautiful!" she breathed, holding the locket by the gold chain and examining it under the lamplight. "Just look at the fine workmanship in the deckled edge of the rim. And see, there is the letter N engraved on the back. That must mean something, surely. Perhaps there is a further clue inside."

"A portrait, perhaps?" suggested Mr. Tomkins.

"Or even a lock of hair," murmured Antoinette, holding her breath as she snapped open the locket.

It was empty.

"Oh!" Antoinette felt numb with disappointment. Wistfully, she turned the locket over in her hands. "Do you imagine this locket could have belonged to my mother, Mr. Tomkins? Is it possible that her name began with an N . . . Naomi, perhaps, or Nicolette?"

Mr. Tomkins spread his hands in a gesture of bewilderment. "I am a lawyer, Miss Aston. I deal in facts, not imaginings. But I should think, yes, it is highly likely that the locket was the property of your mother."

Impulsively, Antoinette slipped the locket around her neck, and fastened the clasp. "I shall never take it off," she declared fervently, "until I have discovered the true identity of my parents!" Then a frown creased her delicate brow. "One thing puzzles me, Mr. Tomkins. How could Dr. Aston have imagined that Miss LeStrange was my mother, when the locket is engraved with an N?"

"Firstly, remember that Dr. Aston had no proof that the locket was your mother's property," replied the lawyer. "She could have inherited it, or even stolen it. Secondly, Miss LeStrange's christian name is Eleanor, but I am given to understand that all her, er . . . acquaintances refer to her as Nell."

"Of course," smiled Antoinette. "How clever of you to deduce that, Mr. Tomkins. My, what a stew poor Dr. Aston must have been in, obliged to explain to his wife that his daughter had just turned up in a basket on the doorstep! Imagine the domestic disharmony he must have endured with Aunt Edith after that! And then, all those years later, to discover it was all for naught, for I was not his kin after all! However, perhaps that blow was not really so bad, for by then I do believe he had truly come to regard me as his niece, and heiress to his house and small fortune."

Mr. Tomkins took out his handkerchief and mopped his brow. Antoinette regarded him with surprise. Despite the fire crackling in the grate, to her mind the drawing room was still uncommonly chill.

"Is something wrong, Mr. Tomkins?" Antoinette inquired solicitously. "You seem somewhat discomposed."

The lawyer turned to face her. "Miss Aston, I fear the mystery of your parentage is not the only shock you will have to bear this afternoon. It is also my unpleasant duty to inform

16

you that you are not, in fact, the principle beneficiary in Dr. Aston's Will."

Stunned, Antoinette sat straight-backed, staring at the lawyer. "You mean . . . I do not inherit the house?"

"I am afraid not," said Mr. Tomkins apologetically. "Nor are there any financial bequests to you."

Antoinette's eyes widened in horror as she grasped the full implication of the lawyer's words. She whispered, "Are you telling me that I am to be left homeless and penniless?"

"Oh dear," murmured the lawyer, "this is all most distressing. *Most* distressing indeed."

"It is Aunt Edith's doing," said Antoinette flatly. "Naturally, she always resented me. Without doubt it was she who persuaded Dr. Aston to cut me from his Will."

"No, no," protested Mr. Tomkins, "things are not as black as all that! You are indeed mentioned in the Will. It clearly states that you are to receive all Mrs. Aston's jewellery."

Antoinette laughed hollowly. "*All* her jewellery? Mr. Tomkins, that amounts to a very small diamond brooch, and a string of second quality pearls. Mrs. Aston was not the sort of woman to be bothered with what she termed, 'fancy clothes and gaudy baubles.' "

"I see," murmured the lawyer, gathering together his papers and shutting them in his case. "So the sale of the jewellery would hardly be likely to keep you in any kind of luxury for the rest of your life. Dear me. It appears, Miss Aston, as if the only course open to you is to throw yourself on the mercy of Dr. Aston's Cousin Cedric."

Antoinette's eyebrows rose. "Cousin Cedric? Who may he be, Mr. Tomkins?"

"He is the person who has inherited Beck Lodge," replied the lawyer. "It is my information that as his present residence in Sheffield is too small for his growing family, he intends moving into Beck Lodge without delay."

Antoinette was beginning to feel as if she had been plunged into a never-ending nightmare. How ironical to think that only a hour ago she had been congratulating herself on being a woman of independent means!

Mr. Tomkins was preparing to take his leave. "I am so very sorry, Miss Aston, to bring you such unpleasant tidings," he said wretchedly.

"It must have been most distressing for you, Mr. Tomkins, to be required to deliver such painful intelligence," said Antoinette, rising to her feet. "I am deeply obliged to you for travelling all this way, in order to break the news to me personally. I shall long remember your kindness and understanding in this very difficult situation."

The lawyer gazed at her with undisguised admiration. That such a lovely young girl should see her world crumble before her, and still retain the style and dignity to accord him the courtesy of such a graceful speech!

He bowed. "Be assured, Miss Aston, that if there is anything I can do to alleviate your circumstances . . . here is my card with the address of my chambers in London. Do feel free to call on me at any time if I can be of any assistance."

Antoinette summoned a smile. "You are most kind."

She rang the bell, and Mr. Tomkins departed in haste to catch the night mail coach back to London. It would be a long time, he knew, before he forgot the golden-haired girl whose future now looked so unbearably bleak.

As the front door closed behind Mr. Tomkins, Antoinette emerged from the drawing room to find Mrs. Hutton standing in the hall, staring at her curiously. Antoinette repressed a wry smile. Naturally, the housekeeper had been listening at the drawing room door. Who could blame her? Of course she was impatient to know what was to become of the Aston household now the doctor and his wife had passed on.

Antoinette had no doubt that within hours, the drawing rooms, kitchens and taverns of Linton village would be buzzing with the intelligence that Miss Antoinette Aston had been disinherited. That a new master was shortly expected at Beck Lodge.

Well, thought Antoinette with a lift of her head, I'll be dashed if I am going to give Mrs. Hutton (and therefore the entire village) the satisfaction of knowing how distressed I feel. Oh, to be sure, I feel like crumpling to the floor and crying till my heart breaks. But I am resolved that no one shall see me weep; no one shall witness my agony of despair.

Accordingly, she turned to Mrs. Hutton and said lightly, "Mr. Tomkins has advised me, Mrs. Hutton, that a Mr. Cedric Aston is the new owner of Beck Lodge. I understand that he is the late doctor's cousin. I imagine that he will be arriving within the next few days to view his property, so perhaps you would be so kind as to prepare the East Wing for his comfort and convenience."

"Yes, Miss Aston. I'll see to that directly," said the housekeeper. She hesitated by the stairs. "Er . . . may I ask if anything further is known about Mr. Cedric Aston . . . with regard to his future intentions, like?"

"I regret I have no further information about the gentleman," replied Antoinette with an equanimity she did not feel. "All I know for sure is that he is married, with a family, and is anxious to take up residence as soon as possible." She smiled at Mrs. Hutton, and declared with admirable conviction, "It will be pleasant, will it not, to hear the sound of childrens' laughter ringing around Beck Lodge?"

And turning away from the astounded housekeeper, Antoinette swept upstairs and locked herself in her bed chamber. Not surprisingly, it was many hours before sleep claimed Antoinette that night.

When she awoke, the sun was streaming into her bed chamber. The frosts had melted, giving way to a day of almost spring-like warmth and brightness. But to Antoinette, it was as if an impenetrable black cloud had descended on Beck Lodge.

Gripped by despair and panic, Antoinette gazed from her window at the sunlit lawns of Beck Lodge. "Gone, all gone," she whispered. "I had imagined that all this—the house, the gardens—would be mine. That although I was now alone in the world, I should at least have the comfort of some material security. But to find that I am now an intruder in the house I call home—oh, that is hard indeed!"

Whereas the night before, Antoinette had lain in bed and given way to wracking sobs over her plight; now, in the harsh light of day, she forced herself resolutely to face facts.

I have no home and no income to call my own, she told

herself. And, heaven help me, I have no name, either! Aston is the name of the man I believed to be my uncle. It does not rightfully belong to me.

She moved to her bedside table, and picked up the gleaming gold locket. For a long time she gazed on the engraved N, willing it to speak to her, to reveal the truth about her parentage.

"Who are you, mysterious, tantalizing N?" she whispered. "And who was my father?"

Fastening the locket around her throat, Antoinette knew she would never rest until she had found her true identity. How terrible life must have been for poor N, she mused. What dreadful events had led this young mother to abandon her precious child on a doctor's doorstep? And what had become of N thereafter? Where was the father! Did he know, or care, that he had sired a baby girl?

So many questions, thought Antoinette sadly. And as yet I can determine the answer to none of them. But somehow, in time, I shall unearth the truth. To be sure, I cannot live the rest of my life without knowing my true identity.

Although Antoinette was extremely hungry, she knew she could not face breakfast at Beck Lodge. Mrs. Hutton would be hovering around, attempting to glean more information about Cedric Aston, and Antoinette's future.

Throwing on a black pelisse and bonnet, Antoinette slipped out of the garden door, and made her way across the bridge which led to the main street of Linton. At the bakery, she stopped and requested a piece of bread of the florid-faced Mr. Burnsall.

The baker looked embarrassed. "Er, beggin' your pardon, Miss Aston, but whose account shall I credit that to?"

Surprised, Antoinette replied, "Why, kindly charge it to my uncle as usual . . ."

Her voice tailed away. He knew. Everyone in the village was aware that Antoinette Aston had been disinherited. That she had no money of her own. That she was dependent for charity on an unknown relative of the late Dr. Aston's who had not yet given his authority for her to charge her expenses to his account.

To make matters worse, the bakery was crowded with people. Some were purchasing bread, others had brought meat to roast in the baker's oven. They were all staring at Antoinette now, their eyes huge with curiosity, sympathy, and relief that they themselves were not burdened with a similar plight.

Suddenly the new baked bread turned to sawdust in Antoinette's mouth. She slapped the remainder of the bread back down on the counter, and ran from the shop. Behind her, the sturdy Mrs. Burnsall took her husband by the shoulders and shook him soundly.

"How could you humiliate the lassy in such a fashion?" she scolded. "Has she not enough troubles to bear without you denying her a simple piece of bread?"

"I didn't think," muttered the baker. "The words just popped out of my mouth. But it's a business I'm running here, woman. Miss Aston is a lovely honest girl, right enough. But I can't go giving credit without the proper authority, can I? It seems to me the sooner the new master of Beck Lodge arrives the better. We'll all know where we are then."

Her eyes stinging with tears, Antoinette ran right through the village and began to climb a winding path that led up into the splendid countryside of the Dales. She adored this landscape. Revelled in the unspoilt beauty of wood and river, dramatically landmarked by soaring limestone scars and cliffs.

Ever since she was a girl, Antoinette had escaped to the Dales whenever she felt angry, afraid or bruised by life. Up here, where the only sounds were the soft baaing of the sheep and the rustle of the wind in the grass, she was able to feel at peace. Gradually, her troubled spirits were soothed, and her courage came flooding back.

There is no point, she told herself firmly, in feeling sorry for yourself. There are thousands of poor unfortunate girls in the world who are far worse off than you. Naturally, you have been in a severe state of shock. Yesterday, you believed your future to be secure. Now it is uncertain. But the basis of your fear lies in the unknown—in not knowing what matter of man Cedric Aston will turn out to be.

Because your "uncle" was such a strict, uncompromising

man, you have been imagining that his cousin Cedric will display the same characteristics. But in all probability you will find that he is a man of kindness, sympathy, even charm. It would be foolish to judge him before you have even set eyes on him. For there is surely no reason why you, he, and his family should not co-exist quite happily under one roof. Beck Lodge is large enough to accommodate a small family. And I should be glad to make myself useful as governess to the children. Why, now I think of it, the future looks quite rosy after all!

Feeling considerably cheered, Antoinette made her way back down the hill and reentered Beck Lodge by the garden door. Her heart was gladdened by the sight of the first crocuses pushing their way through in the wild grass around the apple tree. Winter is nearly over, she thought happily. Soon Spring will be upon us, banishing gloomy thoughts and chilling fancies.

Lightly, she ran upstairs to her bed chamber. Flinging open the door, she froze suddenly on the threshold. A tall, balding man of middle age was standing by the window, examining with a critical eye Antoinette's chipped writing table. He had pulled out the drawer, and was about to remove her journal, in which she occasionally recorded her most private thoughts.

Goaded into action, Antoinette sped across the room and snatched the velvet bound journal from his thin hands. "Who are you?" she demanded angrily. "How dare you enter my room without permission!"

He gazed down at her, a sourly impatient expression in his brown eyes.

"Your room?" he echoed. "I fear you are mistaken, young lady. Every room in this house by right now belongs to me."

Cousin Cedric! Trembling, Antoinette retreated a few steps and hastily introduced herself. Cedric Aston favored her with a cursory bow.

"I confess," he declared, in his dry, humorless voice, "I am surprised to find you still in residence, Miss Aston. I assumed that by now you would at least have been packing your things, ready to quit my house."

"Quit?" whispered Antoinette, her heart beating wildly within her. "But I thought . . . I imagined that I could make myself useful to you. As a governess perhaps for your children . . ."

"My children already have an excellent governess who will be accompanying us here. I have already decided, in fact, to allot her the use of this bed chamber."

"Then . . . wh—where am I to go?" stammered Antoinette.

Cedric Aston shrugged. "Miss Aston. I have six children. I fear there will be no room for you here at Beck Lodge. And I had assumed that you would already have made alternative arrangements."

Antoinette could not believe that he could be so callous, so cold, so unfeeling. "But Beck Lodge is my home!" she protested. "I have nowhere else to go!"

He sighed. "Really, this is all too vexing! Surely, my dear girl, you are not suggesting that it is my place to take financial responsibility for you? I would remind you that there are no ties of kinship that bind us. And I must tell you plain that my lady wife is possessed of an extremely jealous nature. She would not take kindly to having a young, attractive woman like yourself living under the same roof. No, she would certainly not take kindly to that at all!"

Antoinette's head began to spin. She felt as if a great dark pit had suddenly opened up at her feet. She was aware that Cedric Aston was addressing her, but his words seemed to rebound against the dingy walls, making no sense.

Then she heard him say the word almshouse. Instantly, Antoinette was all attention as a wave of terror sent a chill through her bones.

". . . use every influence at my disposal," Cedric Aston was saying, "to have you admitted to the local Fontaine almshouse. It will at least be a roof over your head, and I understand they find work for you—"

"No!" exclaimed Antoinette, her eyes stormy. "Nothing in the world, Mr. Aston, would induce me to enter a poor house. Oh, do not fear," she laughed bitterly as he started to protest, "I shall not impose on your grudging charity. If you would be so good as to leave me alone in this room, I shall pack my things. And I shall quit this house at noon, never to return!"

Her outburst had shamed Cedric Aston. "But where will you go? What will you do?"

"That, as you have made abundantly clear, is my concern, not yours!" Antoinette retorted icily.

Without another word, Cedric Aston turned on his heel and left the room. In a white heat of rage, Antoinette seized a small portmanteau and threw into it her most valued personal possessions.

Then she tore off her black mourning dress and flung it under the bed.

"I have mourned you five whole days, George and Edith Aston," she declared. "That is long enough. Since I am to be turned out of your house, I shall grieve for you no longer."

Defiantly, she selected a dress and pelisse of glowing burgundy red, and a velvet bonnet trimmed with gay pink ribbons. Then she gripped her portmanteau, descended the stairs and bade farewell to Mrs. Hutton.

As the dining room clock struck noon, Antoinette Aston departed from Beck Lodge with her back straight, her head held high and not a single penny piece in her pocket.

Two

Pride and rage propelled Antoinette out of Beck Lodge, and sustained her over the stream, and across the village green. But then her resolution began to falter.

Clutching her portmanteau in her gloved hand, she gazed with despair at the long main street of the village. Oh, how embarrassing, to be obliged to walk the length of the street with all the villagers watching!

I shall be the cynosure of all eyes, the subject of their speculative gossip, thought Antoinette wretchedly. Yet there is nothing for it but to proceed. For this is the shortest route to the highroad.

Squaring her shoulders, Antoinette set forth at a brisk pace, determined to ignore the whispers, the pointing fingers, the curious stares.

She had hardly covered ten yards when a carriage drew up beside her. Recognizing it as the Aston carriage, Antoinette averted her gaze and prepared to march on. But the voice of Hutton, the Aston driver, detained her.

"Just a moment if you please, Miss! Don't be in such a rush. I've come to drive you a little way."

Surprised, Antoinette stared up at the burly Hutton. "Are you declaring that Mr. Cedric Aston sent you with the carriage for me?"

Hutton shook his head. "Bless you, no! As I said to Mrs. Hutton, he's the type of gentleman who'll attend church regular every Sunday, but it'll be a rare event for him to show anyone a little christian charity."

"Mr. Hutton," said Antoinette anxiously, "if you have taken the carriage without his permission, I fear that Mr. Aston may dismiss you!"

"Makes no odds to me," maintained Hutton. "I don't like the man, and I've been offered another job up at Hebdon Hall. Now, in you get, Miss. Where would you like to go?"

Antoinette climbed gratefully into the carriage, and then reflected that she had not given any serious thought to what her destination should be. Her one aim had been to remove herself from Beck Lodge, and the village of Linton, as speedily as possible. But where to now?

London? Antoinette shuddered. She had never been to the capital, but she had heard a legion of sad tales about innocent country girls who arrived there with no money, no friends and no understanding of sophisticated city life. A pitiful fate usually awaited them. No, decided Antoinette, I would be better off in the poor house than cast adrift in London.

Aware that Hutton was looking at her expectantly, awaiting an answer, Antoinette said impulsively, "Would you kindly drive me to the staging post on the highway, Mr. Hutton? I'll pick up a coach there."

"So be it," declared Hutton, cracking his whip. Within minutes, the village of Linton lay behind them. And heaven knows what lies ahead, thought Antoinette tremulously.

When they reached the staging post, Hutton assisted Antoinette from the carriage and inquired after the rest of her luggage.

"When I am settled, I will send word to Beck Lodge for my possessions," replied Antoinette. "Thank you so much for your kindness, Mr. Hutton. I do hope Mr. Aston has not discovered that his carriage is absent!"

Hutton laughed. "No skin off my nose if he does, Miss. Well, I wish you the best of luck. The Sheffield stage is due shortly, if that's any use to you. If you'll take my advice, you'll catch it. That sky don't look too healthy to me."

As Hutton drove back to the Linton road, Antoinette

glanced upward and realized that he was right. The sunshine of the morning had disappeared, and the sky was now covered with a yellowy-gray cloud. Snow clouds that Antoinette recognized with forboding. Having grown up in the Dales, she was all too familiar with the manner in which the weather could change quite drastically in the short space of an hour. She blew on her hands. Yes, the temperature had certainly dropped. All the signs presaged a heavy snowfall—and soon!

It was with considerable relief that Antoinette heard the hornblare of the approaching stage coach. As it crested the brow of the hill, she kept her eyes fixed on the colorful figure of the coachman, splendid in his pink waistcoat and wide skirted green coat, shining with large brass buttons. As if to underline Antoinette's fears about the weather, she noticed that the yellow and green coach carried sturdy snow shovels.

Stepping forward, Antoinette waved an arm as a signal for the coachman to stop. The coach was Sheffield bound, Hutton had said. Antoinette knew next to nothing about the town of Sheffield.

But no matter, she thought. All I desire at the moment is the warmth and security of a carriage roof over my head. That wind sweeping down from the Dales is becoming icier by the minute!

The coach was almost level with her now. But to her dismay, it showed no sign of slowing down. The coachman spotted the solitary girl standing by the roadside, and cupped his hands.

"We are full! Full to overflowing. Sorry, no room!"

And with that, the yellow and green coach sped past toward Sheffield, leaving Antoinette standing forlornly by the staging post.

Oh dear, what is to become of me now, wondered Antoinette in despair. Well, she resolved, there is no point in standing here bewailing my fate. That will bring me no advance. In fact, it will only serve to make me die of exposure if the weather becomes much colder. No, the only thing for it is for me to walk. I am young, and healthy, and at least by stepping it out, I shall make myself as warm as toast.

But which way to take? While she stood there in an agony of indecision, a youth in a battered gig came creaking up the road. He had greasy hair, a thin, foxy face and sharp blue eyes. Antoinette disliked him on sight. But his first words dispelled her antagonism:

"I'm going to Harrogate. Do you want a ride?"

Antoinette sighed with relief. How fortunate, she thought, to be offered two invaluable lifts all in the space of one hour! She smiled at the youth.

"How very kind of you! I should be most grateful."

He said stonily, "It'll cost you."

Antoinette fumbled in her reticule. "Here," she said. "Take these!"

She saw his eyes gleam with greed as he surveyed the pearl necklace she held out. It was, of course, ridiculous to offer a string of pearls in return for a ride to Harrogate. Although the pearls were not first quality, Antoinette was aware that they would still command a fair price, especially in the shady back alleys of Harrogate.

Antoinette had no choice but to offer the pearls as payment, for she had not a single coin upon her person. Before she departed from Beck Lodge, Cedric Aston had emerged from the library and handed her the pearls and diamond brooch bequeathed to her by Edith Aston. They, and the precious gold locket around her neck, represented her total fortune in the entire world.

The oily-haired youth pocketed the pearls, and motioned Antoinette to enter the gig. Then they set off at a cracking pace along the road to Harrogate. Antoinette closed her eyes, feeling weak with a mixture of fatigue and relief. What a strenuous twenty-four hours this had been!

Only this time yesterday, she mused, I was putting on my black bonnet, ready for the funeral of the couple I believed to be my aunt and uncle. And now I find myself cast out of their home, on the road to Harrogate, a town I am completely unfamiliar with! Still, that is better than standing on the lonely roadside with nothing to look forward to other than a snow storm.

Antoinette was so relieved to be on her way at last that

she was oblivious to the bumpiness of the ride . . . and to the dishevelled young man who was about to draw level with them on his foaming, wild-eyed horse.

The unkempt young man waved a pistol in the air, and shouted, "Stand and deliver, I say! Your money or your life!"

Antoinette stared at him scornfully. His theatrical attitude and mode of speech marked him instantly as an amateur adventurer, rather than a genuine gentleman of the road. She turned to the foxy-faced driver of the gig, expecting him to raise his voice in a menacing fashion, and see the imposter off. But foxy-face merely stopped the gig and sat there, waiting.

The young man with the pistol dismounted, and strode toward Antoinette. She gazed disdainfully ahead, refusing to acknowledge his presence. Furiously, he snatched her reticule from her fingers and tore it open.

His eyes lit up. "Ah, you were right, Silas! The lady does have some pretty things upon her. Look at this!" He held aloft Edith Aston's diamond brooch.

Antoinette whirled around and glared at foxy-face. "Why, you are in league with this rogue!" she gasped. She realized what must have happened. No doubt foxy-face and his colleague made a regular practice of waiting by the staging post to pick up unfortunate travellers who, like herself, were unable to board the coach. The second youth would hide by the roadside, waiting for a signal from Silas that the passenger in his gig had rich pickings in money or valuables.

Foxy-face shrugged, completely unabashed. "We all have to scrape a living as best we can, lady. Now what else have you got for us?" Before Antoinette knew what was happening, his grimy fingers had wrenched open the neck of her burgundy pelisse.

"My!" he exclaimed admiringly. "Take a look at this, Ted!"

Frightened now, Antoinette leapt nimbly from the gig and began to race up the road. At all costs, she resolved, they shall not take by locket from me! I would rather die than lose that, my one precious link with my mysterious past!

Antoinette was fleet of foot, but no match for the horse-backed Ted. Within seconds he had caught her up. Dismounting, he seized her roughly by the shoulders and reached out for the locket.

"No!" screamed Antoinette, clawing frantically at his unshaven face. "Leave me be! You shall never take my locket. Never!"

Drawing back her boot, she delivered a hefty kick on Ted's shin. He yelled in agony, but refused to relinquish his grasp on the gold chain of the locket. "You little minx!" he hissed, raising his hand. "I'll teach you to play rough with me!"

Antoinette turned away as the blow fell, but even so he managed to land a heavy smack on her ear, which sent her bonnet tumbling into the road. Dizzy with pain, Antoinette nevertheless contrived to squirm this way and that whilst he attempted to undo the clasp of the locket.

Ted was swiftly running out of patience. "Stay still, damn you! Or I'll hit you so hard you won't recover for days!"

Before Antoinette could voice the defiant retort that sprang to her lips, the foxy-faced Silas let out a warning yell, "Coach approaching over the hill, Ted!"

Ted swore under his breath. "I must have this locket, Silas! It's too good to let go!"

Silas looked scared. "Leave it, man! Let's be gone."

To Antoinette's relief, Ted paid heed to the urgency in his colleague's tone. Roughly, he shoved Antoinette aside, and leaped on his horse. "Don't think you've seen the last of me, lass!" he shouted in a threatening tone. "I'll catch up with you again one day. And I'll have that locket from your sweet white neck!"

And with these menacing words hanging in the cold afternoon air, he and foxy-face rode off. Feeling thoroughly shaken, Antoinette retrieved her bonnet and dusted it down. But before she had time to set it on her tousled curls, the shining dark-blue coach was almost upon her, and a cultured, deep voice was inquiring,

"Can I be of any assistance?"

Antoinette found herself gazing into the concerned gray eyes of a ruggedly handsome man in his early thirties. He went on, "As we crested the hill my driver thought he saw you being set upon by two young rogues."

"They were trying to steal my locket," explained Antoinette, unable to explain to herself why the very sight of this dark gentleman should have started her heart beating so wildly.

"It is dashed unfortunate that we didn't reach you in time!" he declared. "I hope you are not too distressed by the incident?"

"Thank you, no. I am fully recovered," murmured Antoinette.

"Well since I failed so abysmally to see those blackguards off, the least I can do is offer you the convenience of my carriage," said the handsome stranger. "I assume you are on your way to Harrogate?"

"Indeed yes," replied Antoinette slowly, "but I feel it would be best if I did not accept your kind offer. You see, you are the third person today to offer me a lift. The first will most likely lose his job because of it, and then in accepting the second offer, I was robbed, and nearly lost my locket—which is my most treasured possession. So you see, if I ride with you, I dread to think what will befall me!"

The dark-haired gentleman laughed. "My dear young lady, if you continue to stand there on the roadside, what will befall you is an early death from exposure. Are you unaware that it is snowing?"

Sure enough, Antoinette's bare head was already covered with a frosting of snowflakes.

The gentleman in the carriage held open the door. "Come, I will brook no more argument! We shall journey to Harrogate together."

As Antoinette scrambled into the luxuriously upholstered carriage, the driver turned and inquired respectfully, "Has the young lady no luggage, my lord?"

"I really have no notion, Perkins!" declared his master, raising an inquiring eyebrow at Antoinette.

Antoinette let out an inward wail of despair. Her portmanteau! It was still lying in the gig in which foxy-face had beat so hasty a retreat. She was determined, however, to reveal no details of her true plight to the gallant gentleman sitting across from her in the carriage. Although he looked and sounded every inch a gentleman, Antoinette was very well aware that there were those even of highest rank who would not hesitate to take advantage of a girl they knew to be homeless, penniless and friendless.

Accordingly, she said with dignity, "Oh, my things are being sent on. I firmly believe that it is safer to travel without too many encumbrances."

The gray eyes regarded her steadily. "But may I ask what you were doing wandering around the highway on your own? You must have known you were a sitting duck for those blackguards."

"Indeed yes. It was all so unfortunate," said Antoinette airily. "I was intending to catch the Harrogate stage, but stupidly my driver mistook the time, and we arrived too late at the staging post. I was standing there trying to decide what to do, when the two rogues set upon me." Seeing that the dark-haired stranger seemed intent on questioning her further, Antoinette hurriedly sidetracked him by declaring sweetly, "My, we have been travelling together for over five minutes, and I have no notion what your name may be."

He smiled. "The Duke of Lyveden, at your service."

Antoinette's blue eyes widened. A duke! I am sharing a carriage with a real, live duke. My, if only that pompous, superior, overbearing Cedric Aston could see me now!

Gracefully, Antoinette extended her hand. "I am Antoinette Aston—I come from the village of Linton. But if I may say so, you do not sound like a native of Yorkshire."

"No," said the Duke, "I live mainly in London. But much though I love the capital, its charms seemed to have palled for me recently. I thought a change of scene and a change of air would restore my spirits. So I resolved to spend a few months in Yorkshire."

"A wise choice." Antoinette smiled, her eyes discreetly assessing the superb cut of his coat, the lace at his neck, and the laughter lines around his firm mouth. "If you are feeling melancholy, you can rely on the bracing Yorkshire air to blow your cares away high over the Dales."

The Duke nodded. "I have certainly been privileged to enjoy some most unusual entertainment recently. I have been the guest of the Duke of Devonshire, you see. Last night we paid a visit to Grassington. Do you know it?"

"The little lead-miners' town?" asked Antoinette. "Yes of course. I adore the old Tudor hall there, half hidden behind the market square. It gives me such pleasure to stand beneath the gabled windows and imagine the Elizabethan ladies whispering secrets to one another in the window seats."

"Ah, I perceive you are a young lady with a well-developed imagination," remarked the Duke. "I am confident, then, that it would have amused you to have accompanied the Duke of Devonshire and myself last night. We visited the local theatre in Grassington to see a performance by an actor named Edmund Kean."

"I confess, his name is not familiar to me," murmured Antoinette, not caring to admit that she had never in her life entered a theatre. Dr. and Mrs. Aston had not approved of such forms of entertainment.

The Duke raised his ringed left hand and declared, "The Duke of Devonshire is confident that Mr. Kean will in time be one of the greatest actors England has ever known. He was so anxious to see the performance at the rustic Grassington theatre that he put on a tremendous show of appearing touched and honored when we were ushered with great pomp and ceremony into a ducal box improvised from bits of wood decorated with brown paper!"

Antoinette threw back her golden head and laughed. Well satisfied, the Duke of Lyveden sat back in his seat and regarded Antoinette as she retied the pink ribbons of her bonnet.

It was good to see her lovely eyes dancing with merriment, he mused. She had looked so pale and frightened when first she entered the coach. But who the deuce was this beautiful girl with the delicate, heart-shaped face, the dazzling complexion and the brilliant blue eyes?

Her mode of dress, though clean and neat, indicated that she was not a lady of rank. He judged that she was, perhaps, the daughter of a respectable, small town solicitor.

33

And yet—the Duke's gray eyes narrowed—there was a natural dignity and grace about the girl which suggested good breeding. At first sight, thought the Duke, you would take her for a simple country lass. Yet after a few minutes in her company, it is impossible not to be impressed by her charming demeanor, and her unaffectedly elegant manners.

So who is my mystery lady running away from, the dark-haired man wondered. Shrewdly, it had not taken him long to guess that Antoinette was in flight. She had slipped up, when she alleged that she was waiting by the staging post for the Harrogate stage. Although the Duke, being from London, was not familiar with the Yorkshire coach runs, he had overheard his driver, Perkins, remarking that morning that there was no stagecoach or Royal Mail to Harrogate that day. The matter was of considerable concern to Perkins, for many of the stage and Royal Mail coachmen were aggressive characters, blowing their horns, cracking their whips and demanding that any other vehicles draw to the side of the road and let them through.

Crossing his well-muscled legs, the Duke inquired, "Tell me, Miss Aston, what brings you to Harrogate?"

He noticed the flicker of alarm in her eyes, and he admired the poise, the swiftness of her recovery as she replied, "Why, to take to the waters of course, Your Grace."

The Duke laughed. "My, you must be blessed with a strong constitution, Miss Aston. It is my intelligence that the Harrogate waters stink of sulphur. Are you not familiar with the local rhyme,

> *As Satan was flying O'er the Harrogate Well,*
> *His senses were charmed with the heat and the smell;*
> *Says he, 'I don't know what region I roam,*
> *But I guess from the smell that I'm not far from home.' "*

Antoinette replied, with a lift of her eyebrows, "My, Your Grace, for a visitor to the county of Yorkshire you are remarkably well acquainted with the native doggerel."

Perkins listened to his master's delighted laugh with a sinking heart. Whatever is my lord Duke thinking of, he mused, allowing himself to be charmed by a rustic country lass like her?

Perkins considered himself fortunate to be in the employ of the Duke of Lyveden. The Duke owned a fine house in Curzon Street, and a large estate in Hampshire. He was a hard taskmaster, not a man to tolerate insolence, laziness or deceit in his employees. But he's a fair man, admitted Perkins. Do your job right and he'll see you straight. What's more, when there's just the two of us travelling, as on this trip to Yorkshire, he's not too proud to sit down with me for half an hour of an evening and share a jug of ale, and roar with laughter as I regale him with all the local gossip. That's how he learned that rhyme about the Harrogate spa, of course. If I'd known that he would end up repeating it just in order to enchant one of the fair sex, well, I'd never have told him it in the first place. It's not right, a gentleman of his rank consorting with low-born females like her. True, he needs a wife sure enough. Come to that, so do I. But he should be encouraging the attentions of a lady of equal rank to himself. Someone like Lady Anne Monteith, for example. Can't say she's the type of woman I'd choose to spend my life with. I'm not partial to those domineering, hard-eyed types. But its different for the nobility, isn't it? All the Duke needs to do is marry someone well born, capable of giving him heirs to protect the line and then he can leave her at home and enjoy his pleasures elsewhere. That's the civilized way to organize a marriage.

Hearing the Duke roar with laughter again, Perkins decided it was time to intervene. Tapping on the carriage wall, he inquired in a respectful tone, "Where does the young lady require dropping, Sir?"

The Duke gave a start. "There! We have been indulging ourselves in such a merry conversation that we have missed the sight of all the glorious countryside we have passed through. Such moors, and dales and vales! However, the reliable Perkins has jolted us back to harsh reality. Where is your destination in Harrogate, Miss Aston?"

Antoinette sat as if paralyzed. She had been so enjoying her conversation with the Duke she had omitted to give a thought to what lay ahead of her in Harrogate. For the truth was that she had never before visited the town, and knew not a soul there. Helplessly, she gazed into the Duke's handsome face.

Oh, she thought with longing, how safe and secure it is here with you. If only time would stand still. If only we could stay here, warm and snug on the velvet seats, forever.

But already, Perkins was tapping relentlessly on the coach wall. "I beg your pardon, Your Grace, but to what address is the young lady bound?"

Antoinette gathered her wits. The Duke was looking at her expectantly. Somehow, she must conjure an address that would sound valid to his ears.

Suddenly, blessed inspiration struck. There was one person with whom she was acquainted in Harrogate! Well, to be utterly truthful, acquainted was not quite the precise term.

"I should be most grateful," said Antoinette with dignity, "if your driver would take me to the residence of Miss Eleanor LeStrange. Foolishly, I omitted to make an exact note of her address. But perhaps your driver could make inquiries once we reach the vicinity of the town."

The Duke nodded, and called out, "Did you hear that, Perkins? You must inquire of the address of a Miss Eleanor LeStrange."

"I believe I am familiar with the address, Your Grace," replied Perkins.

The Duke smiled. "Excellent! Perkins is quite invaluable, you know. A positive mine of information, even when we're in unfamiliar territory!"

Antoinette sat back in her seat with an inward sigh of relief. What a stroke of inspiration that she should have thought of Miss Eleanor LeStrange! True, Antoinette was not formally acquainted with the lady. They had not even met. But Miss LeStrange was the woman with whom Dr. Aston had become amorously involved—the woman he had believed to be the mother of the child left on his doorstep.

Of course, mused Antoinette, there is no shadow of a doubt but that Miss LeStrange is not, in fact, my mother. But she is the only person whose name I know in Harrogate! And somehow, because of her past liaison with Dr. Aston, I feel a strange affinity with her. Something in my bones tells me that in a strange way I do not fully understand, it is necessary for me to meet Eleanor LeStrange—for my destiny lies within her control.

They were now entering the elegant spa town of Harrogate with its leafy avenues, green squares and delightful vistas of the surrounding Yorkshire countryside.

"Most charming, is it not?" remarked the Duke, gazing from the carriage window.

Antoinette nodded her assent. "Why, it is a town full of the most beautiful flowers and trees. Even now, in February, the squares are gay with crocuses and flowering shrubs. How enchanting it must be in the summer!"

Antoinette's exclamations of delight were interrupted by yet more urgent tapping from Perkins. "Excuse me, Your Grace," he said. "I believe Miss LeStrange resides in Paradise Row. Would you prefer me to drop the young lady at the end of the street rather than drawing up outside the front door?"

The Duke's face darkened. "What the deuce are you on about, Perkins! Naturally, we shall drive Miss Aston to the door! Whatever are you thinking of?"

Perkins' tone was heavy with meaning as he replied, "I would respectfully advise your Grace that it is still daylight."

"Not being senile, blind, or completely mad, I was well aware of that fact, Perkins," retorted the Duke icily.

Perkins bravely continued, "It just seemed to me, Sir, that it might not be fitting for a gentleman of your rank to be seen outside Miss LeStrange's house in daylight!"

Raising his voice, the Duke roared. "What nonsense is this, Perkins! Kindly drive us with no more ado and no more argument to Miss LeStrange's residence in Paradise Row!"

Perkins, who knew better than to argue with his master when he used this tone, obediently cracked his whip and directed the grays through the dignified town toward Paradise Row.

Antoinette had been listening to Perkins with some alarm. Obviously, the driver was party to some intelligence which was denied the Duke and herself. Had she made a terrible mistake in directing the coach to Eleanor LeStrange's? But what else could I do, she thought, desperately. For I know of no one else in this town.

But as the carriage drew to a halt outside number nine Paradise Row, Antoinette was flooded with relief. Miss LeStrange's house was a respectable, bow fronted residence, discreetly fronted by newly painted black railings. The brass door knocker gleamed in the pale afternoon sunlight and a wisp of gray smoke curled welcomingly from the chimney.

Gallantly, the Duke assisted Antoinette from the carriage. Antoinette curtseyed and murmured, "You have been most kind. I am so grateful to you."

"Not at all." He smiled. "The pleasure was all mine, I assure you. Your charming company and delightful conversation transformed a tedious journey into a positive delight. I shall be putting up at the Green Dragon Inn. May I have your permission to wait upon you, within a few days?"

Antoinette's reply was drowned by Perkins, who appeared to be suffering from a sudden and severe fit of choking. The Duke glared at him. "My, that cough sounds quite deadly, Perkins. I do believe instead of a jug of ale tonight, you would do better to imbibe a draught of herbal tea. I will have a word with the innkeeper—can't have you laid up, can we?"

Red-faced, Perkins subsided into silence.

The Duke bowed to Antoinette and with a graceful *au revoir,* took his leave. Antoinette turned to the door, and stretched out a gloved hand toward the knocker. But before she could touch it, the door flew open to reveal a sturdy, round-faced woman dressed in gray.

Behind her, a younger, red-haired lady whispered excitedly. "Who is it, Lake! Is it really the Duke himself?"

"I fear not, Madam," replied the housekeeper, gazing doubtfully at Antoinette.

Summoning a smile, Antoinette declared, "Good day to you. Is Miss Eleanor LeStrange at home?"

Antoinette's sharp ears heard a door slam. The red-haired woman had disappeared.

"I will inquire," said the housekeeper. "What name shall I give?"

Antoinette gave her name and was ushered into an airy, daintily appointed drawing room. It was tastefully decorated in shades of spring green, enlivened with touches of white in the cushions, the marble mantel and the posy of snowdrops adorning the rosewood writing table.

It is definitely the room of an extremely feminine woman, mused Antoinette, seating herself on the comfortable sofa. At that moment the door opened, and a tall, red-haired woman of about forty years entered the room. She was dressed in an elaborate sage green gown, with a heavy silver pendant adorning her throat.

"How do you do, Miss Aston," she said, in her light, amused voice. "I am Eleanor LeStrange."

Antoinete rose to her feet. But as she gazed into Miss LeStrange's gray-green eyes, the room seemed to spin. Suddenly it was as if Miss LeStrange, the rosewood writing table, even the door itself were tilting, sliding out of sight over the horizon.

With a confused sigh, the white-faced Antoinette slumped unconscious at Eleanor LeStrange's elegantly shod feet.

Three

When she regained consciousness, Antoinette found she was lying full length on the sofa. Both Mrs. Lake, the housekeeper, and Miss LeStrange were regarding her anxiously.

As Antoinette's eyelids fluttered open, Mrs. Lake remarked, "Ah, the color's coming back to her cheeks now. I declare, the poor lass was as pale as a ghost! How strange that she should cast one glance at you and go into a dead swoon like that, Madam. What could there have been about you to cause such a reaction?"

Miss LeStrange slipped a cushion behind Antoinette's back as the girl struggled to sit up. "I don't flatter myself that the girl's fainting fit had anything to do with me, Lake," she commented. She cast her shrewd gray-green eyes on Antoinette and inquired, "When did you last eat, child?"

Antoinette gave the matter some thought. She had missed breakfast this morning, she remembered, and of course there had been no opportunity to partake of a midday meal. "I suppose it must have been supper, last night," she ventured.

Throwing up her hands in horror, Mrs. Lake bustled from the room to have a word with the cook. Eleanor LeStrange, meanwhile, drew up a velvet stool and seated herself gracefully beside Antoinette.

"Now, my dear Miss Aston," she smiled warmly, "do tell me how you came to arrive escorted by none other than the Duke of Lyveden himself. I assure you, my entire household is most intrigued!"

"Oh, it is not as you think," demurred Antoinette, encouraged by the friendliness of the older woman's tone. "It is simply that he found me in some distress on the road near Linton—my home, and kindly offered me a lift. I took the liberty of giving him your address because yours was the only name I knew in Harrogate."

Miss LeStrange raised a surprised eyebrow. "Linton," she murmured. "And you say your name is Aston . . ." She smiled suddenly, as if a distant memory had suddenly been rekindled in her mind. But being a woman of tact and considerable experience, she said no more until Mrs. Lake had borne in a tray of steaming soup, cold chicken and a slice of homemade apple pie.

While Antoinette gratefully made her repast, Miss LeStrange made conversation of a purely social nature. She talked of the beauty of the town of Harrogate, of the shops, the parades, and the spacious Forest of Kharesborough with its shady avenues of trees and delightful walks.

Only when Antoinette was replete and sitting at her ease did Miss LeStrange return to the topic that was uppermost in her mind. "Tell me," she said sweetly, "are you by any chance related to a Dr. Aston of the village of Linton?"

Antoinette flushed, and nodded. "For many years I believed myself to be his niece," she began. And as darkness fell, and the lamps were lit, Antoinette told Eleanor LeStrange of the story of her birth, and the devastating revelations of Dr. Aston's Will.

"Why," cried Miss LeStrange at last, "that is outrageous! How callous of Dr. Aston to disinherit you so cruelly. And how dastardly of this Cedric Aston to turn you out of the house!"

Timidly, Antoinette ventured, "Were you and Dr. Aston very much in love?"

"In love?" exclaimed Miss LeStrange in surprise.

"I was given to understand," explained Antoinette, "that you had a romantic liaison with the doctor but that you quarrelled and parted company. That was why he believed the baby on the doorstep to have been put there by you."

"Ah yes," murmured the red-haired woman, a slight smile touching her lips. "I do recall meeting him again many, many years later. I recall that he, somewhat clumsily, brought the conversation around to the matter of children. And when I lightly declared that I considered myself fortunate to have escaped the chains of motherhood, he did look most interested." She sighed. "But as to us being passionately in love, I must confess in all truth that the affection was more on his side than on mine."

Antoinette looked puzzled. "You surprise me, Miss LeStrange. I always found the doctor to be a cold, unfeeling man. It is intriguing to learn that he possessed a tender, vulnerable side to his nature! Do tell me, where were your secret rendezvous? Did he take you for carriage rides after dark or did you enjoy romantic walks up into the Dales together?"

Miss LeStrange arose and said hurriedly, "It was all so long ago, I regret I can hardly recollect the matter at all, now. Besides, it is morbid to dwell on the past." She waved her hands. "What we must discuss is the future, *your* future, Antoinette!"

"I was hoping you might be acquainted with a family who were in need of a governess," suggested Antoinette.

Miss LeStrange stood near the mantelpiece, her white, ringed hands drumming on the smooth marble top. "Ye-es," she said slowly. "I'm sure we'll find something useful for you to do, my child. But for the moment I think the important thing is for you to rest. You have, after all, endured a most traumatic few days." She rang the bell. "I will ask Lake to show you to your room. And tomorrow, I will take you out and show you Harrogate!"

"You are inviting me to stay here with you?" cried Antoinette. "Oh, how very kind! I-am so grateful." Then her hands flew to her face. "But I have no clothes but these I stand up in! And I have no money to buy new ones, or pay you for your board and lodging!"

"Hush, child," soothed Miss LeStrange with a smile. "While you are under my roof I insist that you regard yourself as my guest. While we are out tomorrow we shall take the opportunity to replenish your wardrobe."

"Oh, how shall I ever repay you?" murmured Antoinette.

"No doubt, in time, there will be some small service you can render me," said Miss LeStrange sweetly. She glanced across to the door, where Mrs. Lake stood waiting.

"Ah, Lake. Kindly take Miss Aston up to the blue bed chamber, would you. She has eaten her supper, and now desires to rest."

"Indeed, I feel so much excitement now that my immediate future is assured that my head is buzzing with plans," exclaimed Antoinette. "I am convinced I shall not sleep a wink!"

"And I," laughed Miss LeStrange, "am equally convinced that you will!"

And so it proved. An hour later, when Miss LeStrange and Mrs. Lake entered the blue bed chamber, although it was barely half past seven, Antoinette was sleeping soundly with her lovely golden hair spread across the lace edged pillow. So deep was her slumber that she did not even stir when Mrs. Lake lifted the lamp she was carrying, and shone it full on to Antoinette's face.

For a full minute, Miss LeStrange studied the sleeping girl. Then she gave a contented sigh. "I do believe, Lake, that we have quite a prize here."

The housekeeper nodded. "She is a beautiful girl, Miss LeStrange. And I assure you, the Duke of Lyveden appeared quite entranced with her when they arrived in his carriage."

"I am not surprised," murmured Miss LeStrange. "The Duke is renowned as a connoisseur of beautiful women. His taste is faultless. We must do everything in our power to ensure that he remains captivated by the charms of young Antoinette."

"You propose to ensure that they are much in society together?" inquired Mrs. Lake.

Miss LeStrange shook her head, her gray-green eyes gleaming hard and bright in the lamplight. "Quite the reverse, Lake. I intend to allow him tantalizing glimpses of her—but no more. In no time he will be beating a path to my door, imploring me to allow him access to my golden-haired beauty. And once it is known that the illustrious Duke of Lyveden is a caller here, why, then other titled gentlemen will follow suit."

Mrs. Lake smiled admiringly, "How clever of you, Miss LeStrange!"

"Is it not?" Miss LeStrange moved to the door and went on softly. "As soon as I set eyes on this girl, I knew she would prove invaluable to me. And the ironical thing is, that she is so endearingly desperate to prove herself useful to me! What could be more perfect?"

The sinister laugh of the woman in sage green echoed around the bed chamber. But the innocent girl in the bed slept on, hearing nothing.

The following morning, Antoinette opened her eyes and was immediately conscious of a great sense of peace.

"Oh, how fortunate I am!" she whispered, gazing with delight at the delicately elegant furnishings of the blue saloon. "To think that only yesterday I was without a roof over my head, or a friend in the world. Yet now the kind Miss Le-Strange has invited me to be her guest, and this enchanting room is to be mine for the duration of my stay!"

But Antoinette was not allowed long to contemplate the Wedgwood blue bedhangings and white-bordered sapphire damask curtains. A tap on the door heralded the arrival of a maid bearing a jug of warm water.

Smiling, Antoinette attempted to engage the girl in friendly conversation. She inquired how long the maid had been in Miss LeStrange's service and where her home town might be. But the maid replying in grunts and monosyllables, not once meeting Antoinette's eye, seemed strangely reluctant to answer Antoinette's queries. And Antoinette sensed that it was with relief that at last the maid completed her duties and was able to escape from the room.

Ah well, perhaps she is a very shy girl, thought Antoinette as she bathed her face in the scented water. No doubt in time she will lose her frosty demeanor. And surely, I cannot complain about my reception in this house, for has not Miss LeStrange been the very soul of kindness to me?

When she was dressed, Antoinette made her way downstairs where Mrs. Lake showed her into a sunny breakfast parlor which overlooked the street.

"You'll be taking your repast alone, Miss Aston," said the housekeeper. "Miss LeStrange never rises before eleven and always takes breakfast in her chamber."

Antoinette smiled to herself. My, she thought, how Dr. Aston would have glared with disapproval had he heard of Miss LeStrange's late rising habits. The doctor had no truck with slug-a-beds and insisted that the entire household was up and abroad by seven in the morning.

Antoinette thoroughly enjoyed her breakfast and sat for the next hour contentedly studying the passersby outside in Paradise Row. Having lived all her life in a country village, she was particularly impressed by the elegance of the fashionable ladies parading past the window. With her keen eye, Antoinette was swift to notice every chic new detail, the pearl buttons on the gloves, the tucks on the bodice of the pelisse, the fancy lacing on the boots.

My, she thought enviously, such finery was never available to us in the village of Linton! And Mrs. Aston, as I recall, always declared that she dressed for warmth and comfort, not trivial fashion!

"A penny for your thoughts!" declared a laughing Miss LeStrange from the door. She was dressed from top to toe in the soft silvery green that one sees on lavender bushes in the spring.

Antoinette arose and said, "I was merely admiring the fashions of the ladies passing by. I confess, I feel something of a hayseed in this dull red dress."

"Yes, that color is a little harsh for your delicate coloring," pronounced Miss LeStrange. "And of course, waists are much higher this year. But do not despair. My carriage is at the door and I propose to whisk you straight to my dressmaker. I promise, in no time at all we shall make you the most looked at, most talked about girl in Harrogate!"

"Oh surely not!" demurred Antoinette.

The red-haired woman smiled. But there was no warmth in the gray-green eyes.

Antoinette was surprised that Miss LeStrange elected to take the carriage on the short journey from Paradise Row to the back of Silver Street where the modiste resided. But no doubt, mused Antoinette, Miss LeStrange is merely displaying a kind consideration toward me. She realizes that I am ashamed of my frowsty, travel-stained, red dress, and would not wish to be seen wearing it in the fashionable streets of Harrogate.

The dressmaker was a tall, thin woman with as little to say for herself as the maid who had earlier brought the jug of water to Antoinette's room. While Antoinette happily browsed around the bales of colorful muslins and silks piled around the workroom, Miss LeStrange took the woman aside and spoke to her in a low voice for several minutes. Then the pattern books were brought out. Miss LeStrange confidently chose three or four styles that she declared would suit Antoinette perfectly, and Antoinette was happy to be guided by the older woman.

For day wear, Miss LeStrange ordered for Antoinette a pretty chintz style, printed in gay pink blue, brown and green, with a tucker of white patterned muslin.

"Such a charming, youthful style." The red-haired woman smiled. "Now for evening we desire something a little more sophisticated. I favor a simple style, high in the waist and low in the bosom in a white India muslin with silver thread."

The dressmaker obediently made a note of her client's instructions and measured Antoinette.

"My, such a tiny waist!" she exclaimed. "And such graceful shoulders. She will be a delight to dress, Miss LeStrange."

"Quite so." Eleanor LeStrange nodded, glancing around the workroom. "And now I urgently require a pelisse for Miss Aston. That dark-blue model there looks finished except for the hem. If you will kindly attend to the hem we will take it with us now."

The dressmaker looked flustered. "I regret, Miss LeStrange, that this particular pelisse is promised to Miss Kaye."

Miss LeStrange's mouth hardened. "Are you implying that Miss Kaye's custom is more valuable than mine?" she inquired frostily.

"No, no!" cried the harrassed dressmaker. "It is just that she will be calling for the pelisse this afternoon. Perhaps I can find Miss Aston something else . . ."

"Oh yes!" cried Antoinette, "I should not wish to take a model that belonged to another client!"

"Nonsense," said Miss LeStrange cuttingly. "There is no question of you having another pelisse, Antoinette. That particular blue will set off your eyes in the most spectacular manner. Miss Kaye has dull brown eyes. That blue will not suit her at all." She turned to the dressmaker. "I must insist that we have the pelisse. Otherwise you may consider all my other orders cancelled."

The dressmaker's shoulders drooped. "Very well, Miss LeStrange." And without another word, she fetched needle and thread and set to work taking up the hem.

Half an hour later, with Antoinette attired in the magnificent dark-blue pelisse, the dressmaker ushered the two ladies to the door.

"There is no hurry over the evening dress," declared Miss LeStrange, "but I should be glad if you would deliver the day dress to my home by tomorrow afternoon. Good-day to you!"

As the red-haired woman swept into her carriage, Antoinette could not help but feel a pang of sympathy for the dressmaker. No doubt she had many other orders to attend to, yet Miss LeStrange expected her to ignore all her other work, and make Antoinette's dress in a single day!

"Now," sighed Miss LeStrange, "with our business successfully concluded, I shall take you on a tour of Harrogate. It is only a small town, you know, but I feel that what it lacks in size, it makes up for with natural dignity and beauty."

They drove first around the stray, the two hundred acres of lush grazing land which enclosed on three sides the communities of Low and High Harrogate.

"Quite delightful, is it not?" sighed Miss LeStrange, opening the carriage window and taking deep breaths. "It is such a pleasure to know that even though one resides in a town, one has not far to travel for a draught of pure, country air."

Antoinette hastily turned to gaze out of the other window, to mask the laughter bubbling to her lips. For to Antoinette, a breath of fresh air meant a brisk walk through the glorious countryside of the Dales, not a carriage ride around the outskirts of Harrogate!

After their tour of the stray, Antoinette inquired if it might be possible to visit the celebrated Sulphur Well.

Miss LeStrange wrinkled her nose. "Oh no, it is not the elegant thing for ladies to be seen taking the waters at the Well. Most visitors to the town prefer to have the water sent up to their lodgings, that they may drink it, or even bathe in it, in privacy."

"Indeed, that does seem to be a more convenient manner of taking the cure," agreed Antoinette. "I understand that the waters are a most beneficial aid to the digestion."

"That may be so, but in my experience the people who flock here to take the waters do themselves more harm than good," said Miss LeStrange with a dismissive wave of her gloved hand. "For having dutifully sipped the waters by day, they then crowd into the Green Dragon by night and gorge themselves insensible on hot shoulders of mutton and pigeon pies, punch and ale. So by the morning, they are all out of temper, suffering from severe bouts of indigestion and cursing the water for making them ill!"

"The Green Dragon!" exclaimed Antoinette. "Why, that is where the Duke of Lyveden is residing! Do you imagine if we rode past we might catch a sight of him?"

"Most certainly not!" declared Miss LeStrange emphatically. "I am surprised at you, Antoinette, even to contemplate engaging in such vulgar behavior." And to Antoinette's disappointment, she immediately gave the driver instructions to drive back to Paradise Row.

"I wonder why the Duke is putting up at the Green Dragon?" mused Miss LeStrange. "It is a most respectable inn, of course, but one would have expected someone in the Duke's position to hire a house. I hope this does not mean that he intends to reside in Harrogate only a short time. Did he give you any indication, my dear, of his intentions in this respect?"

Antoinette shook her head. "I regret not. But he did declare a wish to call on me within a few days."

"Indeed?" murmured Miss LeStrange. "Well I am sure we shall all look forward to that!"

The days passed quickly for Antoinette. There were more visits to the dressmaker, shopping excursions, drives to Knareborough Forest, and whole afternoons spent closeted in the blue bed chamber while Miss LeStrange showed Antoinette a score of different ways to dress her hair, to use her fan, to wear her new bonnets. Thanks to Miss LeStrange, and the dilligent dressmaker, Antoinette's wardrobe soon grew to respectable proportions, and before long she had a change of morning and afternoon dresses for every day of the week. To her disappointment, however, her lovely evening dresses remained unworn. It was Miss LeStrange's custom to dine at six on a light meal of just two courses with which she and Antoinette enjoyed a glass of wine. Yet every evening, by seventhirty, Antoinette found it impossible to stop yawning.

"Oh dear, I do apologize," she sighed, as her eyelids began to droop, "but I am finding it most difficult to stay awake. You must think it most impolite of me to fall asleep so early every evening!"

"Not at all." Miss LeStrange smiled sympathetically. "You must remember, Antoinette, that you have suffered a very great shock recently. Two weeks ago, you were a doctor's niece, living a very quiet uneventful life in the country. Now, everything has changed for you. Naturally, it is going to take you some time to adjust. And your sleepiness is Nature's way of helping you to build up your strength. Ah, here is Mrs. Lake come to take you to bed. Good night, my dear, and sleep well."

And as Mrs. Lake put a motherly arm around her and escorted her up the stairs, the sleepy Antoinette felt a surge of gratitude for the mature understanding displayed by Miss LeStrange.

On only one night did she awake before morning. Dimly, through a fog of drowsiness she heard a clock chime two. Feeling desperately thirsty, she opened her bedroom door intending to creep downstairs in search of a glass of water.

Then she stopped in her tracks, listening. Surely that had been the sound of a man's laughter? But where had it come from? It sounded quite near at hand, as if the man was on this very floor of the house.

Confused, Antoinette shook her head. The notion was impossible of course. Clearly, she had been hearing things. Why, in the two weeks she had resided under this roof, Antoinette had not seen Miss LeStrange receive a single visitor, male or female. And naturally, it was quite unthinkable that a respectable lady like Miss LeStrange would entertain a gentleman visitor in her room at two in the morning!

Before Antoinette had time to ponder further on the mystery, she heard a rustle of taffeta behind her. Mrs. Lake, still fully dressed, was advancing down the corridor toward her.

"What are you doing out of bed?" she demanded sharply.

"I . . . I was thirsty . . . I wanted a drink of water," stammered Antoinette, wondering why she should stupidly feel so guilty at being found out of her bedroom.

Mrs. Lake smiled and led Antoinette back to her room. "You should have rung the bell, my dear."

"I imagined every one would be in bed," explained Antoinette, sliding back under the covers. "I did not want to disturb your sleep."

"No cause to worry about that," said the housekeeper, moving to the window and ensuring that the curtains were tightly drawn. "When you reach my age you need only a few hours sleep each night. But you young girls need your rest. Now you lie back and I'll fetch you a soothing drink."

Within a few minutes she returned with a glass of clear, sweet scented liquid. She waited while Antoinette drank it and then watched the girl fall into a peaceful slumber.

As the days wore on and the frosts of February gave way to the sunshine and fresh winds of March, Antoinette's thoughts turned time and time again to Miss LeStrange's strange lack of visitors. Not only were there no callers at the house, but Miss LeStrange made no attempt to visit anyone else in the town. And any excursion from the house, however short, was always performed in the carriage. Miss LeStrange never joined the fashionable ladies promenading up Silver Street or taking the air in one of the pretty, flower-strewn squares.

Only once did she observe Miss LeStrange engage in social conversation and even that was of an extremely brief nature. As the two ladies were emerging from the milliner's one morning, they almost collided with a tall young woman who was strikingly dressed in a red velvet pelisse with a matching bonnet perched at a jaunty angle on her jet black hair. The two ladies bowed and Miss LeStrange murmured some stiff pleasantries about the weather while the dark-haired woman eyed Antoinette with unconcealed interest. But Antoinette was neither introduced nor given the opportunity to converse with her for within a minute Miss LeStrange had swept her into the waiting carriage.

Antoinette was unable to resist inquiring who it was they had just encountered.

"Her name is Lauretta Kaye," said Miss LeStrange disdainfully. "She is a person of no consequence."

Lauretta Kaye, mused Antoinette. I do believe she is the lady for whom my blue pelisse was intended. I recall Miss LeStrange declaring that Miss Kaye had dull brown eyes. Yet from my observation of a moment ago, it would appear that her eyes are not lacklustre at all. They were a deep, rich brown, dancing with life and fun.

That afternoon, observing that Miss LeStrange was in a

good humor after the delivery of a new thyme green bonnet, Antoinette felt emboldened enough to broach the subject of the lack of callers to the house.

Miss LeStrange shrugged. "I am privileged to belong to an extremely select social circle, my dear. It so happens that at the moment most of my acquaintances are out of town. While they are away, I think it best that we remain in our own company rather than resorting to socializing with the second rate of Harrogate."

"Oh, yes of course," murmured Antoinette. "I did not mean to suggest that I am in any way dissatisfied with my life. You have been so kind, so generous! I am ever in your debt."

The red-haired woman smiled. "But I detect that you are becoming a little restless, yes? It is only natural. A young girl like yourself needs companions—of both sexes. I had thought by now that the Duke of Lyveden would have honored his promise to call on you."

Antoinette blushed. "Perhaps he has left town and returned to London?"

"Indeed not. I observed both his carriage and his coachdriver at the Green Dragon when we passed by the other day," said Miss LeStrange. "And yet of the Duke himself there has been no sign. It is most strange, most vexing."

Antoinette could not understand why Miss LeStrange was so concerned. Naturally, she herself had thought a great deal about the handsome Duke since her arrival in Harrogate. How gallant of him to rescue her from a snowstorm and convey her to Harrogate. And yet despite his grand carriage, his title, his elevated position in the world, how companionable he had been on the ride. He had conversed with her in such an easy, friendly manner, making her feel as if she were the one person in the world he desired to be with.

That, decided Antoinette, is the mark of a true gentleman. It must have been obvious to him that I was but a poor country girl. Yet he treated me like a princess.

But as for calling on me, well, it would be fanciful to imagine he would do that. Even with my new clothes and the sophisticated manners taught me by Miss LeStrange, it must still be apparent that he is *ton* and I am not. It would clearly be an embarrassment for him to be seen consorting publicly with me. I should not expect it of him.

And yet, despite these sensible, sober resolutions, Antoinette could not stop herself daydreaming about the Duke. She remembered the exact deep gray of his eyes and the way in which he raised a quizzical dark eyebrow when he uttered one of his sardonic comments. Just the very sound of his name made her heart beat faster and a blush tinge her cheeks. And when she was out with Miss LeStrange, she could not repress a surge of excitement every time a dark-blue carriage came into view.

But the carriage was never the Duke's. She caught not a glimpse of him in Harrogate and still he did not call on her.

A few days later, Miss LeStrange swept into the breakfast parlor and announced, "I have a surprise for you, Antoinette!"

Antoinette's heart leapt as instinctively her thoughts turned to the Duke of Lyveden. Had Miss LeStrange been in contact with him? Had he sent a message to her?

Eleanor LeStrange sat down on the window seat. "Tell me, have you ever heard of an actor called Edmund Kean?"

"Why yes," nodded Antoinette. "I recall the Duke of Lyveden mentioning him. He and the Duke of Devonshire made a special journey to Grassington to see Mr. Kean. The Duke of Devonshire believes that Mr. Kean will shortly be hailed as one of the greatest actors of this country."

Miss LeStrange looked impressed at Antoinette's knowledge of the theatrical world. "Goodness," she murmured, "for a simple country girl, you are remarkably well informed. Well the Duke of Devonshire has been proved right. Mr. Kean has taken London by storm, and next week, he is honoring Harrogate with a visit!"

"He is to perform here?" asked Antoinette, her eyes shining.

"Indeed so." Miss LeStrange smiled. "It will be the most glittering evening. The *ton* of West Yorkshire will be present.

53

I feel it would be a most suitable occasion for you to make your debut into Harrogate society, my dear."

"Oh, I should dearly love to attend!" cried Antoinette. Then her face clouded. "But Miss LeStrange, have you forgotten the difficulty I have staying awake in the evenings? Why, I should be mortified if I dropped off to sleep right in the middle of Mr. Kean's performance! I should never, ever forgive myself!"

Miss LeStrange laughed and fingered the heavy silver pendant at her neck. "Fear not, Antoinette, I am convinced that the excitement of the evening will be sufficient to keep you awake. Now, the main issue to be decided is which of your new evening gowns you are going to wear to Mr. Kean's performance."

Antoinette was almost beside herself with excitement. She had never before attended the theatre, as Dr. and Mrs. Aston had approved neither of theatricals nor the people who were involved in them.

"No gentleman of breeding would take to the boards," Dr. Aston was fond of declaring. "And any woman who chooses to paint her face and display herself in such a vulgar, public fashion is merely inviting trouble."

For days, Antoinette and Miss LeStrange could talk of nothing but Mr. Kean, and which dresses they should wear. For Eleanor LeStrange who was ever only to be seen in shades of green, silver and white, the choice was simple. She would wear her new *eau de nil* silk dress, with the ruched neck and embroidered sleeves.

Antoinette agonized for hours over the pink silk or the white Indian muslin shot with silver thread. Two hours before they were due to set out for the theatre, she had still not come to a decision. She adored the Indian muslin but was the neckline cut too low? Yet the pink silk, though gloriously pretty, was a little loose around the waist.

It was Miss LeStrange who finally swept into the blue bed chamber and decreed in an authoritative tone that Antoinette would look best in the white muslin. Then she rustled out again, leaving the sullen maid to assist Antoinette in the completion of her toilette.

An hour later, with her golden curls brushed into a silken halo around her head, Antoinette turned to look at herself in the long glass. She uttered a gasp of dismay. The white muslin dress was without doubt a beautiful creation, with the silver threads reflecting the light like finest gossamer.

"But the neckline!" fretted Antoinette. "It is far too low! I should be put to the blush appearing in public with so much of myself in view!"

She hastened to the tallboy, and drew out a length of pretty lace, which she inserted into the bosom of the dress. Much relieved, she fastened her gold locket and feeling well satisfied with her appearance, descended the stairs to await Miss LeStrange in the drawing room.

When at last Miss LeStrange entered the room, the smile on the face froze to an expression of dismay.

"My dear!" she exclaimed, "why have you ruined that beautiful dress?"

And before Antoinette could protest, she had stretched out an imperious hand and wrenched the lace from the neck of the white muslin.

Antoinette flushed. "I felt that the neckline was too exposed," she said defensively. "I have never before in my life owned a dress cut as low as this!"

Miss LeStrange smiled knowingly. "You have a beautiful bosom, my dear. It would be foolish not to show it off. So many girls of your slender build possess thin, scrawny shoulders and bosoms. You are fortunate to be so well rounded."

She laughed as Antoinette's cheeks burned poppy red. "There, I have embarrassed you! But you know, it is an important lesson in life to learn how to make the most of your assets. It is foolish to be shy, or diffident about those physical attributes which are truly exceptional."

Realizing that Miss LeStrange was not to be moved on the subject of the dress, Antoinette said no more, but resolved to keep her evening shawl close around her shoulders for as long as possible at the theatre.

Delighted that she had managed to stay awake past her usual bedtime of seven-thirty, Antoinette was anxious to set forth from the house. But Miss LeStrange was still regarding her with a critical eye.

"That gold locket," she declared at last. "I notice that you always wear it, Antoinette. Of course I quite understand that you own no other jewellery, but I feel that it is a little too heavy to enhance that delicate white muslin. It would be best if I lend you my pearls to wear tonight."

Already, her hand was reaching for the bell to summon Mrs. Lake with the pearls. Hastily, Antoinette exclaimed.

"It is most kind of you to offer to lend me your pearls, Miss LeStrange, I hope you will not be offended if I refuse . . . it is just that you have been so generous to me. This lovely dress, my fan, my shoes—I am indebted to you for them all. I am sure you understand that I have a sentimental longing to wear just one item that truly belongs to me."

Afterward, Antoinette wondered what innate instinct forbade her from telling Miss LeStrange her true reason for refusing to take off the locket. Although she had revealed to the older woman the story of how she was found as a baby on the steps of Beck Lodge, Antoinette had never said one word about the gold locket. She was convinced that the locket belonged to her mother. But she found it too painful, too emotive a subject to discuss with anyone else in the world. She knew someday she would discover the true identity of her mother, and thereby, of herself. But it was a private quest, one that she was determined to undertake in utmost secrecy.

Fortunately, Miss LeStrange, having won the battle of Antoinette's neckline, was prepared to give way over the matter of the locket.

"Ah well," she said lightly, "wear the locket if you wish. It is a pretty trinket. Unusual, too, with that delicately deckled edge."

Antoinette stood immobile by the fireplace, dreading the moment when Miss LeStrange would examine the locket more closely, and discover the engraved letter N on the back. A score of explanations flooded Antoinette's mind. She could say that Mrs. Aston had given her the locket and pretend that the lady's Christian name had begun with an N . . . she could allege that as a child she had been unable to say Antoinette, and had been known by the nickname of Netta . . .

Happily for Antoinette, as Miss LeStrange stood staring curiously at the locket, the footman entered to announce that the carriage was at the door. The evening at the theatre had begun!

Antoinette's blue eyes sparkled as bright as sapphires as she regarded the glittering foyer in the elegant theatre to the east of Church Square. As they stood in the crush, Miss LeStrange pointed out some celebrated faces to Antoinette. "See, there is Lord Rothsey. Such a distinguished looking gentleman, is he not? Oh, and the Duke of Devonshire has just made his entrance." She pouted. "How vexing! I had anticipated that the Duke of Lyveden would be in his party. But there appears to be no sign of him."

Antoinette, too, was feeling disappointed that the Duke of Lyveden had not made an appearance at the theatre. How she longed to see him just once more! But, she reasoned sensibly, if he did come to see Mr. Kean, he would most likely be escorting some beautiful, titled lady. And how jealous I should feel! Perhaps it is best, then, that he has stayed away. Now I shall not be tortured by the sight of him paying court to a celebrated beauty.

To divert her mind from such unwelcome thoughts, Antoinette declared, sotto voce to Miss LeStrange, "Why, there is Miss Kaye—the lady from whom I stole the blue pelisse, she looks in high spirits tonight."

Lauretta Kaye was indeed in sparkling form. Surrounded by four handsome young blades, she swept to her box in a blaze of peacock-blue silk. More peacock feathers adorned the coiled black hair, and her smiling red lips were enhanced by a liberal application of carmine.

"What a dreadfully common sight she looks!" shuddered Miss LeStrange. "So vulgar! So overdressed! Come, Antoinette, it is time we took our places. And I shall ensure that we seat ourselves as far as possible from the spectacle of Miss Lauretta Kaye!"

Dutifully, Antoinette followed Miss LeStrange to a box on the opposite side of the theatre from the raven-haired beauty. Despite Miss LeStrange's disparaging comments, Antoinette found herself unable to tear her eyes away from Lauretta Kaye. It had to be admitted she was garishly dressed. Yet this did not appear to deter her male admirers one whit. She was soon surrounded by a throng of gentlemen of all ages, and she laughed, conversed and flirted with them all. They seemed positively delighted with her.

Observing Antoinette's interest, Miss LeStrange said cuttingly, "Miss Kaye resides, you know, in *Low* Harrogate. No one from our side of town would dream of setting foot there. But to my mind even Low Harrogate is too respectable a place for one such as Miss Kaye. I am surprised she does not favor one of the other, more vulgar Spa towns."

"Which one would you recommend for Miss Kaye?" inquired Antoinette with deceptive innocence. Although she did not understand the reason for the rivalry between the two women, she was beginning to enjoy it to the full.

Miss LeStrange said disdainfully, "I believe New Tunbridge Wells would suit Miss Kaye most admirably. I recollect my mother telling me that at that Spa bizarre entertainment is provided as one takes the water. There is a Musick-house with concerts of kettle drums, acrobatic turns and rope dancers. I must remember to mention it to Miss Kaye next time she engages me in conversation."

As Antoinette raised her fan to mask her smile, the buzz of chatter among the audience died away. The orchestra struck up and the red velvet curtain rose on the commanding figure of Edmund Kean.

The ladies in the audience gasped in admiration as they regarded his saturnine good looks—the coal-black eyes, the noble mouth, the tragic expression. With a swirl of his black cape, he subdued the audience into hushed submission as he declaimed in deep, haunting tones. *"To be or not to be. That is the question . . ."*

But the remainder of Hamlet's agonized soliloquy was lost on Antoinette. Distracted by a movement of bright peacock feathers on the other side of the theatre, she suddenly realized that none other than the Duke of Lyveden himself was sitting in the box beside Lauretta Kaye. He was wearing a superbly cut dark-blue evening frock and sat with his chin resting on his hand, clearly absorbed in appreciation of the brilliant performer on stage.

Lauretta Kaye, however, appeared not a whit interested in the art of Mr. Kean. Realizing that the Duke was sitting near her, she was employing every flirtatious tactic at her command to gain his attention.

Languidly, she raised a rounded white arm to stroke the feathers in her hair. She tossed her head, turning this way and that to give the Duke the benefit of her enviable profile. She fluttered a scented lace handkerchief. She even sighed and then glanced quickly around to see if the Duke was regarding her with rapt admiration.

He was not. To Antoinette's amusement, he kept his fine gray eyes fixed firmly on Mr. Kean. It was as if poor Lauretta simply did not exist. Antoinette noticed the look of chagrin on Miss Kaye's face and wondered what device the lady would employ next. From the determined set of her chin, Antoinette judged that Miss Kaye was not a lady easily deterred in her pursuit of a man.

Antoinette had to wait no longer than the interval for an answer to Miss Kaye's dilemma. The audience left their boxes and descended to the lower floor, preparing to adjourn into the Supper Room. Antoinette watched as Miss Kaye was among the first to make her way up the side aisle. To Antoinette's surprise, she did not so much as glance at the Duke of Lyveden as she passed which was fortunate, as the Duke happened to be looking the other way.

But at the top of the aisle, Miss Kaye stopped and was soon engaged in laughing conversation with a bevy of her admirers.

"The sign of an ill-bred woman," declared Miss Le-Strange, glaring across the audience at Miss Kaye, "is one who laughs loudly in public. Come, Antoinette. Let us repair to the Supper Room. After the trauma of Mr. Kean's performance I am much in need of a reviving glass of wine."

As they proceeded up the aisle, Antoinette noticed the athletic figure of the Duke of Lyveden about ten yards ahead of them. It was then that she understood Lauretta Kaye's strategy. For the dark-haired woman and her band of young blades were blocking the way to the Supper Room. In order to gain entrance to the room, the Duke would be obliged to request Miss Kaye to make way for him. And naturally, mused Antoinette with a wry smile, Miss Kaye would lose no opportunity of taking advantage of this encounter with the Duke.

But the Duke of Lyveden was a man with a mind of his own. Observing the situation at the entrance to the supper room, he suddenly turned on his heel and began to walk back down the aisle toward Antoinette and Miss LeStrange. As he approached, Antoinette's heart seemed to turn a series of somersaults. His lean, rugged good looks and imposing figure affected her as had no man ever before.

Oh please, she prayed, let him recognize me! How I long to hear the sound of his voice once more!

He was nearly upon her. Miss LeStrange's pressure on her arm reminded her to curtsey and demurely lower her eyes in the presence of the Duke. As she arose, trembling from head to foot, she heard him declare,

"Good evening, Miss Aston."

Antoinette could not believe it. He sounded so cold, so distant toward her! Was this the same man who had laughed and conversed with her with such warmth and ease on the road from Linton to Harrogate?

She murmured, "Good evening, Your Grace," and raised her blue eyes to his. No, she had not been mistaken by his tone. His eyes, too, were steely gray. Horrified, Antoinette realized that he was regarding her with scorn, and contempt. Could it be disappointment?

"I trust you are profiting from your sojourn in Harrogate, Miss Aston," he said coolly. "Now if you will excuse me . . ."

He bowed and with a final dismissive glance, made his way to join the Duke of Devonshire's party. Antoinette stood ashen faced, suddenly uneasily conscious of her low cut gown and her revealing expanse of bosom.

Then Miss LeStrange's ice cold fingers were gripping her arm and propelling her not toward the Supper Room but to the street door.

"You fool!" hissed Miss LeStrange with venom in her tone. "You stupied ungrateful little bitch!"

Amazed, Antoinette could only stammer. "But . . . but why are you so angry with me? Where are we going? It is only the interval . . ."

"We are going home," spat Miss LeStrange, her face contorted with rage. "I have heard enough of Mr. Kean. For the rest of the evening you are going to listen to me. It is time for you to learn a few home truths about your future, my girl!"

Four

Miss LeStrange sat tight lipped in the carriage and said not a word on the journey back to Paradise Row. Terrified by the grim expression on her benefactor's face, Antoinette shrank into a corner and tried to determine what exactly she had done to incur Miss LeStrange's wrath.

She was sweetness and light, mused Antoinette thoughtfully, until my brief encounter with the Duke of Lyveden. Could it be that she imagines I put myself forward in some manner by speaking to him?

Antoinette felt perplexed. But it was the Duke who first addressed me, not to have replied would have been extremely impolite.

Or could it be that Miss LeStrange is feeling piqued because I did not present her to the Duke? Surely she realizes that our conversation was of such a short duration, there was no opportunity for me to effect an introduction for her.

Ah well, thought Antoinette, studying Miss LeStrange's glacial eyes, no doubt I shall discover soon enough what my sins are!

When they reached Paradise Row Antoinette had expected to be summoned into the drawing room for her painful interview with Miss LeStrange. But to her surprise, the red-haired woman snapped. "Follow me," and led the way up to her own bed chamber.

Despite her anxiety at the encounter to come, Antoinette nevertheless felt intrigued. She had never before been permitted a glimpse of Miss LeStrange's personal apartments. Antoinette had no doubt that Miss LeStrange's bed chamber would be furnished in the same quietly elegant taste that distinguished the rest of the house. She predicted that the wall hangings would be in palest green, as that was Miss LeStrange's favorite color.

The red-haired woman flung open the doors of her apartment and quickly lit the lamps. Antoinette stood on the threshold and staring around her in disbelief. She rubbed her eyes. She found herself totally lost for words.

She was gazing on a room which was garishly decorated in red, black and silver. The scarlet bed and curtain hangings contrasted with a silver-edged-black bed coverlet and dark carpet. Laid out on the bed was a filmy nightgown which to Antoinette's amazement appeared to have no front, just a few silver ribbons tying the sides together. She turned away to hide her blush, but her embarrassment reflected in the myriad of silver-framed mirrors placed all around the room.

Miss LeStrange gave a low chuckle, "Exquisite is it not?"

"I . . . well, it is certainly most unusual," hedged Antoinette desperately.

"My dear, there is no cause to be coy. It is without doubt the most vulgar room you have ever set eyes on," declared Miss LeStrange, motioning Antoinette toward a black velvet chair heaped with red cushions.

"I do not understand," said Antoinette, with a sense of foreboding. Nervously, she perched on the edge of the black velvet chair. Every instinct warned her that she should flee from this room, from this house, before it was too late. But Miss LeStrange was standing between herself and the door. And there was a strange, hard gleam in the red-haired woman's eyes which compelled Antoinette to sit quietly, and not dare move.

"This," declared Miss LeStrange with a wave of her hand, "is what you could call my workroom. This is where I earn my daily bread. Or perhaps I should say nightly bread, to be more accurate."

She laughed again as she watched the truth dawning on Antoinette's lovely face.

"You mean . . . you are telling me that you are a woman who . . . a woman of . . ." stuttered the appalled Antoinette.

"Courtesan is the word you are groping for," said Miss LeStrange pleasantly. "It has a more graceful ring to it than some of the other descriptions of my profession."

Antoinette sat rigid, numb with shock. And then, as her senses returned, she felt anger at herself.

How could I have been so naive, she berated herself. Why did I not stop and think? All the signs were there for me to read; and stupidly, I ignored them all.

When Miss LeStrange offered to take me in, I should have paused and wondered why she should display such generosity to a perfect stranger. And I should have pondered further on Miss LeStrange's revealing lack of social activity. To think that I believed her when she told me her *elite circle of acquaintances* were unfortunately out of town! Clearly, the reason she has no callers is that the cream of Harrogate shuns her company.

And then there was the man's laughter I heard within the house that night. He must have been here, within this very room! No wonder Mrs. Lake hurried me back to bed with such speed. She must have been terrified that I would start asking awkward questions.

At this point, Antoinette turned to Miss LeStrange and challenged, "You drugged my wine at dinner every night, did you not?"

Miss LeStrange affected a sorrowful smile. "I regret that it was necessary. You see, it was not politic for you to be aware at that time of the nocturnal activities of the house."

Conscious of the malicious note in Miss LeStrange's voice, Antoinette felt herself beginning to tremble with fear. In all her life she had never felt as terrified as she did now. Even that demoralizing scene with Cedric Aston when he declared that he was turning her out of Beck Lodge, had not frightened her as much as the knowledge that she was now firmly within the grip of a ruthless, immoral woman.

Yet from some deep, inner well, Antoinette managed to summon an armory of courage, strength and dignity. I would die rather than show her I am afraid, she thought fiercely.

Instinctively, her hand flew to the gold locket around her neck. Her thumb traced the delicate engraved N on the back of the locket.

Please, mysterious N, prayed Antoinette. Whoever you are, wherever you are—give me the wit and the will to face this woman. Do not let me wilt and stutter in a feeble, cowardly manner!

Miraculously, as if her veins were suffused with fire, and power she held the gold in her hand. Lifting her head, Antoinette heard herself say, in tones of magnificent disdain.

"So, Miss LeStrange! For almost a month you have gone to great pains to keep your *profession* secret from me. Why then am I privileged tonight to be admitted into your tawdry inner sanctum?"

The gray-green eyes flickered in surprise at the venom of Antoinette's unexpected attack. But Miss LeStrange was a seasoned campaigner. She recovered quickly and lashed back.

"Because tonight, my *pretty* little girl, you undermined all my plans. Everything I have worked for in the past is now destroyed. But I was never one to give up that easily. As one strategy has failed, I shall now resort to a second. Which is why you are sitting here in this delightful room, tonight!"

Once again Antoinette experienced a frisson of fear running down her spine.

Miss LeStrange walked around her bed chamber flicking the folds of the scarlet bedhangings, smoothing the black coverlet, appraising herself in the long silver-framed mirror. "I remarked to you earlier this evening that it is important in life to capitalize on your assets. Now look at me." She paused in front of a long glass. "I am quite obviously no longer in the first flush of youth. My face is lined. My body, despite the discipline of constant attention to diet, is beginning to sag. When I bend down to pick up a fallen fan, I creak, like a frigate buffeted by storms."

Miss LeStrange continued in a matter-of-fact tone. "However, until recently I was able to overcome these . . . disadvantages. As you will have noticed, I dress well, to disguise my figure faults. When my clients visit me here, they find the room lit by soft, flattering lamps. I am experienced at my craft. I may no longer be young but I know how to please a man."

Antoinette lowered her eyes in an attempt to blot out the mental picture of Miss LeStrange lying between the red bedcurtains in intimate embrace with her gentleman caller.

"But a year ago," hissed Miss LeStrange, in a voice laced with malice, "Lauretta Kaye took up residence in Harrogate."

Antoinette gasped. So Miss Kaye was also a woman of easy virtue! Oh, thought Antoinette despairingly, how foolish of me not to have realized! But how could I have known? In the little village of Linton, such women were talked about in whispers. But we did not have such a lady in residence in the vicinity. When I arrived in Harrogate, I had no notion how one could recognize a courtesan. Nevertheless, she admitted, I should have given the matter more thought. It is absurd that I did not realize the basis for the rivalry between Miss Le-Strange and Lauretta Kaye!

"Lauretta Kaye," Miss LeStrange went on in icy tones, "is young, and pretty and captivating. After six months I was appalled to find that all my best clients—those with titles, wealth and influence—were deserting me and flocking to her door. All I was left with were the coarse farmers, the red-faced squires, the mean-eyed mill owners. I freely confess, I was in despair at my plight." She smiled suddenly at the golden-haired girl. "And then, my dear, fortune smiled on *me*. *You* came knocking on my door."

How well Antoinette remembered that fateful afternoon. With what youthful optimism had she lifted the brass door-knocker! If only, she thought, I had sought another destination. But where else was I to go? I knew of no one else in Harrogate. If I had not thrown myself on Miss LeStrange's mercy, I should have been picked up by the Watch and thrown into the poor house as a vagrant.

"When I learned that the Duke of Lyveden had taken an interest in you, I believed that Fate had dealt me a trump card," said Miss LeStrange. "You see, I knew that once he learned of my profession, he would probably not desire to call at the house. The Duke is a devastatingly attractive man, as no doubt you are aware. All the eligible heiresses in London are setting their caps at him. He has no need of the services of women like myself."

Antoinette was unable to repress a sudden spurt of jealousy as she thought of the London beauties competing for the Duke's favors. If only I were a rich heiress, she thought wistfully. Oh, to be sure, I should not rest until he courted me to the exclusion of all others!

Antoinette said coolly to Miss LeStrange, "As I am patently neither rich nor titled, how did you believe that my arrival would be to your advantage with regard to the Duke?"

Miss LeStrange appraised the slender girl in the black velvet chair. "True, you have neither wealth nor family. But you are blessed with outstanding beauty. My plan was to allow the Duke tantalizing glimpses of you. If I had set you loose on Harrogate society, to attend balls, routs, soirées, he would soon have engaged you in conversation, and possibly grown tired of you. He is ten years older than you and inevitably he would have found the chatter of a country girl like yourself fatiguingly naive after a while."

Antoinette bit her lip to bite back the hot retort. How dare Miss LeStrange imply that she was nothing but a decorative hayseed? Why, in the coach coming to Harrogate, she and the Duke had conversed with great ease and equality on a whole host of subjects. And many times, Antoinette recalled, I made him shout with laughter. I wonder if his sophisticated London beauties are as adept at amusing him?

Oblivious of the rage burning within Antoinette, Miss LeStrange continued blithely. "No, by permitting the Duke only occasional sights of you. I hoped to inflame him to such an extent that he would ignore all talk of my, er, dubious reputation, and call here at Paradise Row."

Antoinette nodded. "And no doubt, once word spread that none other than the Duke of Lyveden had called here, then this would be enough to lure other gentlemen of title and influence to cross your threshold."

Miss LeStrange clapped her hands. "Exactly! You, my dear, were to be the bait to lure my best clients back from Lauretta Kaye. However"—her brow darkened—"I had reckoned without two things. First, for the past few weeks there has been no sight of the person of the Duke in Harrogate. I frequently observed his carriage and his driver, Perkins. But the Duke himself appeared to have disappeared. Then, when he does at last put in an appearance tonight to see Mr. Kean, he goes out of his way to speak to you. And what happens? You bungle it!"

"But he said only a few words to me!" protested Antoinette. "I replied in a polite, modest manner."

"You stared at him like a frightened rabbit!" declared Miss LeStrange. "You were shaking from head to foot!"

"I beg your pardon," retorted Antoinette. "I had no notion that you desired me to purse my lips, thrust forward my bosom and generally play the vamp!"

Miss LeStrange raised her hand and struck Antoinette hard across the cheek. "Impertinent minx! I did everything I could to ensure the Duke would regard you with lustful eyes. Why do you imagine I chose this low-cut dress for you?"

Still smarting from the smack on her cheek, Antoinette cringed even more from the memory of the Duke's scornful eyes raking over her exposed figure . . . his sarcastic tone as he commented, "I trust you are profiting from your sojourn in Harrogate, Miss Aston."

Profiting! Antoinette swayed in her chair overcome with shame and embarrassment. Of course, she saw it all now. The Duke, observing her in such an immodest gown, and in the company of Eleanor LeStrange, believed her to be a loose woman! No wonder he was in such haste to disassociate himself from her!

Miss LeStrange, however, clearly viewed the encounter in a different light. "Here was your golden opportunity! The Duke's favors lay within your grasp. And what did you do? You stood there, simpering like a country milkmaid. You bored him with your naive, girlish ways. No wonder he turned on his heel and left you!"

Overcome with despair, Antoinette closed her eyes. The Duke was the only man she had met in her life whom she admired without reservation. Although she accepted that he belonged to a social elite to which she could never aspire, his good opinion mattered enormously to her. And now she knew she had lost his respect forever.

Relentlessly, Miss LeStrange shook the golden-haired girl by the shoulders. "Kindly pay attention when I am talking to you! If you dare to close your eyes once more in that dismissive manner, I will take a stick and beat you black and blue!"

Antoinette's fighting spirit was aroused. She lashed back. "But surely it would not be in your best interests to inflict ugly bruises on my tender white flesh, Miss LeStrange. Our gentlemen callers would not be at all pleased by the sight of damaged goods!"

Miss LeStrange turned white with fury. But she controlled herself, and muttered through clenched teeth, "My, Antoinette, I had no idea you were such a firebrand. Well, that is all to the good. My rough farmer clients prefer a woman with a passionate nature."

Antoinette's throat tightened. She was beginning to regret her impetuous outburst. "You are not seriously suggesting that I should join you in this . . . this activity?" she whispered.

The gray-green eyes glittered cruelly. "Indeed I am. I have invested a great deal of time and money in you, Antoinette. I have no intention of seeing it all go to waste. You will start work tomorrow night. Squire Bulton is my regular Thursday night client. You may find him a little rowdy in his approach, but he'll soon put you through your paces. And I will inform you over dinner of his particular likes and dislikes."

Antoinette leaped to her feet. "How dare you suggest such a thing? I won't do it! I won't!"

Miss LeStrange said languidly, "My dear, you have no choice. Tonight, you will be locked in your chamber. And even if you did attempt to run away, where would you go? You have no money, no friends, nothing!"

"I would rather walk the streets than remain in your evil clutches!" cried Antoinette, dashing for the door.

But Miss LeStrange was too swift for her. She siezed hold of the kicking, struggling girl, and called for the housekeeper. Together, the two women dragged the screaming Antoinette back to the blue bed chamber and flung her on to the bed.

Antoinette heard the scrape of the key in the lock and hurled herself at the oak door. "Let me out!" she hammered. "Let me free this instant! You cannot keep me here against my will. It is against the law!"

But her only answer was a chilling laugh and the slam of a door as Miss LeStrange returned to her red, black and silver boudoir.

Antoinette flung herself down on her bed and wept bitter tears of anger and self-reproach. Again and again she chastised herself for having been so gullible, so naive.

Everything they say about country girls is true, she accused herself. You arrived at this house dewy with innocent sincerity, and foolishly prepared to fall into the clutches of anyone who smiled and said a kind word for you. Foolish Antoinette!

After a while, Antoinette dried her tears and sat up. Well, she thought grimly, this dreadful predicament is all of my own making. So it is up to me to extricate myself from the situation. For one thing is sure—there is no one else in the whole world who can help me now!

Her first instinct was to escape. Somehow, she must find a means to flee the house.

But how, pondered Antoinette, absently twisting a curl of hair around her finger. My chamber door is locked as, no doubt, are the outer doors downstairs. And none of those tight-lipped servants will come to my aid. They are all totally loyal to Miss LeStrange. No doubt she pays them handsomely to guarantee their silence.

Antoinette scrambled off the bed and investigated the drop from the window. But one look was enough to convince her that it was hopeless. She was two storeys up, and even if she did summon the suicidal courage to jump, her fall would be broken by the spikey black iron railings fronting the house.

Sheets! thought Antoinette. Perhaps if I tied them together I could make a descent out of the window?

Then her shoulders drooped. No, it would not do. Her

descent would take her past Mrs. Lake's chamber and the housekeeper had stated on many occasions that she slept only a few hours each night.

Sighing, Antoinette subsided on to the window seat. Engulfed with despair, she thought with dread of tomorrow evening, when she would be forced into the lascivious embrace of the coarse Squire Bulton. Desperately, Antoinette fingered the gold locket around her neck.

"Oh what am I to do?" she whispered. "What is to become of me?"

Breakfast tray in hand, Mrs. Lake approached the blue bed chamber with considerable apprehension. Young Miss Aston was a strong, healthy girl. After a night's sleep, she could be refreshed and most likely in fighting form. Mrs. Lake did not relish the prospect of having her ankles kicked and hair torn out by a furious miss being held against her will.

However, Miss LeStrange had explained that they were to regard Miss Aston as an investment.

"It has to be faced, Lake. I am not getting any younger. I intend to groom Miss Aston to take over from me. She is young and beautiful. Men will flock to compete for her favors. And after her initial outraged reaction, she will soon grow accustomed to the work."

"Do you believe so, Miss LeStrange?" Mrs. Lake had remarked doubtfully. "She seems a girl of high principles to me."

"So were we all, once," laughed Miss LeStrange. "But you mark my words. When she realizes how much of a fortune there is to be made simply by pleasing men, she will soon forget her fancy principles. Greed, Lake, corrupts us all in the end."

Mrs. Lake still looked unconvinced. "But even if you are right, Miss LeStrange, what is to stop her going off and setting up her own establishment? Where is the gain to us then?"

"That is a gamble we must take," agreed the red-haired woman. "At first, of course, Miss Aston will resent me. That is only natural. But after a while, I think she will come to appreciate my value to her. I shall be able to show her all the er, tricks of the trade, as it were. And as I am familiar with all the clients, I shall take on the responsibility of weeding them out, so she is not bothered with anyone who cannot pay, or is likely to become violent. Yes, I do believe that in time, Miss Aston and I will become if not friends, then mutually compatible business partners."

Unfortunately, thought Mrs. Lake, inserting the key into the lock of the blue bed chamber, the day when Miss Aston would once more smile on Miss LeStrange was a long way off. At the moment, the girl was doubtless seething with anger, lying in wait to ambush the hapless housekeeper.

Taking a deep breath, and adopting her most intimidating expression, Mrs. Lake pushed open the door and marched purposefully into the chamber. To her surprise, she found Antoinette sitting demurely on the window seat.

Mrs. Lake blinked. Why, the girl was wearing her new pink silk evening gown. At ten o'clock in the morning!

Antoinette looked up, and gave Mrs. Lake a dazzling smile. "Good day to you! Isn't it a lovely morning? Oh, and you have brought hot rolls for my breakfast. That is indeed kind of you."

"Er . . . how are you this morning, Miss Aston?" inquired a puzzled Mrs. Lake. "Are you feeling quite well? No touch of fever . . . ?"

Antoinette spread her arms. "I am feeling wonderful! I wonder if you would be so good as to advise Miss LeStrange that I should like to wait on her, in her boudoir at her earliest convenience."

"Yes of course," said the amazed Mrs. Lake, setting down the breakfast tray. "I will go and tell her directly."

Mrs. Lake was well aware that her employer never opened an eye until well past ten-thirty. Nevertheless, such was her state of agitation that she burst into the red, black and silver chamber and shook Miss LeStrange awake.

Half an hour later, Mrs. Lake unlocked the blue bed chamber door and informed Antoinette that Miss LeStrange would see her immediately. Never had Miss LeStrange risen and dressed with such speed in the morning! But she was so incredulous at Mrs. Lake's report on Antoinette that she could not wait to inspect the girl for herself.

Mrs. Lake went on, "I expect you would like to change into a day dress, Miss Aston. Shall I lay out the blue sprigged muslin for you?"

"Thank you, no," said Antoinette, setting down her coffee cup. "I am quite content with my appearance."

Mrs. Lake was beginning to fear that the dramatic events of last night had seriously deranged the golden-haired girl. "But Miss Aston, with respect, that is an evening gown you are wearing!"

"I am quite well aware of that, Mrs. Lake," replied Antoinette haughtily. "Now would you kindly escort me to Miss LeStrange's room?"

Escort her, thought the outraged Mrs. Lake. Why, from her imperious manner anyone would think she was the Princess of Wales herself, rather than a little nobody here under lock and key!

Antoinette swept into Miss LeStrange's bed chamber and sat down, uninvited, in the black velvet chair.

"Good day to you," she smiled at the astonished Miss LeStrange. "I am so sorry to disturb you so early. Perhaps Mrs. Lake would be good enough to bring you some of her excellent hot rolls. They are particularly delicious this morning, I do assure you."

Motioning the housekeeper to withdraw, Miss LeStrange, who was clad in a light morning robe, discreetly clutched her bedpost for support, and inquired, "You are in good health, Antoinette? You were not plagued by bad dreams, nightmares?"

Antoinette laughed. "My, what concern everyone is displaying for the state of my health today! I am in excellent spirits, I assure you." Her blue eyes shone with sincerity as they gazed on the red-haired woman and she continued, "I am here so early because I wanted to apologize without delay for my appalling behavior last night."

The perplexed Miss LeStrange could only echo. "Your appalling behavior . . . ?"

Antoinette clasped her hands, and said earnestly, "You

must forgive me. When you told me about your profession, and the nature of this house, I behaved like a priggish young milksop. Yes, I was shocked, horrified, scandalized. I admit it."

The gray-green eyes were scrutinizing Antoinette carefully, analyzing every word, every gesture, every slight change of facial expression. Antoinette's tone hardened, "But I thought long and hard about the matter through the night. And I realized that I have much to thank you for. After all, who am I? I am a simple country miss, with no home of my own, no fortune, no family. My sole assets are quick wits and passable good looks."

Miss LeStrange smiled at the girl's modesty. Antoinette was, without doubt, one of the most beautiful girls in the entire county of Yorkshire!

She said encouragingly, "And no doubt you began to consider how you could best turn those assets to your advantage?"

"Exactly!" beamed Antoinette, smoothing down the skirt of the soft pink evening gown. "Naturally, for a girl from such a sheltered background as myself, the notion of adopting your profession is abhorrent. But when one gives the matter more thought, well, then it appears that one's initial fears are really girlishly naive."

Miss LeStrange was no fool. She inquired cautiously. "And what, exactly, led you to that conclusion?"

Antoinette stood up and moved across the room so that both women were reflected together in one of the full length mirrors.

"Consider," she said, waving a hand at their mirror images. "I am young, attractive and inexperienced in the ways of men. This last feature is a double edged sword. On the one hand, it is likely to make me more desirable to the gentlemen concerned. But on the other, it means that I shall be lacking in confidence and the required degree of sophistication . . . unless, that is, I have the benefit of a more experienced woman to guide me."

Miss LeStrange raised an admiring eyebrow. "My, Antoinette, I had no idea that your pretty little head was capable of such shrewd calculations."

"Oh, I have always been a quick learner," said Antoinette with a conspiratorial smile. Then like a flash, the smile had gone and the hard edge was back in her voice. "It seemed to me, Miss LeStrange, that you and I would make an excellent partnership . . . You would supply the expertise, and experience, while I would use my physical charms to lure these gullible men to part with their sovereigns."

Miss LeStrange smoothed back her red hair. She was impressed by what she had heard. So, she mused triumphantly, I was right! These apparently simple country girls may be lacking in worldliness, but they do possess a primitive, animal cunning.

But Miss LeStrange, too, was a shrewd sophisticate. It did not suit her purposes to reveal that she was convinced quite so easily. She wanted every wrinkle ironed out before she would accept Antoinette's words at face value. After all, she reasoned that only last night the girl had been kicking and screaming, yelling that she would cut her throat rather than sell her virginal body. Yet in a bare twelve hours, her attitude had completely changed. Understandably, Miss LeStrange was wary.

"Tell me my dear," she said lightly, "why are you wearing your evening gown?"

Antoinette's eyes danced. "Oh, poor Mrs. Lake was quite mystified to see me dressed thus! But you see, Miss LeStrange, if we are to be business partners, I thought it best that I should come to you this morning and ask you for some lessons in how to best prepare myself for the . . . the work of the evening. That is why I am wearing this evening gown. If you are to teach me how to divest myself of a gown in the most alluring manner, it seems fitting that I practice on the proper garment, rather than a muslin-sprigged day dress."

My, thought Miss LeStrange, the girl really is taking this profession seriously! It appears that she earnestly desires to learn all the skills of her craft. And who better to advise her than I?

But the wary Miss LeStrange still had one more test for Antoinette. Crossing to her bedside table, she picked up a sheet of paper and declared, "I am delighted to hear of your change of heart, Antoinette. And I have excellent news for you. Instead of Squire Bulton I have found a far more illustrious person for your first client."

She noticed the flicker of relief in Antoinette's blue eyes. Well, who can blame her, thought Miss LeStrange. I have to confess even I find Squire Bulton the most revolting creature! She went on.

"This letter arrived for you this morning. Naturally, Mrs. Lake brought it to me when I awoke. I decided to open it myself rather than tax you with it after your disturbed night."

Antoinette nodded, and inquired levelly, "Who is the letter from, Miss LeStrange?"

"From none other than the Earl of Rothsey!" exclaimed Eleanor LeStrange. "He expresses a desire to call on you tomorrow afternoon, *to discuss a matter of a particularly delicate nature!*" She laughed. "What a sweet, old fashioned manner the Earl has! But are you not overwhelmed with delight that such an illustrious personage should desire your favors?"

Antoinette looked radiant. "I can hardly believe it!" she cried joyously. "That I should be singled out by none other than an earl! Tell me, was he present at the theatre last night?"

"Indeed he was," replied Miss LeStrange. "He was obviously captivated by your charm and beauty. Of course, it has to be admitted that the Earl is old enough to be your grandfather; nevertheless, I am sure you will find him a most considerate client. And what a catch for your first venture into the profession! My, Lauretta Kaye would be spitting with rage if she knew!"

Laughing, Antoinette seized her around the waist, and whirled her around. "When the Earl of Rothsey sets foot over the threshold tomorrow night, it will mark the beginning of a profitable partnership between us, Miss LeStrange!"

"Yes," agreed Miss LeStrange, all doubts now swept aside. "I will send word to Squire Bulton cancelling his visit tonight. He will be disappointed, of course, but you can make it up to him next week. I know he will be dazed with delight when he is finally allowed to be alone with you!"

Antoinette's expression was businesslike. "May I suggest that we set to work without delay, Miss LeStrange? I have so much to learn with so little time before the earl's visit tomorrow afternoon. I do not want to disappoint him or disgrace you!"

"My!" laughed Miss LeStrange, "what a delightfully eager pupil you are, Antoinette! Allow me to dress and consume my breakfast, and then we shall closet ourselves in here and I shall teach you everything I know!"

Eleanor LeStrange was as good as her word. For the remainder of the day, Miss LeStrange showed Antoinette how to paint her face, how to receive a strange man into her bed chamber, and how to remove her clothes in the most graceful, alluring manner.

"All men are different," Miss LeStrange informed Antoinette. "Some find it exciting to watch a lady undress. Always remember to sit down to unroll your stockings, my dear. There is nothing more ungainly than the sight of a girl balancing precariously on one leg."

She watched with an approvingly critical eye as Antoinette sat in the black velvet chair, lifted her petticoats and sensuously removed first one silk stocking, then the other.

"Good! That's excellent. I admire the disdainful flourish as you fling them to the floor. An excellent touch, that!" Miss LeStrange crossed to her tallboy and opened one of the drawers.

"Of course, not all men appreciate the delay of the undressing ritual. They may prefer you to be in a more immediate state of readiness for them. For such clients, I have assembled a ravishing collection of night attire. Here, take your pick from these. I had most of them specially made in Paris."

She threw onto the bed an assortment of fine gossamer nightgowns. Antoinette gasped with delight as she held up first one, then another. They were all most cunningly styled with criss-cross fronts to reveal the bosom, and lace and ribbon side ties to show rounded curves and long slender legs to their best advantage.

"They are exquisite," she breathed. Then her face clouded. "But I fear that if I am so beautifully attired, and presenting such a graceful image, I shall find it extremely hard to broach with the client the delicate question of my, er, fee."

Miss LeStrange raised a hand and said reassuringly, "You have no need to worry about such sordid details. That is my job. I shall come to a mutually satisfactory arrangement with the client over finance. By the time he arrives at your boudoir, all that sort of thing will be over. You will give him a glass of wine and converse charmingly for a few minutes, and before long he will have completely forgotten that he is paying handsomely for your favors."

"How I do admire your expertise," murmured Antoinette. "You appear to have thought of everything. It is so comforting to know I can rely on you. And I am confident, too, that the clients you select for me will be perfect gentlemen, and not given to violence of any kind."

Miss LeStrange cleared her throat, and would not meet Antoinette's eye. "Yes . . . well I shall do my best in that direction of course. But you must understand that men are by nature aggressive creatures. In the heat of their passion they may sometimes become a little rough . . ."

"But what do you recommend me to do?" inquired the wide-eyed Antoinette. "I should not wish to offend the client by refusing his advances. Yet if he bruises my body, it would not look well to the gentleman who followed him."

"No," agreed Miss LeStrange thoughtfully. After a moment's pause she reached into a tortoise-shell box on her dressing table. "Take these," she said, handing Antoinette some small sachets. "If a gentlemen becomes in any way difficult, offer him a glass of wine, and slip one of these in it. Within minutes, he will be sleeping like a baby."

Antoinette laughed delightedly. "Ah! I do believe I am already familiar with these lethal little powders!"

Miss LeStrange had the grace to blush. "You must understand that it was necessary—" she began.

"Oh, have no fear—I am not in the least vexed by the matter," Antoinette assured her, slipping the powders into her reticule. "I am sure that in your position I would have done the same."

Miss LeStrange looked relieved. "How you have changed in the last twenty-four hours, Antoinette! Why, you are now quite the woman of the world. I am very proud of you." She glanced at the clock on the mantel. "Heavens, it is almost five! How time has flown. I suggest we dress for dinner now, and continue your course of instruction tomorrow morning. Then after luncheon you must rest for an hour in preparation for the Earl of Rothsey's visit!"

In a companionable spirit, the older woman accompanied Antoinette back to her room. Mrs. Lake was just emerging from the blue bed chamber and swung open the door to permit Antoinette to enter.

"I have made a start on the changes you ordered for the decor," Mrs. Lake informed Miss LeStrange. "I will complete the preparations tomorrow morning."

"Excellent." Miss LeStrange smiled. She turned to Antoinette and ushered her into the chamber. The room was still predominantly blue but now the color scheme was charged with touches of red. The pretty blue bedhangings had been replaced by scarlet drapes, and a bright red rug had been laid on the floor. On the bedside table was set a decanter of wine and two glasses, while the wall opposite the bed was now lined with mirrors.

Antoinette clapped her hands delightedly. "Oh, how magnificent it looks! Mrs. Lake, you have really worked wonders. My, how I shall enjoy entertaining in this splendid chamber."

Mrs. Lake and Miss LeStrange exchanged approving glances. "I will leave you now to change for dinner," said Miss LeStrange. "If you require anything, Antoinette, just ring the bell. Mrs. Lake will always be near at hand to attend to your needs."

"How very kind," smiled Antoinette. "And thank you so much for such an instructive day, Miss LeStrange; I declare, I really cannot wait for tomorrow to dawn—that I may put all my new learned skills into practice!"

Well satisfied, the two older women left the room, softly

closing the door behind them. Antoinette listened to their footsteps receeding down the corridor.

The smile vanished from her face. With a shudder, she closed her eyes against the blue and scarlet vulgarity of the bed chamber. Then she sank down onto the rug and buried her head in her hands.

Five

A tap on the door. Antoinette leaped to her feet and hastily composed her features. "Is that you, Mary? Do enter!"

Mary, the sullen fair-haired maid, entered with a jug of warm scented water. While the maid set down the jug on the marble-topped washstand, Antoinette crossed to the bedside table and poured two small glasses of wine.

Turning, she offered one to Mary, exclaiming gaily, "Will you share a glass of wine and a secret with me, Mary?"

The girl hesitated. "Oh I don't think I ought, Miss. Mrs. Lake would throw me out on the street if she caught me drinking on duty."

"But there is no reason for Mrs. Lake to know anything about it." Antoinette smiled. "I am surely not going to tell her! Besides, today is my birthday. I should be so glad if you would join me in a celebration glass of wine."

Mary eyed the glass which Antoinette held out. But she still looked doubtful.

Antoinette went on encouragingly. "You see, I did not want to reveal to Miss LeStrange that it was my birthday. She has been so generous to me, I did not want to burden her with the feeling that she must buy me a birthday gift. So I have kept it a secret." She sighed wistfully. "But I should so like to mark the day in some small, special way. It seems such a pity to let one's birthday slip away as if it were just an ordinary day of the week."

Mary nodded and suddenly held out her red hand for the

glass. "You're right, Miss. Thank you very much. But I can't stay long, mind! Mrs. Lake will be suspicious if I'm not back below stairs soon."

Smiling, Antoinette raised her glass. "Good luck!"

"And many happy returns to you, Miss." Mary raised the glass to her lips and swallowed the wine in one gulp. "Now I must be off."

Antoinette crossed to the door and stood with her hand lightly on the handle. "Doesn't this room look splendid now, Mary? I do so love all these touches of red. So much brighter and more interesting than that plain drab blue, don't you think? Of course, being fair, I expect blue is your favorite color. I am very fond of it myself for my dresses, but I do feel in a room it can look a little cold; unless of course the chamber has a southern or westerly aspect, in which case the sun would be streaming in . . ."

But Mary was not listening to Antoinette's opinions on color and decor. Her eyes were beginning to close and she was swaying dangerously in the middle of the red rug.

Antoinette ran forward and caught her as she fell. "Dear me, Mary," murmured Antoinette, pulling her onto the bed, "we don't want any nasty loud thumps of bodies landing on the floor, do we? No doubt you are unaccustomed to drinking wine. Strange how just one glass can affect some girls in the most remarkable manner."

As she spoke, Antoinette was busy pulling off Mary's cap, apron, and plain blue working dress. She found it harder work than she had anticipated, for Mary was a dead weight. It was an unwieldy business tugging her leaden arms out of tight sleeves, and heaving the folds of material up and over her head.

When at last the maid was clad only in her camisole and petticoat, Antoinette sank into a chair and rewarded herself with a few sips of wine. What a long, exhausting day this has been, she thought. I never realized before how fatiguing it is to maintain a deceit. My poor fair face aches with all the smiling and delighted exclaiming I have done today as Miss LeStrange instructed me on the arts of the courtesan.

Antoinette blushed as she recalled some of the secrets

Eleanor LeStrange had divulged to her. Who would have dreamt that such things ever took place between a man and a woman? And how ironical that I, an unmarried girl, now know—in theory, at least—just as much if not more than many women who are approaching their silver wedding anniversaries!

But of course, thought Antoinette with a sigh, it is all so different if you are married and in love. How repugnant it was listening to Miss LeStrange realizing that she seriously expected me to surrender myself to perfect strangers . . . men with brandy breath, coarse unwashed bodies; men with wives and families at home; men old enough to be my grandfather . . .

Although she had concealed it well, Antoinette had been amazed to learn that the Earl of Rothsey desired to purchase her favors. She recalled a fleeting glimpse of him at the theatre. Although no longer young, he was an extremely distinguished-looking gentleman with silver hair, a kindly face and penetrating blue eyes. Of all the men in Harrogate, he was the last Antoinette would have expected to call on a courtesan.

But then had not Miss LeStrange emphasized that this was often the way. That her most regular clients were not the flamboyant, roguish types, but serious, quiet, outwardly respectable men like lawyers, accountants, doctors.

Men like Dr. Aston, in fact, realized Antoinette. She smiled wryly. How foolish I was to have been taken in over his relationship with Miss LeStrange. Clearly, Mr. Tomkins the lawyer was attempting to spare my blushes when he told me that the doctor had fallen in love with one of his patients. I doubt very much if Miss LeStrange was a patient at all. Clearly, she was practicing her profession then, and Dr. Aston was a frequent visitor.

What an extraordinary thought! If only I had known of this while I was living under Dr. Aston's roof, thought Antoinette wickedly. He would never more have had the power to silence me with a wrathful glance, or frighten my beaux away, or beat me and send me to bed without any supper.

Hastily, Antoinette set down her glass. How foolish of her to sit here wasting time like this! If she was ever to escape from this house then she must act, and quickly.

Hurriedly, she shed her own gown, and slipped on Mary's dress and apron. The blue dress was four inches too long but Antoinette solved that problem by gathering up the excess material over the girdle at her waist. With the apron tied over it, Antoinette looked far from her slender self but that was all to the good, she reasoned, as Mary was markedly thick around the waist.

Antoinette gazed down at the unconscious girl. Thank heavens Miss LeStrange had risen to the bait and given her those sleeping powders! Without those, admitted Antoinette, my plans would have been scuttled. Poor Mary, I am sorry to do this to you, for although you have never been really friendly toward me, you have never done me any harm. But you will not suffer. You will sleep now until morning and awake totally refreshed—if somewhat puzzled!

Thank heavens the girl was gullible enough to believe my story about it being my birthday today, thought Antoinette, pulling Mary's mob cap tight around her head. In truth, my birthday is not until November. Oh, I wonder where I shall be, and what will have befallen me by then?

Picking up Mary's tray, Antoinette surveyed herself in the long glass mirror. She was not dissatisfied with her appearance. She and Mary were of the same height, and although Mary possessed a bigger, plumper face, Antoinette was confident that with the mob cap pulled well down she would pass at a distance for the fair-haired maid.

Carefully and quietly, Antoinette opened the door of the blue bed chamber. The main test, she knew, would be avoiding Mrs. Lake's eagle eye. If I can only scurry past her, thought Antoinette anxiously, I shall be home and dry!

It had not escaped her notice that although Miss LeStrange had omitted to order the blue bed chamber to be locked, she had stationed Mrs. Lake in a room at the top of the stairs: *If you require anything, Antoinette, just ring the bell. Mrs. Lake will always be near at hand to attend to your needs.*

To ensure that I am not attempting to flee the house most like, Antoinette realized. For although I believe I convinced Miss LeStrange of my eagerness to join her profession, she must have been afraid that I might wish to shrug off her protection and set up on my own. And that would not have suited her at all. Far better to have me working under her roof, while she remained firmly in control of the purse strings!

Antoinette's heart began to beat rapidly as she hurried along the corridor and approached the top of the stairs. Just as she was about to make her descent the housekeeper's door opened and Mrs. Lake peered out.

"Ah, is that you, Mary? Has Miss Aston anything she requires?"

Antoinette took a deep breath, and lowered her voice to Mary's sullen mutter: "Yes, ma'am." Antoinette was almost numb with apprehension. What shall I do, she panicked, if Mrs. Lake orders me into her room to stoke up the fire, or remove a tea tray? She has only to take one full look at my face to know that I am an imposter!

Keeping her head down, and carefully in shadow, Antoinette waited. Then Mrs. Lake said, "Well don't just stand there, girl! Hurry on downstairs, it is time the dining room lamps were lit."

With an inward sigh of relief, Antoinette made her way down to the green baize door. But she did not pass through it, into the servants' domain below. Instead, she flung down her tray, and dashed along the corridor, past the flower room and the china room, until she reached the garden door.

It took but a moment to draw back the bolts. Praying that the door would not creak, she pushed it open, and made a dash for the gate. Fortunately it was now growing dark, so she was unlikely to be observed by anyone watching from the house.

Almost sobbing with triumph Antoinette wrenched open the garden gate and stepped into the lane which ran up to Paradise Row. Thankfully, she took great breaths of the still night air.

"I am free!" she whispered joyously. "Oh praise be, I am free at last!"

But now she had made her escape, where could she go? Antoinette knew it would be fatal to tarry long in the vicinity of Paradise Row. She decided that the most cunning course of action would be to take a nearby footpath across to Low Harrogate. Miss LeStrange had declared a score of times that no lady of quality would dream of setting foot in Low Harrogate.

Antoinette had no notion whether this was true or not. What she did know for sure was that Miss Lauretta Kaye resided in Low Harrogate, and it was for this reason alone that Miss LeStrange shunned the area.

Her mind made up, Antoinette made haste toward the footpath. It would not be an easy route for the path was unlit, and she suspected that she would be obliged to cross part of the Common on the way.

But anything is better than remaining under Miss LeStrange's roof, determined Antoinette, turning on to the rough footpath. And when I reach Low Harrogate I shall be safe. Miss LeStrange never ventures into that part of the world. But to make doubly sure, I shall make my way to the nearest church and place myself under the protection of the minister. No harm can come to me then.

As her eyes strained in the darkness to pick out overhanging branches, thorn bushes and deep ruts in the path, it occurred to Antoinette that there had been another solution open to her. Why had she not run straight up to the Green Dragon Inn, and explained her plight to the Duke of Lyveden?

But Antoinette's steps did not falter. Resolutely, she kept on toward her chosen destination of Low Harrogate. She knew she would never forget the look of scorn in the Duke's eyes when he had regarded her at the theatre. Antoinette was not prepared to risk incurring such blistering contempt again.

How can I be sure that he would believe my story, she thought. It is plain that he is ready to believe me to be a woman of low morals. And who can blame him? He finds me wandering alone on the highway with no luggage, no chaperone or protector. And when next he sets eyes on me, I am in the company of High Harrogate's most notorious courtesan! Is it likely then, that he would believe my tale . . .

that I did not realize the nature of Miss LeStrange's profession . . . that I was held at the house by force . . . Oh, how farfetched it sounds!

Oh, no doubt the Duke would be kind. He would reach into his velvet jacket and hand me some silver. Then he would instruct Perkins, his sharp-eyed driver, to find me suitable lodgings for the night. I should be taken into the kitchen, quizzed by the inn staff, pawed by the stable boys . . . Antoinette's cheeks flamed.

No, I could not bear it! It is better by far that I aim for Low Harrogate where no one knows me. Somehow, I must make a fresh start. And this time, I must have my eyes wide open and my wits about me!

Antoinette shivered with apprehension as the footpath led her into a stretch of the open Common. Far away into the distance she could see the welcoming lights of Low Harrogate. But first there was this menacing Common to be crossed.

Fortunately for Antoinette, it was too early in the evening for drunken revellers to be abroad. Her few fellow travellers across the Common were honest workers who had completed their day's toil and were intent on hurrying home to their supper.

A loud quacking alerted Antoinette to the fact that she must now be passing the local pond. Some way ahead she was able to discern the sign of the White Hart. I wonder if I dare call at the inn, she mused, to ascertain where the nearest church may be?

It was then that Antoinette realized she was not alone. Two men carrying fishing tackle had emerged from the pond path and had fallen into step with her.

"Evenin'!" said one cheerfully. "Goin' far are you, sweetness?"

It was too dark to see his face, but the voice sounded familiar to Antoinette. She was trembling with fear at this sudden intrusion. Without thinking, she adopted a line of defense which had always proved successful against the rough village lads in Linton, when they had shouted impertinent remarks at her.

She simply lifted her head, adopted her most frosty

tone, and said haughtily, "Kindly allow me to proceed. I am in an extreme hurry."

But as soon as the words were out of her mouth Antoinette realized her mistake. These were no naive village lads, easily cowed by the sound of a cut-glass accent.

"Well, well!" exclaimed the first young man. "Who have we here, then? She sounds like a lady, doesn't she, Silas? But what's a lady doing walking by herself across the Common at night? A most unwise move, I would have thought. You never know what ruffians you might get yourself involved with."

They both laughed, and seizing Antoinette by the arms, pulled her up the road and into the light of the White Hart lamp.

" 'Tis nought but a young maidservant, Ted," said the lad named Silas. "Yet why was she talking in such a society accent?"

"Perhaps because she ain't a servant at all," suggested Ted. Roughly, his hand closed around Antoinette's chin and tilted her face up to the light. As he gazed into her terrified eyes, there was for man and girl a sudden dawning of recognition.

Heaven help me, thought Antoinette, her heart beating wildly. It is the two ruffians who stole my jewellery on the highroad near Linton!

A slow smile spread across Ted's pock-marked face. "Well, well! Didn't I say I'd catch up with you again some day?" He drew her close, his broad hands pinioning her arms to her side. "I have a room here at the White Hart, my pretty lass. I propose that you and I spend the night there. I seem to recall that last time we met, you tore at my face like a wild cat. Well this time, sweetheart, it'll be you screaming for mercy!"

"No!" gasped Antoinette as he dragged her toward the inn door. Desperately, she writhed, kicked and struggled. "I won't go with you! I'd rather die!"

As she struggled with the strong, grinning Ted, Silas suddenly intervened.

"Hold back a moment, Ted. I've just had a thought," he said urgently.

Ted roared with laughter. "My! Did you hear that, pretty lass! Silas here has been doin' some thinking! Shall we tell the minister to ring the church bells in celebration?"

Silas grabbed hold of his companion's arm. "Listen will you! You know I've been walking out with that pert young kitchenmaid from Paradise Row? Well she was telling me that Miss LeStrange has a new girl who she's secretly training to take over her clients."

" 'Bout time too," nodded Ted. "That LeStrange woman's getting too long in the tooth for that kind of carry on. But what's all that got to do with our golden-haired beauty here?" He pinched Antoinette's cheek and slid an exploring hand under her apron.

"The girl," said Silas, "is blonde, blue-eyed, young and beautiful. She always wears a gold locket 'round her neck. And the story goes that she's unused to Miss LeStrange's kind of work. All the below-stairs staff are wondering how she'll take to it."

Before Antoinette could move, Ted ripped open the high neck of the blue serving girl's dress. His eyes gleamed as he observed the gold locket adorning her white throat.

"So! It is you!" he exulted. "You've borrowed, or stolen that maid's uniform, and run away, haven't you?"

Antoinette glared at him, determined to say not one more word than was necessary to these blackguards. She knew she must conserve all her strength, keep her wits about her and seize the first opportunity to make her escape.

Ted went on softly. "It seems to me, Silas, that Miss LeStrange would pay handsomely for the return of her protegée."

"Shall we take the girl straight back to Paradise Row then?" asked foxy-faced Silas eagerly.

"No," cautioned Ted. "We shall not let her set eyes on the girl until she's agreed to our price. I'll stay here with the hostage, Silas, and you go and bargain with Miss LeStrange. And don't tell her where the girl is until she's agreed to pay in gold!"

Silas nodded, and disappeared into the stables of the White Hart to saddle up his horse. When he reappeared, he paused by the couple under the lamp.

"Just one thing, Ted," he said warningly. "Remember Miss LeStrange won't pay as much for damaged goods. The whole point of this girl is that she's a maiden. Miss LeStrange will be able to demand a sensational price from the client who deflowers her. So you keep your hands off, Ted!"

Antoinette's cheeks were burning. Oh, the indignity, the embarrassment of being discussed in such a manner! It is as if, she thought wretchedly, I am to be put up for auction, and knocked down to the highest bidder.

Ted scowled. "Oh, all right," he said reluctantly. "I swear I'll not lay a finger on her. Be on your way then, Silas. And remember! That LeStrange woman drives a hard bargain. Don't let her make you agree to a cheap price. It's a prize we've got here, my lad, and don't you forget it!"

When Silas had cantered off toward High Harrogate, Ted took Antoinete around the back of the White Hart and directed her up a flimsy ladder to a room above the stables.

"Hardly the kind of elegant boudoir you're accustomed to," he smirked, lighting a small lamp.

Antoinette sank down onto a bale of straw, and said nothing. Her mind was racing with feverish plans of escape and flight. I must get away, she thought desperately. If Miss LeStrange recaptures me, I shall be in her evil clutches for ever! She will keep me locked up like a caged bird. If I don't make my bid for freedom now, I shall never have another chance!

Suppressing her repugnance of the rogue who was her jailor, Antoinette summoned a smile, and said with a sigh, "Well, since all this has come to pass, I suppose we should make the best of the situation. There is no point in us continuing to be hostile toward one another."

"That's the spirit!" agreed Ted, hanging up the lamp on a beam hook.

"I must confess, I am most awfully hungry," said Antoinette plaintively. "Do you think they have any bread and cheese in the inn?"

Ted grinned. "Oh no! You'll not catch me with that one, lass! Even if we both starve, neither of us is going to move from this spot until Silas returns. You can be sure of that!"

And to Antoinette's dismay, he hauled up the ladder and tucked it neatly against the wall. Then he stretched out on the straw about two feet away from Antoinette.

"That locket," he said firmly, "hand it over."

Antoinette froze. What was she to do? She was alone with this ruffian. He was ten times stronger than she. What defence could she offer?

Ted went on. "Come on, now lass! You can count yourself fortunate that I've decided not to ravish you. I'm tempted, mind. I freely admit it. But at the moment I happen to be very short of funds, and Miss LeStrange's gold will come in very useful. But I don't see why I shouldn't have something extra for my pains. I haven't forgotten that you clawed my face, you bitch. Now give me that locket! Or do I have to take it for myself?"

Antoinette was petrified with fear. He must not take her locket, her one precious link with her past. Never, never would she give it up or cease to wear it around her neck until the day that she discovered her true parentage, her legitimate identity.

As the rogue advanced toward her, Antoinette's first instinct was to claw, tear, kick and bite, but she had come a long way since her first fateful encounter with Ted on the highroad near Linton. She had followed her instincts then, and attacked him physically.

But four weeks under the roof of Eleanor LeStrange had taught Antoinette more subtle strategies. As Ted's grimy hand reached out to wrench the locket from her neck, Antoinette summoned a triumphant laugh.

"Fool's gold, Ted!" she cried merrily. "I warn you, if you dare to lay a finger on this locket, you will not receive so much as a penny piece from Miss LeStrange!"

He hesitated. "What nonsense is this you talk, lass?"

Calmly, Antoinette turned over the locket, held it under the lamp. She beckoned Ted toward her. "Come, see the engraving on the back."

He stumbled toward her and examined the back of the locket. "Why, it is engraved, very prettily, with the letter N. What significance has that?" he challenged.

"You are clearly unaware," replied Antoinette, "that Miss LeStrange's Christian name is Eleanor. Her intimates know her as Nell. Some months ago, she visited the small village where I grew up. She went walking in the Dales and had the misfortune to sprain her ankle. I happened upon her, and assisted her to the local doctor. As a small token of her gratitude, she gave me this locket."

Antoinette held her breath, wondering if Ted would believe her story.

To her relief, he nodded, and took a few paces back. "Ah. I wondered how you first became acquainted with such a woman as Miss LeStrange." He slumped down on the straw once more. "So. I'm forbidden to touch you, or your precious locket. Well, I just hope Silas is wringing a good price from Miss LeStrange. I don't think I've ever in my life known such a frustrating evening!"

Antoinette lowered her eyes, feeling relieved that he had not taken her locket—but frightened, too, at the prospect of what would befall her if she did not escape before Eleanor LeStrange arrived. Feverishly, she considered plan after plan. Clearly, it would be foolish to attempt to overpower the burly Ted. But if the lamp were overturned and extinguished— could she jump down into the stableyard and make a dash for freedom?

But even as Antoinette inched her way toward the lamp, there came the sound of carriage wheels turning into the yard. They screeched to a halt and a few moments later a horrified Antoinette heard the unmistakeably imperious tones of Miss LeStrange:

"You up there! Put down the ladder this instant!"

"Do as she says, Ted!" called Silas. "She's agreed to pay us the gold!"

Ted scrambled to his feet, and threw down the ladder. Antoinette shrank into a corner as the nimble Miss LeStrange ascended the ladder and strode into the loft. Ignoring Ted, she rushed across to Antoinette and hauled the girl to her feet. The gray-green eyes were blazing with fury.

With her hands gripping Antoinette's shoulders, she hissed, "Tell me the truth now, Antoinette, did either of these two ruffians lay a finger on you? Are you still a vir—"

"Fear not, Miss LeStrange," spat Antoinette with a disdainful toss of her golden head. "I am still intact, I assure you."

Miss LeStrange sighed with relief. Turning to Ted, she flung down a heavy velvet bag which Antoinette guessed must contain a fair amount of gold coins. As Ted greedily grabbed the bag, Miss LeStrange hustled Antoinette toward the ladder.

While Miss LeStrange pushed Antoinette into the waiting carriage, Ted called down from above, "A short meeting, sweetheart, but a profitable one! I trust we meet again some day—in more mutually agreeable circumstances!"

"I sincerely hope not!" muttered Miss LeStrange, snapping her fingers at the driver. As the carriage rolled out of the White Hart yard, Miss LeStrange began to vent her fury on Antoinette.

"You stupid, ungrateful, deceitful girl! Oh, you are clearly not the simple country lass I took you for! Yes, you gulled me completely!" She turned in her seat and viciously pulled off the servant's mob cap from Antoinette's head. "Very clever, drugging the foolish Mary and escaping from the house dressed as a maid! Well you shall not have the chance to outwit me again, I can assure you of that!"

Antoinette retorted hotly, "You are a cruel, merciless woman. You have no right to hold me against my will!"

"I shall do as I please!" Miss LeStrange laughed mirthlessly. "There is no one who will come to your aid. Who in the world cares about a little nobody like you? No, you are now totally under my dominance. And believe me, I shall make you work for your keep!"

Antoinette shuddered at the menace in her tone. Tears sprang to her eyes as the older woman dug her long nails into her hand. But she bit her lip to stop herself crying out. She would not allow this evil woman to reduce her to a cowed, pleading state!

"Do you realize that I had to pay those ruffians a fortune in gold to get you back?" demanded Miss LeStrange indignantly. "My, I am heartily sorry I sent word to Squire Bulton cancelling his appointment for tonight. I should have relished the prospect of him going to work on you! As it is, you will most like have a comparatively easy time of it with the Earl of Rothsey tomorrow afternoon. He is an old man, and will inevitably be lacking in vigor. However, I shall ensure that he pays me a top price for your favors. After the trouble you've caused me tonight, I deserve just recompense. For quite apart from the physical inconvenience to myself, I shall no doubt be obliged to increase Mary's wages to encourage her to keep her mouth shut over the incident."

Despite her grave plight, Antoinette could not help but smile at this last remark. How galling for Miss LeStrange if her arch rival Lauretta Kaye discovered the details of tonight's episode.

But Antoinette's smile soon turned to despair as the carriage arrived in the ironically named Paradise Row. The door was opened by a grim faced Mrs. Lake. Antoinette was hustled unceremoniously up the stairs and pushed into the dreaded blue bed chamber.

"I shall return after luncheon tomorrow," declared Miss LeStrange, "and personally supervise your toilette for the Earl of Rothsey's visit. And do not waste your time concocting any more ingenious schemes of escape, my dear. Your door and all the outer doors will be firmly locked. And in addition, Mrs. Lake will remain on guard outside your chamber."

The door slammed. The key grated in the lock.

With a sob of despair, Antoinette flung herself down on the bed. She noticed that the flask of wine and the sleeping powders had been removed in her absence. Antoinette could not help but feel a pang of sympathy for the maid, Mary. No doubt when she awoke from her drugged sleep she would undergo a very unpleasant interrogation from Mrs. Lake and Miss LeStrange.

Wearily, Antoinette removed her dress and apron. It had been a long, fatiguing day. And all for nothing, thought Antoinette, crawling into bed. Oh, with what high hopes did I watch this morning dawn! I was so convinced, then, that I could outwit Miss LeStrange. I should have succeeded, too, if I had not had the extreme ill luck to fall into the hands of those two blackguards.

Antoinette pulled the covers up to her chin and blew out the candle. She could not bear the sight of the garish red bedhangings, the mirrors, the scarlet rug—they were too painful a reminder of what was to happen tomorrow.

Surely, thought Antoinette desperately, if I explain to the Earl of Rothsey that I am being held in my house against my will . . . if I tell him that I am being forced to give my favors . . . he is an honorable gentleman. Surely he will help me?

But by the time he reaches my boudoir, he will have paid Miss LeStrange a great deal of money, Antoinette realized. He will demand value. And it has to be admitted that lust dishonors even the most distinguished gentlemen. After all, despite his noble bearing and kindly face, he was in almost indecent haste with his written request to call on me.

No, wept Antoinette, there will be no help to be gained from the Earl of Rothsey. It seems that I am doomed. By this time tomorrow night I shall be a fallen woman. With my reputation in tatters, I shall be well and truly in the clutches of the dreadful Miss LeStrange!

Six

"Wake up, Antoinette! Hurry girl. Rouse yourself!"

Antoinette opened her eyes and was amazed to see Miss LeStrange herself standing over her.

"What . . . what hour is it?" inquired Antoinette sleepily. An icy chill struck her heart. Remembering that Miss LeStrange never arose until eleven, Antoinette wondered if she had overslept to such an extent that it must be now almost midday. No doubt the cruel Miss LeStrange had come to prepare her for the visit of the Earl of Rothsey in a few hours time.

Antoinette closed her eyes, feeling sick with terror. Miss LeStrange took her by the shoulders, and shook her.

"It is nine o'clock!" she declared. "You must hurry and dress. There is a gentleman downstairs who desires to inspect you."

Inspect me, indeed, thought Antoinette with a surge of anger. How dare they treat me like a piece of prize horseflesh!

Raising a scornful eyebrow, she inquired disdainfully, "And may I ask who this gentleman may be who is so eager to see me that he calls here so early in the day?"

Miss LeStrange had moved into the adjoining dressing room and was hastily raking through Antoinette's collection of day dresses. "Too early in the morning for green, gives the skin an unhealthy tinge," she murmured. "The pink is pretty but the lace is curling at the neck. I do believe the blue muslin would be best. It will show up your eyes and make you look fresh, young and virginal. The Duke will be impressed by that."

"The Duke of where?" demanded Antoinette, slipping into her petticoat.

Miss LeStrange seized the blue muslin from the rail and threw it at Antoinette. "The Duke of Lyveden of course," she said impatiently. "Now don't stand there staring at me! Hurry! He is downstairs waiting for you!"

With trembling fingers, Antoinette drew on the blue dress. Her heart ached with disappointment. So, it seemed that the Duke of Lyveden was just like other men after all. She had imagined him to be a man of integrity and honor. A man who would not stoop to calling on women of low morals. But here he was, so eager that he was knocking on the Paradise Row door at nine in the morning! And to think, mused Antoinette sadly, that I admired him so greatly! How foolish. How naive.

Miss LeStrange herself took charge of brushing Antoinette's hair. Antoinette winced as the red-haired woman tugged her curls into a pretty Grecian style around her head. "I must confess, Miss LeStrange, I am a little confused," said Antoinette dryly. "Why am I getting dressed? And why is the Duke waiting below? Would it not be more in order for me to receive him here, in my bed chamber?"

Miss LeStrange was so intent on her task that she missed the sarcasm in Antoinette's tone. "Don't you see," she said excitedly, "the Duke must have heard that the Earl of Rothsey was to be your very first client. You mind how competitive menfolk are. The Duke has obviously come here hotfoot this morning to look you over in the clear light of day. If you pass muster in the cold hard light of the north drawing room, he will make a bid for you. I shall then have the delightful task of setting his bid against that of the Earl of Rothsey. Whichever man wins, you can be sure it will be an extremely profitable day for us!"

A strange, blessed numbness was beginning to affect Antoinette. The situation in which she found herself was so terrifying, so bizarre, that she found it impossible to believe it was really happening to her. It was as if the real Antoinette Aston was standing on the other side of the room watching a golden-haired girl shake out the folds of her blue dress and prepare to go downstairs to be inspected by a duke.

As they approached the drawing room, Miss LeStrange murmured urgent instructions to Antoinette. "Leave all the talking to me. You are not required to say anything at all. Maidenly modesty is extremely becoming, but don't keep your eyes cast down all the time. Make it plain as you look at the Duke that you find him attractive. A shy smile would be most effective. You've got excellent teeth, thank heavens. Don't be alarmed if he requires you to take a turn around the room. He will be inspecting your figure . . ."

My, thought Antoinette, no doubt I shall also be required to trot around the paddock and bare my gums for inspection!

The Duke was standing near the window impatiently tapping his riding crop against his well-muscled thigh. Despite her contempt of his character, Antoinette nevertheless experienced a surge of admiration as she rose from her curtsey and regarded him. How handsome he was! In the sunlight, his dark hair glinted blue-black. A chocolate-brown morning coat fitted his broad shoulders to perfection. His breeches were immaculately wrinkle free, while his boots were polished to a chestnut shine.

But the gray eyes were cold and businesslike. Antoinette refused to flinch from their gaze. Boldly, she met his glance. Steely gray challenged icy blue. Neither would give way. No doubt, thought Antoinette, I should drop my eyes modestly to the floor. But I won't! He shall not have the satisfaction of imagining he has cowed me. He may have come here to buy me, but I'll be dashed if I'll simper and affect to be grateful for the privilege!

Miss LeStrange broke the silence. "Well, here she is, Your Grace," she said with a gay little laugh. "Is she not enchanting? She is nineteen years old and a total innocent. Turn around now, Antoinette, that the Duke may observe how charmingly you move."

"I do not require a parade of inspection," said the Duke curtly. He went on, speaking directly to Antoinette, "I should be obliged if you would ring for your outdoor clothes. I should like us to take a turn around the Common in my carriage."

"Oh, how delightful!" exclaimed Miss LeStrange, pulling the bell. When Mrs. Lake appeared, she instructed, "Kindly fetch bonnets, pelisses and gloves for Miss Aston and myself."

When Mrs. Lake had withdrawn, the Duke addressed Miss LeStrange. "I am sure you have many important things to occupy you this morning, Miss LeStrange. I have no desire to impose on your time. In short, there is really no necessity for you to accompany Miss Aston and myself on our ride."

Miss LeStrange fluttered her hands. She laughed. But her eyes were frosty. "Oh, but Your Grace, I fear I could not possibly allow dear Antoinette out on her own! She is under my care and protection you know. And I am a woman who takes my responsibilities seriously."

"I assure you," replied the Duke coldly. "Miss Aston will come to no harm while she is in my company."

"I am so sorry, Your Grace," Miss LeStrange smiled sweetly, "but I must insist on accompanying her as chaperone. You would prefer that, would you not, Antoinette?"

But Antoinette, who had been instructed to leave all the talking to Miss LeStrange, looked vaguely out of the window and said nothing. Mrs. Lake entered and assisted Antoinette into the dark blue pelisse and a lovely bonnet decorated with silk cornflowers.

The Duke took a pace forward and inquired in a pleasant tone, "You are Miss Aston's legal guardian, I take it, Miss LeStrange?"

Miss LeStrange paled. "Not exactly . . . I am more in the nature of her protector." She directed a meaningful look at Antoinette. "The dear girl is such an innocent, she desperately requires a mature woman to guide her. Otherwise, she is likely to fall into bad company. Why, only last night—"

"I hope," said the Duke in whiplash tones, "you are not inferring that I am bad company?"

Miss LeStrange choked. "Why no. Of course not, Your Grace. What I meant was—"

But the Duke was no longer listening. With an imperious wave of his arm he swept Antoinette from the room. Before the furious Miss LeStrange realized what was happening, the

Duke and Antoinette were entering his imposing dark-blue carriage.

"To the Common, Perkins!" instructed the Duke.

The carriage set off down Paradise Row, leaving Eleanor LeStrange ready to tear out her dyed red hair with rage.

Antoinette sat straight back on the velvet-lined seat of the carriage. She was deeply relieved to be away from the presence of Miss LeStrange. But why, she wondered, was the Duke so anxious to remove me from Paradise Row? Can it be, she blushed, that he desires to come to some private financial arrangement with me?

She averted her head, gazing out at the race course so the Duke should not observe her burning cheeks. A string of horses were cantering around the course, ridden by fresh-faced stable boys. Antoinette envied their freedom, their youthful high spirits. How she longed to jump from the carriage, leap onto a horse and ride away into the glorious Dales!

It was then that she became aware that the Duke was addressing her. Armoring herself for what was to come, Antoinette composed her features and gazed across into his impenetrable gray eyes.

"I must apologize," began the Duke courteously, "for arriving at such an early hour. I fear I disrupted the household and disturbed your sleep."

"It was of no consequence," replied Antoinette distantly. Then her impish sense of humor asserted itself, and her eyes danced. "Though no doubt poor Miss LeStrange was most discomposed. She is utterly averse, you see, to rising before eleven. So your arrival at nine must seriously have disturbed her equilibrium."

The Duke smiled grimly. "That was my intention, Miss Aston. I had heard that Miss LeStrange was a notoriously late riser. I hoped that by calling early she would be too befuddled with sleep to notice that I was sweeping you off without a chaperone."

Antoinette regarded him steadily. So it was as she had ascertained! He had virtually abducted her with the purpose of arriving at a private financial arrangement. Antoinette's fury and embarrassment was however tempered with a certain degree of admiration for the cool manner in which he had outwitted Miss LeStrange.

She turned and glanced fearfully out of the window. What if Miss LeStrange had summoned her own carriage with the intention of giving chase? But no, the race course road was clear behind them. Miss LeStrange must be feeling sufficiently bruised from her encounter with the Duke not to risk incurring his displeasure further.

The Duke leaned forward in his seat. Antoinette shrank back, alarmed. Surely he would not be so crass as to make advances to her here, in his carriage, with the sharp-eared Perkins alert for every scream?

As if realizing what was in her mind, the Duke smiled and said gently, "Do not be afraid, Miss Aston. I have invited you to ride with me, unchaperoned because I have a proposition to put to you."

Antoinette sat very still. Suddenly, she could not meet his eye. Oh if only, she thought wildly, I did not find him so overwhelmingly attractive! If only circumstances were different and we were able to meet and converse as social equals. How delightful it would be to be in the company of this devastating man!

The Duke seemed ill at ease. He brushed back a lock of black hair and flicked a speck of dust from his morning coat. Then he said, "I will come straight to the point, Miss Aston. I am leaving for London this afternoon. I should like you to accompany me—as my fiancée."

Antoinette's heart appeared to stop. She felt curiously lightheaded, dizzy, and breathless. Had she heard right? Surely her ears must be deceiving her?

"Did . . . did you say . . . as . . . your fiancée?" she stammered tremulously.

He nodded. "Those were indeed my very words, Miss Aston."

Antoinette took a deep breath, and bit her lip to prevent herself singing out loud for pure joy. Somehow, just when she least expected it, a miracle had happened. All her wildest dreams had come true! Unbelievably, the Duke of Lyveden, a man of fortune, position, and influence; the man to whom she was attracted above all others—he had expressed a desire to marry her! She, Antoinette Aston, a lowly orphan with no family, no dowry, no home, was destined to become the Duchess of Lyveden!

Of course, it had to be admitted that the Duke had uttered no words of love, no romantic avowals or promises to cherish her above all others. But perhaps he feels that this is neither the time nor place, decided Antoinette. In due course, as we walk through his London garden in the moonlight, then will be the appropriate occasion for tender sentiments to be murmured between us.

Hastily, aware of the lengthening silence, Antoinette summoned her wits to reply. She still felt dazed, unable to believe that this was really happening to her. But she knew she must give him her answer in the most graceful terms. To fling her arms around his neck and exclaim, "Oh yes, yes I will marry you!" would hardly be an action fitting for a future Duchess!

As she drew breath to reply, the Duke continued, "Naturally, it will be a purely business arrangement and I do not intend to presume upon your time for longer than six months."

The light died in Antoinette's blue eyes. "A business arrangement?" she faltered. "I do not understand."

The Duke frowned. "I am thirty-years-old, Miss Aston. For various good reasons which I will not bore you with, I have decided that it is time I was wed. It appears," he continued dryly, "that various young ladies and their mothers in London have come to the same conclusion."

This Antoinette could well imagine. The handsome Duke was clearly one of the most eligible bachelors in all England. Naturally, every heiress in the land would be setting her cap at him.

And to imagine, she thought sadly, that I was such a fool as to imagine that he had chosen me! Oh Antoinette, she accused herself, why will you always let your dreams take possession of you? When will you learn to face reality?

Steeling herself to take the bit between the teeth, Antoinette inquired, "And is there no young lady whom you regard with particular affection, or love?"

The Duke sat back, crossed his long legs and said briefly, "Frankly, no." His eyes softened for a moment, and he murmured, "There was one girl who touched my heart in a manner I had never before experienced, but . . . it was not to be."

Antoinette listened, intrigued. Had the one love of his life married another? Or perhaps she had died, so tragically young.

"To return to the point," said the Duke, matter-of-factly, "I find myself in an extremely difficult position, Miss Aston. There are in London three ladies each of whom common sense advises me would make an excellent wife and Duchess, but I am finding it devilish hard to come to a decision . . ."

He spread his hands, and Antoinette realized that modesty forbade him from continuing. She said with a smile, "You mean all three ladies are vying so ardently for your attention that you cannot choose between them?"

"That is exactly the position," he replied. "Please understand, Miss Aston, that I do not speak thus out of vanity. I may be a Duke but I fear I shall make an impossible husband. I have a fearful temper and I do not suffer fools gladly. In fact my sister Emma has often declared that she will feel nothing but pity for the poor girl who agrees to become my bride!"

Antoinette retied the ribbons on her bonnet and said thoughtfully, "Nevertheless, I can appreciate the complexity of your situation. Having decided that it is timely to choose a bride, you find that your critical faculties are blunted by the behavior of the ladies themselves. No doubt they are at all times charming, witty, gay and dressed in their best. They are careful always to reveal to you the most sympathetic side of their natures. So you have no opportunity to see them in their true colors."

"Miss Aston, you have summed up my predicament exactly!" exclaimed the Duke. "Believe me, I have seen it happen so many times that a fellow leads down the aisle a lady he believes to be the most sweet-natured creature in the whole world. And then he returns from his wedding tour, closets himself in whites and bemoans his fate in marrying a cold-hearted, extravagant shrew!"

Antoinette smoothed the fingers of her gloves and murmured, "So as I understand it, your intention is to employ me as a decoy?"

The Duke's tone was hard. "It occurs to me that if I arrive back in London with a fiancée on my arm, I shall then have the perfect opportunity to judge the true characters of the three ladies from the manner in which they respond to you."

"How neat," said Antoinette icily. "And when the cream has risen to the top and you and I suddenly become disengaged, what then is to become of me?"

"Naturally, I shall make generous financial provisions for you," the Duke said briskly. "Of course, it would not be fitting for you to remain in London but you could choose where you wished to go—Lyme Regis perhaps, or Bath—and I should settle a proper sum upon you."

He has thought of everything, Antoinette realized contemptuously. He has even calculated the details of how I am to be disposed of when I am no longer of use to him. I wonder if I will be permitted to stand in the gutter and throw rose petals at his society wedding?

"May I ask," said Antoinette sarcastically, "why *I* have been selected for this role? It is clear to me that you require a girl whose face was unknown in London. But as must be apparent, I was not born a lady, Your Grace. How will you explain to London society that you have become engaged to a mere commoner?"

The Duke drummed his long fingers on the window pane as his gray eyes critically surveyed Antoinette's face and figure. "True, you may not have been born a lady, Miss Aston. But I believe you will pass for one in London. It is not just a matter of elegant turns of speech or a certain manner of dressing. No," he continued thoughtfully, "you do possess a naturally well bred air, Miss Aston. You carry yourself well and there is a natural dignity in your manners and demeanor."

Antoinette's inner glow of pleasure at this unexpected compliment was ruthlessly extinguished as the Duke went on.

"So you see, that was the first good reason for selecting you. Another important factor, of course, is that you are available. You appear to have no family ties restricting you. And from what I have observed from your character and mode of living, it occurred to me that you would not be affronted by my suggestion of a business proposition."

Antoinette turned away to hide the tears stinging her eyes. Oh, but this was hateful! Because of her association with Eleanor LeStrange, the Duke obviously regarded her as a woman of low morals, a female who lived on her wits, prepared to turn her hand to anything however shady or dishonorable.

I must tell him the truth about myself and my origin, realized Antoinette desperately. Once he learns how I came to find myself in this sorry situation, then he will view me in a more kindly light.

She began falteringly, "Your Grace, there are certain facts about myself, and my life, which I should like you to know. You see—"

He silenced her with a wave of his hand. "Forgive me, Miss Aston, but I do believe it would be best if we kept this arrangement on a purely business level. I have no urge to pry into your private life or your past. My proposal is that we pose as an engaged couple for six months; after which time we shall go our separate ways and never set eyes on one another again. Now what is your answer? Will you accompany me to London?"

Antoinette was seething with anger. How dare he dismiss her life, her past, with an airy wave of his hand? It is as if I have no significance at all, she thought hotly, except as some sort of pretty puppet whom he will direct in the role of his fiancée. But as a real live person, a human being, I do not exist at all in his eyes!

What a bonehead I was to admire him so much! Why, in his own fashion he is as cold and ruthless as Miss LeStrange herself. He is anxious to be wed. Yet he has no thoughts of love or affection for his intended. No, he intends to parade me as his fiancée and meanwhile coolly appraise the behavior and character of the three most fancied fillies. No wonder his sister Lady Emma said she pitied any girl who agreed to marry him!

And yet, mused Antoinette with an inward sigh, it has to be admitted, that I am in no position to allow high principles to direct my decision. For the plain fact is that if I am to escape from Miss LeStrange, I must flee from Harrogate. I cannot leave on my own for I have not a penny to my name. So I am left with no choice.

The Duke said impatiently, "Miss Aston, I am waiting for your answer."

Antoinette sat straight backed, her pretty head held high. "Yes, Your Grace," she said with dignity, "I will come with you to London."

He slapped his thigh. "Capital! I had an instinct that I could rely on you, Miss Aston. Now, I propose that we drive straight to the Green Dragon to collect my luggage, and then proceed immediately toward London. I take it that there is nothing you desire to collect from the house of Miss LeStrange?"

"Oh no!" cried Antoinette with relief, delighted at the prospect of never being obliged to set eyes on Miss LeStrange again. The morning sun was streaming in through the carriage window. Antoinette leaned back in her seat, enjoying the sensation of the sun on her face and the knowledge that she was soon to leave Miss LeStrange miles behind her.

Feeling warm, she loosened the ribbon fastening the neck of the blue muslin dress. As her fingers played around her throat, she felt suddenly sick with panic. A dreadful chill swept over her as she realized that her locket, her most treasured possession, was not in its accustomed place around her neck.

Frantically, she thought back over the events of the morning. When Miss LeStrange had shaken her awake, she remembered observing the gold locket in its accustomed place in the velvet box on her bedside table.

But with Miss LeStrange hustling me to get dressed, I forgot to put the locket on, realized Antoinette in despair. It must still be lying on the bedside table in Paradise Row!

Urgently, Antoinette caught hold of the Duke's arm. "I

have just remembered—there is something I left—we must return to Paradise Row!" she exclaimed jerkily.

He raised a surprised elbow but said immediately, "Very well, I shall leave you there and proceed to the Green Dragon. As it happens, I have some correspondence to attend to which will occupy me for about an hour. I will send Perkins for you at mid-day exactly."

As the carriage drew up outside Miss LeStrange's house, Antoinette felt a fearful sense of forboding as she left the safety of the Duke's presence. How she dreaded encountering Miss LeStrange again! But I must have that locket, Antoinette told herself. There is no question of my quitting Harrogate without it.

To Antoinette's relief, a footman answered the door. There was no sign of either Miss LeStrange or Mrs. Lake. Swiftly, Antoinette ran up the stairs and crept along the corridor to the blue bed chamber. Her spirits soared as she pushed open the door and espied the gold locket glinting in its velvet box on the bedside table. Smiling, she ran across the room and hastily fastened the chain around her neck.

Never again will I forget to put the locket on in the morning, she vowed—not until I have discovered my true identity and unravelled the mystery of my past. Who knows, perhaps in London I may stumble across a vital clue . . . anything is possible. I shall certainly call on the Astons' lawyer, Mr. Tomkins. He seemed a sympathetic man. It may be that since his visit to Beck Lodge to tell me the terms of Dr. Aston's Will, fresh intelligence has come to light on my chequered ancestry.

But of one thing am I determined: I shall reveal to no one the nature of my quest. It is a task I shall undertake alone. For I have learned since I left Linton that it is foolish to put your trust or confidence in others. Inevitably, they will betray or deceive you. Even a man like the Duke of Lyveden who at first sight appeared to be gallant, noble and wise, now reveals himself as a self-centered, arrogant individual with no scruples about manipulating others for his own ends.

Antoinette crossed to the door and cast a final glance around the blue bed chamber. Farewell, hateful room, she exulted. I shall never set eyes on you again! I am so glad to be leaving you forever for I shall retain not a single fond memory of the nights spent within your walls!

The house was still bathed in silence. Unable to believe her luck, Antoinette ran along the corridor and began her descent of the long, curved staircase. She had decided not to wait for Perkins to call with the carriage. Far better to bid a thankful adieu to Paradise Row and make her own way up Silver Street to the Green Dragon Inn.

Antoinette rounded the curve of the stairs and then stopped, her heart hammering wildly. At the bottom, barring her way to the front door, stood a grim faced Miss LeStrange and Mrs. Lake.

"And where might you be going in such a hurry, Antoinette?" demanded Miss LeStrange.

Antoinette thought quickly. In time, she realized, every drawing room in England would be buzzing with the intelligence that the Duke of Lyveden was engaged to a Yorkshire lass, Antoinette Aston. It occurred to Antoinette that this news was her best line of defence against Miss LeStrange. Surely the red-haired woman would not dare bar the exit to the house to the fiancée of the Duke of Lyveden!

Accordingly, Antoinette said with grave composure, "I wish you to know, Miss LeStrange, that the Duke of Lyveden has proposed to me, and I have accepted."

Miss LeStrange stood at the bottom of the stairs, apparently struck dumb. Her gray-green eyes bored into Antoinette. Then she spread her hands and burst out laughing.

"Why, if that is not the most amusing tale I have ever heard! The Duke! Engaged to you! My, how droll!"

"I assure you, it is the truth," said Antoinette quietly.

The laughter died from Miss LeStrange's eyes. "You are seriously telling me that he has asked you to marry him?" she demanded.

"Yes." Calmly, Antoinette descended the stairs noting that the implacable Mrs. Lake was standing firmly in front of the door.

Miss LeStrange took a pace forward and hissed. "No. You have gone too far this time, my dear. Remember, I have been gulled before by your innocent expression and ingenious lies. Why, it is preposterous! Why should the Duke of Lyveden, one of the most eligible bachelors in England, choose to marry a common country girl like you?"

To which Antoinette had no answer. For she could hardly tell Miss LeStrange the Duke's true reason for desiring to present her as his fiancée. However, she was determined not to quail before Miss LeStrange's blistering scorn.

"I realize, Miss LeStrange," said Antoinette loftily, "that the word love is a stranger to your vocabulary. Nevertheless, it is something which still exists in the world." Modestly, she cast down her eyes. "The intelligence came as something of a shock to me, I must confess. But it transpires that the Duke of Lyveden has fallen in love with me and——"

She was interrupted by a derisive burst of laughter from Miss LeStrange. "Stuff and nonsense! Have you taken leave of your sense, girl? That the Duke may find himself captivated by your physical charms I readily admit. You are an outstandingly beautiful girl. But love? Marriage? Never!"

"I fear you will be forced to eat your words when his carriage arrives here to collect me at mid-day," retorted Antoinette angrily.

Miss LeStrange paled and Antoinette realized her mistake. Panic stricken, she flew down the stairs and turned to run toward the garden door. But Miss LeStrange was too swift for her. Calling to Mrs. Lake to assist her, she seized Antoinette's arms and pinioned them behind her back.

"Call the carriage; Lake!" ordered the panting Miss LeStrange, holding Antoinette in a vice-like grip despite the girl's frantic struggles. "Tell the driver to bring it to the garden door."

As Mrs. Lake flew to obey her mistress, Miss LeStrange pushed Antoinette ahead of her toward the garden door. "If the Duke's carriage does call here at mid-day, they will find you not at home, my dear. I shall put you into hiding. But rest assured, we shall return later this afternoon, that you may keep your appointment with the Earl of Rothsey. I have no intention of allowing you to disappoint him. And no intention of allowing you to thwart me in the fortune I shall extract from him for your youthful favors!"

With the carriage at the gate, Miss LeStrange was mercilessly thorough. Antoinette was dragged through the garden to the carriage with a scarf tied around her mouth to prevent her from screaming.

As the carriage set off, Mrs. Lake and Miss LeStrange sat staunchly on either side of her, each firmly gripping one of her arms. The blinds were drawn and the terrified Antoinette had no notion in which direction they were proceeding. It was only when her sharp ears detected the quacking of some ducks that Antoinette had a glimmering of where they might be.

Could they be passing the pond in Low Harrogate? She recalled that it was here that she had been set upon by Ted and Silas when they were returning from their fishing expedition. Yet Miss LeStrange had always declared that she regarded Low Harrogate as socially beyond the pale. Why then would she have brought her captive here? And to what destination?

This last question was soon answered. When the carriage halted, Antoinette was escorted into the street and observed that they were stationed outside a tall, white painted house in Wellington Terrace. The three women were speedily ushered inside and Antoinette found herself in a small, over-decorated drawing room, crammed with sofas, ornate gilt framed mirrors and cheap objects d'art.

Before she had time to draw breath, the drawing room doors opened to admit a tall, raven-haired young woman. Antoinette gasped. It was none other than Lauretta Kaye, Miss LeStrange's declared rival!

Miss Kaye, dressed in a peacock blue morning gown, laughed at Antoinette's bewildered expression. "The child is confused, Nell," she informed Miss LeStrange. "No doubt she expected us to be tearing one another's throats out!"

Miss LeStrange smiled grimly and turned to Mrs. Lake. "You must return immediately to Paradise Row. If the Duke or his driver should call, you must be polite but doltish. Inform them that Miss Aston has left the house for good and of her own free will. You have no notion where she has gone, or why. Is that understood?"

"Yes, Miss LeStrange," replied the housekeeper, hurrying from the room.

The red-haired woman then took Lauretta Kaye aside and conversed with her in whispers for several minutes. Miss Kaye nodded seriously. "You did right to bring her here, Nell. It is the last place anyone would dream of looking!"

She whirled around to regard Antoinette who was sitting in stunned silence on the sofa. "My, but she is a beauty! No wonder you were reluctant to let her go!"

Antoinette's eyes blazed. "You are in league, both of you!" she accused, "You merely pretend to be enemies!"

Miss LeStrange laughed. "My dear Antoinette, we are astute business women, making our living as best we can in a hard, cruel world. Naturally, it suits our purposes for Lauretta and I to pretend to be at daggers drawn. It means that if ever the watch become too vigilant at either of our establishments, we can take cover at the house of the other. A perfect situation, is it not?"

Antoinette recoiled, frozen with horror at finding herself enmeshed in such a nightmarish situation. These were without doubt the most menacing, the most ruthless women she had ever had the misfortune to encounter. It had been hard enough to summon the wit to outface the evil Miss LeStrange. But to discover that Miss LeStrange was in league with an equally malicious accomplice brought Antoinette to the brink of despair. What chance had an unsophisticated nineteen-year-old girl of escaping from this black hearted pair?

Chilled with the numb acceptance of defeat, Antoinette sank back on the sofa. She was doomed, she knew it. These two dreadful women had ensnared her and driven her to the end of her tether. She had used every ounce of strength and mental agility to foil Miss LeStrange and she had failed.

The Duke's driver would be told that she had left Paradise Row. The Duke would assume that she had had second thoughts about their bargain and had run away. He would snap his aristocratic fingers and return to London, giving her not a second thought apart from a passing curse at causing him such inconvenience.

I am trapped! Antoinette whispered to herself. *There is no one who can help me now.*

And then the silence in Lauretta Kaye's drawing room was shattered by a loud, insistent hammering on the front door.

Seven

Miss LeStrange and Lauretta Kaye exchanged alarmed glances. In the second that their attention was distracted, Antoinette saw her chance and seized it.

Taking a firm hold on the tasteless china figurine on the table beside her, Antoinette hurled it with all her might at the gilt framed mirror over the fireplace. While the two older women recoiled in shock and horror as the shattered glass crashed into the marble hearth, Antoinette shot past them and made a dash for the door.

Ignoring Eleanor LeStrange's outraged scream of protest, Antoinette flew down the hall toward the front door, outside which the mysterious caller was still beating a relentless tattoo. Antoinette had no notion of who Miss Kaye's visitor might be. She knew only that he had provided a most welcome diversion. This was her last opportunity to escape. If she failed now, her future looked bleak indeed.

With a sob of relief, she wrenched open the heavy front door. To her amazement the Duke of Lyveden was standing on the step. He was splendidly attired in a dark brown travelling cloak. He looked tall, distinguished, and very angry indeed.

He motioned to his waiting carriage. "Get in," he instructed Antoinette curtly.

"But—"

"Do as I say, damn you!"

Petrified by the furious expression on his handsome face,

Antoinette hurried into the carriage. Meanwhile, Miss Le-Strange had appeared at the door. Her fury fully matched that of the Duke of Lyveden.

"How dare you barge in here and take that girl in such a high-handed fashion!" she stormed.

The Duke's eyes were the color of the sea on a cold, wintry day. "You deserve to be horsewhipped, Madam!" he lashed. "You are an inhuman, unfeeling, merciless creature."

He took a step toward her. Miss LeStrange paled at the grim expression on his face. "You—you would not harm a weak, defenceless woman!" She quavered, clinging pathetically to the doorpost.

"Fortunately for you, I am in great haste to return to London," snapped the Duke, "and I have no time to waste on reptilian objects like yourself."

He turned on his heel and marched toward his carriage. Miss LeStrange drew a deep breath. "Why you arrogant—"

But her outburst was stilled by Lauretta Kaye who laid a warning hand on her arm and murmured, "Nell! What are you thinking of? To cause such a ruck right here on the door-step with the entire street enjoying the spectacle! If you are not careful we shall have the law upon us!"

"Drive on, Perkins!" ordered the Duke, slamming the carriage door shut and seating himself opposite the trembling Antoinette. She stole a glance from the window and was rewarded with a last glimpse of Eleanor LeStrange's face, contorted with rage as she watched Antoinette disappearing from her life forever.

At least, I hope it is forever, shuddered Antoinette. I hope and pray I shall never have the misfortune to set eyes on Eleanor LeStrange again!

She turned to the Duke and said hesitantly, "I thank you from the bottom of my heart for arriving when you did. But how did you know where she had taken me?"

The Duke frowned. "I blame myself for not accompanying you back to Miss LeStrange's house in Paradise Row. But I had some urgent correspondence to attend to before I left Harrogate. However, I instructed Perkins to keep an eye on the house, and you."

Antoinette was touched at his concern. "Perkins performed his duties most thoroughly," she remarked, "for I was taken from the house via the garden gate in the adjoining lane. How clever of Perkins not to have merely watched the front door."

"Ah, I do believe Perkins somewhat favors his skills as a sleuth," smiled the Duke. "He saw you being bundled into Miss LeStrange's carriage, and followed you to Low Harrogate. Then he raced back to the Green Dragon to give me the news that you were being held in Wellington Terrace."

Antoinette touched the locket at her neck. "I am sorry to have given you so much trouble," she murmured.

"No doubt it is my fault for letting you out of my sight," said the Duke. "I do believe that for the remainder of our journey, I must keep you firmly in view!" He gazed out of the window and cursed under his breath. "Just look at that sky!" he declared.

As the carriage proceeded onto the main highway to Leeds, the sky gradually became overcast with yellow gray clouds. "There is snow on the way," predicted Antoinette, casting an experienced eye over the distant Dales. "It'll be a heavy fall, too, by the looks of it. The farmers will be out now rounding up their sheep."

"It makes travelling so difficult," commented the Duke. "We've had an appallingly cold winter down south. And a few weeks ago when I made the journey from Harrogate to London, the snow was so bad we had the shovels out every morning and afternoon. It took me four days to do the journey one way."

"I had not realized you had been back to London so recently," said Antoinette.

The Duke replied curtly, "I was called back suddenly on urgent family business."

Antoinette laughed. "Poor Miss LeStrange! She was hunting for you all over Harrogate. She espied your driver and carriage at the Green Dragon and naturally assumed that you too were still residing there! She was furious when each day we returned from our ride without having set eyes on you."

"Mmm. I left Perkins here with the carriage quite

deliberately, as I wished my London visit to remain quite private, and unremarked," commented the Duke intriguingly. Then he continued, in a tone which brooked no argument. "And it would please me, Antoinette, if you would do me the courtesy of never again referring to that LeStrange woman. I wish to hear no more about her. Is that understood?"

"Y . . . yes, of course," stammered Antoinette. "I shall never mention her name again."

The Duke then sat back in his seat and soon appeared lost in thought. Antoinette was glad of his silence, for it had suddenly struck her that she was leaving Yorkshire. Her homeland. The countryside she had grown up in and loved so much was slipping past before her eyes. Heaven knew when, if ever, she would set eyes on it all again.

Misty eyed, she gazed out of the carriage window and whispered a wistful farewell to the clusters of stone houses built on the hillsides that led down to the mills and collieries in the valley. She bid adieu to the green hills of the Dales where she had walked so often as a young girl. And she wiped away a tear as the snow began to fall on the springy turf of the moorlands, those vast tracts of rugged land where the wind blew keen and fresh, the vistas were gloriously endless, and the water leapt clean and cold from the countless springs.

How pure and honest it all is, she thought. I have never been to London but I have no doubt it will differ vastly from Yorkshire.

Up on the driver's seat, Perkins could be heard cursing as he urged the horses to greater efforts in a desperate bid to beat the worst of the snow. Antoinette huddled back in her seat, shivering with cold. She was still wearing her thin blue muslin dress and a light pelisse which provided no defence against this unseasonal weather.

The Duke suddenly emerged from his reverie and slapped a hand against his burnished boot. "Dash me, Antoinette!" he exclaimed, "I've been so immersed in my own thoughts that I haven't given a thought to your clothes. You must be petrified with cold in those thin garments!"

Antoinette was indeed so numb that she had hardly the strength to reply. With no more ado, the Duke ordered Perkins to draw up at the first sizeable clothing establishment in Leeds. Within half an hour, Antoinette was fitted with a warm wool travelling coat and a matching beaver hat and muff.

"It is really most kind of you," murmured Antoinette, snuggling her fingers into the cosy muff. "I feel much revived now."

"You must not be shy, you know, about telling me what you need," instructed the Duke as they proceeded toward Wakefield. "As I told you before, I am now responsible for all your needs. But you cannot expect a bachelor like myself to be familiar with feminine finery. When we arrive in London the whole matter will be easily resolved, as you will simply buy what you require and charge it to my account."

Antoinette hid a smile at the Duke's description of himself as a bachelor, unversed in the ways of women. Unmarried he may be, thought Antoinette, but I have heard enough of him from Miss LeStrange to know that he has always found the feminine sex highly attractive. Miss LeStrange was an avid reader of the society pages and often declared that there was not a single beautiful girl in London who had not at one time or another been escorted by the dashing Duke of Lyveden.

Darkness fell. Perkins lit the coaching lamps and the carriage rolled on through the snowy hills and vales, until at last they were greeted by the welcoming lights of the Angel Inn at Chesterfield. While Perkins attended to the weary horses, the Duke engaged two rooms and a private dining room. Antoinette was most impressed at the Duke's concern that she should not be allocated a chamber over the noisy tap-room below. With the landlord hovering in obsequious attendance, the Duke inspected six rooms before declaring that the chamber on the quiet west side would be the most suitable for Miss Aston.

When she had brushed her hair and refreshed her face after the long journey, Antoinette joined the Duke in their private room for dinner. A huge log fire crackled in the grate, and the hungry Antoinette was more than ready for the tasty roast pork, raspberry pie and good sharp English cheeses which were served to them.

As the Duke poured two glowing glasses of red wine, he commented, "I trust you have no objection to dining alone with me, Antoinette? No doubt propriety would dictate that we should sup in one of the public rooms; but after the wearying journey I selfishly felt I could not face a rabble of boisterous merrymakers."

"Oh, I quite agree," Antoinette assured him, warming her hands by the fire. She felt perfectly secure with the Duke. She was in her own mind utterly convinced that a man of his age and experience must have enjoyed many pleasant dalliances with the beautiful society ladies of London. But she knew he was too gallant to take advantage of his seclusion with her. Besides, she thought with a wry smile. Am I not now his fiancée? No doubt he is anxious to lead a virgin from the altar!

The question of their alleged engagement brought to the surface something which had been troubling Antoinette.

"Your Grace," she ventured, "when our engagement is announced in London, it seems likely that people will be unable to restrain themselves from quizzing us about my background. Whatever are we to say?"

"Ah yes," nodded the Duke, laying down his knife. "Obviously, I cannot just produce you from midair. You must have a respectable family, a background . . ." He pushed back his dark hair and thought for a moment. Then he smiled. "How does this sound to you? I was travelling through the Yorkshire Dales one bright sunny day when suddenly my horse went lame and I was forced to seek refuge at a large, lonely house—"

He broke off, looking somewhat aggrieved as Antoinette threw back her golden head and laughed merrily. "What is so amusing about that?" he demanded.

Antoinette sipped her wine. "Forgive me, but to have a horse going lame is such a cliché! It happens in just about every novel I have ever read."

The Duke said loftily, "Since you are so quick to criticize,

Antoinette, no doubt you can equally speedily suggest a more credible story?"

"The mist," said Antoinette readily, leaning forward as she developed her theme. "Even on the sunniest day in the Dales, that lethal mist can come swirling down at a moment's notice. In a trice, you found yourself marooned in strange territory, with not a signpost, a light or a friendly face to guide you.'"

"And how, may I ask, did our intrepid adventurer find his way to your door?" demanded the Duke sceptically.

Antoinette smiled. "Ah. You are a man of ingenuity. Not one to give up at the first setback." The Duke's mouth twitched with amusement. Antoinette went on triumphantly. "You found your way by following the stream. Water always flows downwards, so by taking its route, you knew you were coming down from the Dales, instead of heading upward into thicker mist and danger."

The Duke sat back in his chair and gazed at her with frank admiration. "Capital!" he exclaimed. "My, what an inventive minx you are, Antoinette! So, drawn by the lights of your house, I knocked and asked the way. The mist was so thick that your kindly grandmother offered me shelter for the night."

"My grandmother?" queried Antoinette. "Have I no parents then?"

The Duke frowned. "I think not. If we give you a hale and hearty father, there may be suspicious people in London who might try to find out more about him. No, we shall say you are the daughter of a wealthy Yorkshire squire, who was unfortunately orphaned at birth. You were brought up by your grandmother, and you have led an extremely sheltered life."

To mask her embarrassment at what must come next, Antoinette said crisply, "So you arrived at the house. You fell headlong in love with me. You proposed. I accepted."

"Er, yes," muttered the Duke, avoiding her eye. He waved a hand. "I understand that in these novels you appear to be so fond of, these whirlwind romances happen all the time."

Not to men like you, thought Antoinette grimly. You have too cold a heart, my lord Duke, ever to be captivated at first sight by a woman.

Antoinette nibbled on a cube of cheese. "There is just one problem. Is it likely that my devoted Granny Aston would allow me to set forth with you to London without a maid, or a chaperone?"

But the Duke was ready with his answer. "Your loyal maid is a simple Yorkshire lass who is too frightened to set foot in the sinful capital. And as for your grandmother, well, she has always longed to travel, and visit her brother in Italy. Now that the war against the French is over, it is safe for her to journey across Europe, and she is determined to seize the opportunity before she becomes too old to undertake such an adventure."

Antoinette sighed. "What a gritty old lady! How one admires her!"

"But our fictional grandmother is quite in character," laughed the Duke. "For during my sojourn in Yorkshire I have encountered any number of indomitable elderly ladies."

"Yes, there is something about the bracing northern air which makes us disinclined to languish palely on sofas," agreed Antoinette.

The Duke nodded. "Of course, your grandmother will be secure in the knowledge that you will be residing not with me but with my sister Emma. I own two adjoining houses on Curzon Street thus enabling Emma to have her own establishment."

Thus ensuring that your sister is not forever under your feet, keeping a watchful eye on your activities, surmised Antoinette shrewdly. Aloud she inquired, "How old is the Lady Emma?"

"She is fifteen years," said the Duke. "Her mother died years ago and she has been cared for by our faithful housekeeper, Mrs. Reynolds, and a governess, Miss Welch. Unfortunately, the latter has recently proved untrustworthy and I was obliged to dismiss her."

Antoinette was curious to hear more. But the Duke

pushed back his chair and abruptly suggested that it was time for Antoinette to retire.

"We have a long journey ahead of us tomorrow," he said. "And if this snow continues, the roads will be treacherous, if not impassable."

In the morning, Perkins greeted his master with the intelligence that although more snow had fallen during the night, he was confident that they would be able to proceed.

"The mail coaches have been getting through, Your Grace, and the snow boys are out with shovels."

"How about the horses?" inquired the Duke. "Are they well rested?"

Perkins nodded. "They're rarin' to go, Sir. Yesterday I was worried because one of them didn't seem to be running too well. But it was only a stone lodged in the shoe. I'd feared she might be lame."

Perkins looked bewildered as the Duke and Antoinette burst into laughter and as the carriage rolled out of the inn yard he was still scratching his head, wondering what was so amusing about a horse going lame.

Nottingham . . . Melton Mowbray . . . Northamptonshire . . . as the miles rolled by Antoinette sat entranced by the change in landscape. Although the countryside was covered with snow, Antoinette could still observe that as they travelled further south, the terrain became less rugged than that of her native Yorkshire. Now they had left the industrial mills and collieries far behind them, along with the grandeur of the moorlands and the breezy peaks of the fells.

As they approached Bedford, where they were to stay their second night, Antoinette was delighted by the gentle spread of farm lands and the elm trees, winter-bare, sparkling with snow in the late afternoon sunlight.

They were up soon after dawn to begin the last stage of their journey. Now that London was a bare day's ride away, Antoinette was beginning to feel distinctly nervous about the life that awaited her. That she, plain Antoinette Aston, an orphan from a tiny Yorkshire village, should presume to masquerade as the Duke of Lyveden's fiancée! Oh, the effrontery of it all quite terrified her. How would she cope when faced by the cream of London society? Surely they would soon reveal her for the nobody she really was?

My manners will appear so rustic to those fine ladies, thought Antoinette wretchedly. I shall never be able to compete with their wit, their sophistication—I am convinced I shall make one foolish blunder after another. And how they will laugh at me!

As if sensing her growing alarm, the Duke sought to divert her attention by talking about his own travels. Antoinette was particularly interested to learn about the Grand Tour he had undertaken as a young man. She sat rapt as he described the gaiety of Paris and the splendor of Versailles. He described in terrifying detail how he and his party crossed the Alps and made their way to Florence. There, he said, they danced by blazing candlelight to the intoxicating music of viols and harpsichord. And when they tired of dancing, they walked in scented arbors and the ladies ate deliciously iced fruits while they listened to the strains of the music floating through the warm night air.

As they approached Barnet, they were delayed for an hour by a stage coach which had overturned in the snow.

"Dashed nuisance," murmured the Duke. "I was hoping to give you your first view of London by daylight. But now it will most certainly be dark when we arrive."

Antoinette said helplessly, "I feel so stupidly ignorant about the capital. I always longed to go there, of course, but I never imagined my dreams would come true so rapidly or in such a strange fashion!" She sighed. "No doubt it will seem monstrously large to me. But I have no notion even of how many people dwell there."

"About nine hundred thousand, I believe," replied the Duke. "It is a fascinating city. A place of contrast. To the east along the banks of the River Thames, the streets are dark and narrow, thronged with sailors and the men who work constructing the ships for our great navy. Yet to the west, one is greeted by a vista of elegant squares, graceful wide streets and tall, imposing houses."

Antoinette fell silent, her hands clasped nervously in her fur muff. Part of her longed to be back in the familiar little village of Linton, a child again, building a snowman in the grounds of Beck Lodge. But that life is behind me now, forever, she thought sadly. In a few hours, I shall be required to take my place in fashionable London society as the betrothed of the Duke of Lyveden. I shall be a woman of consequence, of position. There is no turning back. But how terrifying it all seems!

Overcome with fatigue and anxiety, Antoinette closed her eyes and slept. The next she knew was that the Duke was shaking her awake.

"Wake up, Antoinette! Or you will lose your first opportunity to see St. Paul's."

Antoinette sat up with a start. Although it was dark outside, the gas lights illuminated the soaring dome and glittering cross of St. Paul's cathedral. On the steps sat a pale faced girl of about the same age as Antoinette. She clutched a large flat bottomed basket and sang out in a sweet, plaintive voice:

> Come buy my fine matches, come buy 'em of me:
> They are the best matches that e'er you see.
> My Mother she lives in Rosemary-Lane,
> She makes all my matches, and I sells the same.
> For lighting of candles, or kindling the fire,
> They are the best matches that you can desire.
> All you that has money, and I that have none,
> Come buy all my matches, and let me go home.

"Oh that poor girl!" exclaimed Antoinette. "How thin and undernourished she looks. May we not buy some of her matches so she can go home to bed?"

"What a soft-hearted creature you are," smiled the Duke. He leaned from the carriage window and called to the girl, "How many boxes have you yet to sell?"

"Twenty, sir!"

The Duke flicked a silver coin into the air. The girl reached up and caught it expertly. Her face lit up and she ran across to the carriage.

"Thank you kindly, Sir!" she cried, and tipped her basket of matches through the window, on to the carriage floor. Then she rushed off to a nearby stall, and ordered for herself a cup of steaming hot elder wine, poured from a gleaming copper urn.

"Oh dear," murmured Antoinette, as she and the Duke sat ankle deep in match boxes. "I had no idea she would take you seriously about buying all the matches, Your Grace."

"No matter," he replied amiably. "The servants will be glad of them in the kitchen. And by the by, Antoinette. Do you not think it would be a good idea if you stopped addressing me as Your Grace? It sounds somewhat formal, coming from my fiancée!"

Antoinette tilted her pretty head and regarded him. It suddenly occurred to her that she had no notion what his Christian name might be. She pondered the matter, considering which name would suit him.

George? No . . . he was too athletically built to fit that name. Frederick was too pompous. The Duke possessed a searing temper, right enough, but he also displayed a redeeming sense of humor. Henry? Dear me no, decided Antoinette. That name has too many overtones of the self-indulgent King Henry VIII.

The Duke leaned forward. "My name is Alexander," he informed her.

"I will try to remember to call you that," murmured Antoinette, her heart beginning to beat wildly as she realized they were now entering Curzon Street. They were almost at their destination!

Within minutes, the carriage pulled up outside a pair of tall, imposing white houses. The next quarter of an hour passed in a blur for Antoinette. She was aware of a flurry of servants, all wearing the Duke's dark blue and gold livery. There was pine panelling in the hall, and an impressive carved staircase. She was introduced to Mrs. Reynolds, the housekeeper, a motherly looking woman who dipped a curtsey and said, "I expect you are exhausted after your long journey, Miss Aston. Would you care to take a late supper in your room? I will have one of the footmen take up your luggage immediately."

Before Antoinette could stutter a reply, the Duke smoothly intervened. "I'm afraid I was in such haste to show Miss Aston London that I whirled her away from Yorkshire without so much as a hairbrush, Mrs. Reynolds. Her luggage will be following on later. Meanwhile, perhaps you could make her comfortable with some of my sister's toilette things?"

"Oh yes, Your Grace," said Mrs. Reynolds, her eyes shining as she gazed up at the Duke. Antoinette could readily imagine what was going through her head. How romantic, that the Duke was so much in love with the young lady that he could not wait to bring her to London to make her the toast of the town!

Mrs. Reynolds went on: "The Lady Emma very reluctantly retired to bed. Naturally, she was anxious to stay up and greet Miss Aston but I told her it would be better to wait until morning when the young lady was rested."

"Most thoughtful of you, Mrs. Reynolds," agreed the Duke. Turning to Antoinette, he said, "I will leave Mrs. Reynolds to show you to your room, Antoinette. I shall return tomorrow after breakfast, and then I shall show you the sights of London. Goodnight then, my dear. And sleep well."

With that, to Mrs. Reynolds' obvious delight, the Duke leaned down and kissed Antoinette most tenderly on the forehead. She blushed, suddenly aware that this was the first physical contact ever to take place between them.

Rising to the occasion and conscious that all the servants were listening, Antoinette smiled and whispered, "Goodnight, Alexander. I shall be waiting for you tomorrow morning!"

Sternly repressing the urge to laugh with admiration at Antoinette's excellent imitation of a girl in love, the Duke turned and strode out into the night. Mrs. Reynolds wasted no time in conducting Antoinette to her room.

"I hope everything is to your satisfaction, Miss Aston," said the housekeeper, throwing open the door. "Lady Emma has been hopping in and out of here all day, moving a vase here, changing the flowers there, worrying that the colors of the hangings might not suit you."

Antoinette's eyes widened with delight as she regarded the room. Light and airy, it was decorated in gold and green, with a figured velvet bedspread and white satin curtains tied back with deep pink ribbons.

"You brought no maid with you? No doubt she was frightened of making the long journey from Yorkshire," Mrs. Reynolds chattered on, busily untying the bedcurtains. "I'll ask Lady Emma's maid Ellie to attend to you for the time being . . ."

Antoinette fell into bed that night with her mind in a whirl. To think that six weeks ago she had been a simple village girl, to whom London was simply a dot on the map, a place she yearned to visit once in her life before she died. And now, here she was in none other than Curzon Street, one of the most fashionable areas of the capital. Not only that, thought Antoinette incredulously, but I, a destitute orphan who seemed destined for the poor house, am now to have my own maid to attend me! How eventful life has unexpectedly become. I wonder what fresh surprises await me tomorrow!

"Tabitha! Oh you naughty girl. Come here this instant, you rascal!"

Antoinette awoke with a start as something small, black and furry pranced across her bed, followed an instant later by a sprawl of pink muslin tangled around long, youthful arms and legs.

The new arrival on the bed sat up, laughing breathlessly. She was a girl of about fifteen years, with a tumble of glossy dark curls, merry gray eyes and dazzling white skin.

"Oh dear. I am so sorry to wake you, Miss Aston! I'm afraid I could not resist peeking in to gain a first glimpse of you, and my new kitten insisted on skipping in here to explore." The girl dived between the bedcurtains and emerged clutching a tiny, green-eyed kitten.

Antoinette smiled. "You must be the Lady Emma. I am

126

delighted to make your acquaintance—even if it is under such unorthodox conditions!"

Lady Emma looked anxious. "Oh, I do hope you will not tell my brother about my undignified entrance! He impressed upon me most strongly that I must not be a nuisance to you. But I was so anxious to meet you, Miss Aston! Or may I call you Antoinette as we are so soon to become sisters."

"Yes, I should be much happier to be called Antoinette," said the golden-haired girl, warming to the frank and friendly nature of the Lady Emma. What a charming, open girl she is, mused Antoinette sadly, suddenly hating the masquerade to which she was committed herself. How delightful it would be if we were really to become sisters by marriage. I shall hate deceiving Lady Emma. And even on this short acquaintance, I know I shall be deeply sorry to lose her friendship when the time comes for me to depart this house and disappear into the depths of the countryside.

Lady Emma ran across the room and pulled the bell. "May we have breakfast together in your bedchamber, Antoinette? It will be such a treat! Alexander will rarely allow it. He says it shows a lack of discipline to lie abed in the mornings. He likes to see me up and working at my lessons by ten."

"I've no doubt he will excuse you just this once," Antoinette assured her, stroking the kitten's silky black head.

When Lady Emma had ordered their breakfast, she drew up a gold velvet stool and remarked, "How lovely you are, Antoinette! I have never before seen eyes of such a deep blue. And your skin has such a pretty bloom to it! Oh, I am so glad Alexander fell in love with you. I have always been afraid he would choose that haughty Lady Anne Monteith as his bride. Or worse, Lady Susannah Clegg with her simpering ways and affected airs."

Antoinette pricked up her ears. So, it appeared that the Lady Anne and Lady Susannah were two of the ladies who would be "under trial" during his fake engagement to herself. Antoinette felt a pang of pity for them. How terrible to imagine that your chances of becoming Duchess of Lyveden had been dashed by an unknown girl from Yorkshire—and worse, not to know that your every gesture, word and action were under careful scrutiny by the cold-hearted Duke. Which one of them would pass the test and be rewarded so unexpectedly with the Lyveden family tiara?

But wait—had not the Duke mentioned a third girl from whom he was to make his choice? Antoinette wondered who she could be.

The maid brought in hot coffee, rolls, ham, toast, jam and marmalade. Lady Emma poured a saucerful of milk for the kitten and confided, "I can't tell you how relieved I am that Alexander has actually fallen in love. You see, when he told me he was to be wed I feared that he had committed himself to someone purely because of my own wild behavior."

"I do not understand," said Antoinette, sipping her coffee. "How would your actions affect something so serious as the Duke—as Alexander's wedding plans?"

Lady Emma was silent for a moment. Then she burst out: "It all came to pass because Alexander will insist on treating me as a child! I shall be sixteen in six months' time, Antoinette. Yet he will not allow me to attend a single ball or supper party. My day is filled with lessons, dancing classes, and rides with my governess in the park. Then after an early supper I am packed off to bed. It is so unfair! Lady Susannah's sister is the same age as I, yet she is practically *Out*. Whereas I am allowed no social life whatsoever."

"That does sound a little harsh," agreed Antoinette. "But no doubt your brother has only your best interests in mind. No doubt he desires to protect you. Although I am a stranger myself to London society, I understand that for a young, unsophisticated girl the fashionable whirl can be extremely taxing."

"But I wanted to see for myself," protested Lady Emma. Her gray eyes twinkled mischievously as she went on: "So when Alexander went north, I seized my chance. My governess's brother, Ralph Welch, invited me to go with him to the Frost Fair. And I agreed!"

"The Frost Fair?" inquired Antoinette. "What is that?"

"Oh, it is a very rare happening," explained the dark-haired girl taking the sleepy kitten onto her lap. "Because of the severe winter, the River Thames froze right over between London Bridge and Blackfriars. Well, it is in the character of Londoners you know, to take full advantage of every situation. So they set up a fair on the ice."

"How very novel," smiled Antoinette. "Were there swings and skittle stalls?"

"Yes! And pedlars, ballad hawkers, pie-men and even a wheel of fortune. At night they lit torches along the edge of the ice. So pretty! Ralph called for me here after supper, and we spent three hours at the fair. I drank mulled wine and we danced across the ice. Oh, it was such fun!"

"But surely you did not accompany Mr. Welch without a chaperone?" demanded Antoinette.

Lady Emma shrugged. "I know it was wrong of me, Antoinette. Miss Welch, my governess, would have accompanied us but she felt unwell that evening. Rather than disappoint me, she allowed me to go alone with her brother. And I came to no harm—I was safely home by half past ten."

Antoinette was shocked at the irresponsible behavior of the governess. To have allowed her charge to leave the house at night and unchaperoned, was rash indeed. No wonder the Duke had dismissed her.

"Alexander might never have discovered the truth of the matter, but Mrs. Reynolds sent word up to him. He came galloping back from Harrogate in the most fearful rage!" Lady Emma shuddered at the memory. "Miss Welch was cast from the house and I was treated to a severe spanking. Be warned, Antoinette! My brother is a wonderful man in many ways but when his temper is up he is quite terrifying!"

Indeed? thought Antoinette hotly. Well if he dares raise his hand to me he'll receive full measure in return. He may be a peer of the realm, and I a poor orphan, but I'll teach him to treat me with respect!

Lady Emma went on: "Then the next day, he called me into the library for a long talk. He told me he was worried because since our parents died I have had no proper family life, no parental control or correction. He disappeared back to Harrogate and then, only yesterday, I received his letter telling me that he was betrothed!"

So that was the urgent correspondence which had taken him back to the Green Dragon instead of accompanying me to Paradise Row when I went to collect my locket, thought Antoinette. He must have written his letter and instructed the messenger to ride night and day to Lady Emma in London.

"You can imagine my consternation," declared Lady Emma, her gray eyes wide. "I thought I was to be confronted by some hard-faced northern woman as my future sister. But as soon as I set eyes on you I knew my brother must have fallen headlong in love with you! Do tell me how you met. What were your very first words to my brother? Oh, it is all so romantic!"

Whilst Antoinette recounted the fictional tale of her meeting with the Duke at her grandmother's lonely house in the Dales, her mind was following a different track. So, she mused, the real reason behind the Duke's urgent desire to wed is his wish to provide a secure family background for his sister Emma. She is soon to come *Out*. With her striking good looks, and the Lyveden name and fortune, she will no doubt speedily attract a score of beaux. And with the best will in the world, it will not be possible for the Duke to supervise her every moment of the day. She is young and clearly impressionable. It would only need one rogue of a fortune hunter to sweep her off her feet and abduct her to Gretna Green, and her life would be ruined. But with a married sister to act as guide and chaperone, the Duke would feel easier in his mind as Lady Emma embarked on her first season.

With breakfast over, Lady Emma withdrew while Antoinette dressed and completed her toilette. Then Antoinette made her way down to the cream and gold morning room where Lady Emma was kneeling in front of the fire attempting to read the latest issue of *La Belle Assemblee*. Every time she turned a page, Tabitha leaped upon it and tore a hole in the paper.

Laughing, Antoinette took the girdle from her waist and ran it snake-like along the carpet. The kitten eagerly gave chase and soon the two girls and the kitten were racing around the room, ending in a tumbled, laughing heap on the floor.

Neither noticed the door open, and the entrance of a tall, auburn-haired young woman. She was fashionably dressed in a chestnut colored morning dress, adorned with a beautiful amber necklace.

Impatiently, she rapped on the walnut writing table. The two girls whirled around, the laughter dying on their lips as she declared icily, "What is this unseemly spectacle?" She glared at Antoinette. "Are you unaware that the Duke insists on his sister being seated in the schoolroom by no later than ten a.m.? He will hardly regard this fracas in the morning room as an auspicious beginning to your first day as governess!"

Eight

Slowly, Antoinette rose to her feet. She was painfully conscious of her limp, travel-stained, blue muslin gown, and her hair, in disarray after the romp with the kitten. Little wonder that this tall, elegantly dressed lady had mistaken her for Lady Emma's new governess! How shaming, thought Antoinette wretchedly. Thank heavens the Duke is not present to witness the scene!

Before Antoinette could utter a word, there was a peal of laughter from Lady Emma. "Lady Anne, what a droll sense of humor you have! Of course Miss Aston is not my new governess. Alexander only returned from Harrogate last night and he has not yet had the opportunity to interview any harridans for the position."

"Impudent minx!" declared the Duke of Lyveden with mock severity at the door. "Just for that, I have a good mind to employ a real tartar as your new governess." He strode across the room and kissed first his sister, and then Antoinette on the cheek.

Antoinette could not meet his eyes. Heavens, she thought, if I am to pose successfully as the Duke's fiancée for the next six months, I must stop blushing every time he kisses me good-day. What is it, I wonder, about the physical presence of this man which whirls me into such a confused state?

The Duke turned and bowed to the auburn-haired woman. "Good morning, Anne. I am delighted to have the pleasure of introducing you to Miss Aston. Antoinette, may I present Lady Anne Monteith."

The two ladies bowed. The Duke continued with a smile. "You are the first outside the family to hear the news, Anne. Miss Aston has done me the honor of agreeing to become my wife."

Lady Anne Monteith blanched. "She . . . she is your fiancée?" she gasped, her ice-blue eyes boring into Antoinette.

Antoinette gazed steadily back. So this was the Lady Anne who had hoped herself to become Duchess of Lyveden! How would she react, Antoinette wondered, now that she imagined her chances of wedding the Duke were dashed? Antoinette was aware that the Duke, while affecting to tease the playful kitten, was in fact quietly regarding Lady Anne with keen interest.

Although Antoinette had taken an instant dislike to the auburn-haired woman, she could not but admire the speed and grace of her recovery. She had clearly been shocked to the core by the news of the engagement. But within seconds, she was smiling broadly and had advanced across the room to embrace Antoinette.

"My dear! I am delighted for you. Let me be the first to congratulate you."

The Duke looked impressed at such generosity of spirit. But his sister had all her wits about her. "Why, Lady Anne!" she protested, laughing, "what are you thinking of? Surely it is correct to congratulate the *gentleman* on his engagement—not the lady!"

Antoinette repressed a smile. She realized that Lady Anne had made no slip of the tongue.

But Lady Anne Monteith was too skilful a campaigner to lose her poise at the hands of a mere fifteen-year-old girl. She waved a careless hand and replied lightly, "My, Emma, how prosaic you are becoming! Naturally, I included both Alexander and Miss Aston in my sentiments. Alexander is to be congratulated in finding himself such a beautiful bride, while Miss Aston is to be commended for having the good sense to accept him." She smiled at the Duke, and inquired sweetly, "Is it to be a Spring wedding, Alexander? Miss Aston would make the most enchanting May bride!"

Again, the barb was not lost on Antoinette. Were not May weddings regarded as notoriously unlucky? She detected a flash of relief cross the Lady Anne's pale blue eyes as the Duke said, "We shall set the day at about six months hence, Anne. Miss Aston is fresh down from Yorkshire and will need time to adjust to London life."

"Ah yes, of course," murmured Lady Anne. "She is so sweet, so docile, Alexander! Tell me, do all Yorkshire girls have so little to say for themselves?"

Oh how Antoinette longed to wring Lady Anne's aristocratic neck! But she steeled herself to reply pleasantly, "I find it a good rule in life, Lady Anne, never to waste my breath unless I have something worthwhile to say."

"Then to be sure," smiled Lady Anne, moving hastily aside as the kitten made a dive for her ankles, "we shall all wait with bated breath for the pearls of wisdom to drop from your lips."

Lady Emma bent to rescue the kitten from Lady Anne's boot and inquired of her brother. "Shall we have an engagement ball, Alexander? Oh do say yes! It would be such fun!"

Antoinette felt a stab of alarm at the prospect. A society ball with herself as the prize exhibit. Oh, what a terrifying thought. Especially if all the ladies of the *haute monde* were cast in the same supercilious mold as Lady Anne.

To her relief, the Duke shook his head. "What a transparent little creature you are, Emma! Admit it, the main reason you would like me to hold a ball is to enable yourself to attend!"

"Yes that is quite true," pouted Lady Emma. "I am fifteen-years-old, Alexander, and I do so long for the day to come when I may wear my very first ball gown and put my hair up. I am so tired of my schoolgirl smocks, and lessons, and being sent to bed every night after supper!"

The Duke frowned. "I have told you before, Emma! I will not have my sister coming *Out* into society at the tender age of fifteen. Now kindly remove yourself to the schoolroom and attend to your lessons. Have you completed that task I set you on the varying climates of all the European countries?"

The dark-haired girl hung her head. "It is so tedious, Alexander! I was hoping you would allow me to go shopping with Antoinette. After all, she is new in London and will need a guide, and it would be boring for you to trail around milliners and dressmakers in Bond Street."

"Your brother is right," said Lady Anne, laying a hand on the girl's arm. "You would do best to attend to your lessons. Why, you have years and years ahead of you yet for shopping and dancing till dawn! And if you are agreeable, Alexander, I should be delighted to offer myself as a guide for your fiancée."

The Duke smiled warmly at Lady Anne. "That is most handsome of you. You have excellent taste and I know I can rely on you to introduce Antoinette to establishments of quality and flair."

With that, he led a sulky Lady Emma away to supervise the beginning of her day's studies. Antoinette envied the girl. She would far rather have sat snugly in a schoolroom than endured a morning's shopping with the patronizing Lady Anne.

"Shall we away?" asked Lady Anne. "My carriage is outside." Then she hesitated by the door and cast an amused glance at Antoinette's mud splashed blue muslin dress. "Oh—but no doubt you are anxious to change your gown before we depart?"

Antoinette decided that it was high time she threw herself whole-heartedly into her role as the Duke's betrothed. If I allow Lady Anne to get the better of me now, Antoinette realized, she will regard me as easy prey and make my life a misery for the next six months.

With a gay laugh, Antoinette flicked the folds of the blue muslin. "My dear, I know it seems impossible to believe. But the fact is that this is the only dress I have in London to my name!"

Taking Lady Anne's arm, Antoinette guided her toward the door, declaring conspiratorally, "Alexander is such a romantic! He positively carried me off from my grandmother's house in the Dales before my maid had time to pack for me.

'But what about my clothes,' I protested. 'Buy some more in the capital,' he instructed me. 'I can't wait to whisk you to London to introduce you to my sister!' Now tell me, Lady Anne, is that not the most devastating thing you ever heard?"

"Extraordinary," commented Lady Anne as they entered her well-appointed carriage. "But then Alexander is a most unusual person. One can never be sure quite what he will do next. I have known him all my life, you know. We are dear, dear friends." She gave the driver instructions to proceed to Bond Street and then remarked thoughtfully, "You say your people are from the Dales? You must be acquainted, then, with my cousin Frederick—Lord Hebdon of Hebdon Hall?"

Antoinette's heart sank. Was she to be exposed as an imposter so speedily? Of course she had heard of Lord Hebdon. His residence, Hebdon Hall, was celebrated throughout all Yorkshire as the venue for the most splendid hunt ball of the season. One year, Dr. Aston had been called to the Hall on the night of the ball to attend to a lady with a sprained ankle. He had returned quivering with fury, denouncing the extravagance of the scene.

"No less than four orchestras, I tell you, Edith," he had ranted to his wife. "And all the chandeliers blazing, twenty courses served at dinner, and ladies with gowns cut so low that even I, a medical man, was put to the blush!"

Antoinette bent dutifully over the sampler she was embroidering, sighing with envy. How she had longed to attend such a glittering occasion!

Lady Anne raised a languid hand in greeting to Lady Holland as she swept past in her pale blue carriage, and probed further: "Unfortunately, pressing engagements in London prevented me travelling north to Frederick's last hunt ball. But I understand everyone, but everyone was there?"

"So I believe," replied Antoinette, calmly, her mind racing. "Regrettably, I have never had the opportunity to attend balls as my grandmother possessed this quaint notion that crowds alarm me. I believe that as a child I was taken to the opera and fainted in the crush. My dear grandmother refused to believe that I had grown out of the affliction and has ever since encouraged me to partake in only tranquil entertainments."

Antoinette drew an inward breath at the enormity of this falsehood. How lightly the phrase, *I was taken to the opera*, had tripped off her tongue. When in truth, the only dramatic event she had attended in her life had been to see Edmund Kean, accompanied by the odious Miss LeStrange!

Lady Anne raised a surprised eyebrow. "But did you not rebel? Never to attend a ball! Why that is harsh indeed on a young girl."

"No doubt it sounds so," smiled Antoinette serenely, "but you see, I would never do anything to vex my grandmother. Since my poor parents died when I was so young, she has been a tower of strength and kindness to me. She devoted herself to me and I would not dream of repaying that affection by acting against her wishes."

Inevitably, Lady Anne was curious for details on how Antoinette had met the Duke. When Antoinette had recounted the tale of how the Duke had found himself lost in the mist, Lady Anne remarked archly, "My, it is fortunate then that the Duke arrived alone, and was not accompanied by the Duke of Devonshire and a boisterous party. With your grandmother's aversion to crowds, he would most like have been turned away at the door and hence missed the glorious opportunity of falling in love with you!"

"Yes, that would have been tragic indeed," sighed Antoinette, lowering her eyes to conceal her merriment.

Lady Anne seemed unable to leave the subject alone. Like a terrier worrying at a bone, she went on: "It is obvious to me now why Alexander found himself so speedily captivated by you. With your sheltered upbringing he clearly imagined that you would be a good influence on his sister." She laughed spitefully. "Poor little Emma! Wait until she hears that you are nineteen and have never attended a ball. If the Duke abdures her to follow your example, Emma will be tearing out her pretty black curls with rage!"

Now the carriage was turning into Bond Street. Never in her life had Antoinette witnessed such an array of elegant, fashionably dressed ladies and gentlemen. At last the snows had melted and the long hard winter was over. And it seemed to Antoinette as if the entire *haute monde* had dressed in their best and thronged into Bond Street to enjoy promenading in the welcome April sunshine.

As Lady Anne's carriage drew to a halt, Antoinette observed the admiring eyes of many young bucks turned in the direction of the auburn-haired woman. The regal Lady Anne ignored them all. Briskly, she swept Antoinette from the dressmaker to the haberdasher, to the milliner and the mercer. At each establishment Lady Anne was greeted with the respect due to a long-standing and influential patron.

At first, Antoinette was happy to stand quietly by and allow Lady Anne to take complete charge. Confidently, Lady Anne consulted with the dressmaker and chose for Antoinette a dazzling selection of carriage dresses, walking clothes, riding habits, day, afternoon and evening gowns. What a fortune this must be costing, thought Antoinette, unable to restrain a *frisson* of pride as she heard Lady Anne casually instruct the dressmaker to send the account to the Duke of Lyveden in Curzon Street.

But it was at the mercers, however, that Antoinette began to feel a prickle of unease. They had come to inspect the bales of muslins, silks and velvets, and to choose the fabrics which would be sent around to the dressmaker making Antoinette's new wardrobe. Once again, Lady Anne strode purposefully around the shop making her selection while the mercer hurriedly scribbled down her instructions.

"We will take the turquoise blue sarsonet, and that pretty green silk. Then for Miss Aston's riding habit, I think the dark burgundy wool—"

"No," interrupted Antoinette, suddenly coming to her senses. "With respect, Lady Anne, I do not believe those colors are at all suitable."

Lady Anne smiled indulgently. "My dear Miss Aston, I do feel it would be best if you allowed yourself to be guided by me in these matters. I appreciate that coming from the north as you do, you are not familiar with the range and variety of fabrics and colors which are available to us here in the capital."

But Antoinette was not going to be put down by a remark intended to make her feel like an ignorant hayseed. She saw now what a subtle game Lady Anne was playing. At the dressmakers, Lady Anne had been careful to choose for Antoinette styles which suited to perfection her slim frame and golden coloring. Having gained Antoinette's confidence in the quality of her taste, Lady Anne was now attempting to undermine the beauty of the styles by selecting fabrics which would look ill against Antoinette's fair skin.

Antoinette walked across to the laden shelves, and cast an eye over the materials. "That turquoise blue and the lime green silk are too vivid for my complexion," she said firmly. "And as for that dark burgundy wool, why it would make me look positively consumptive."

Lady Anne laid a hand on her arm, and said in an amused tone which did not marry with the frosty expression in her blue eyes, "My, how forthright you Yorkshire girls are! So delightfully opinionated! Thank heavens I am here to advise you. You see, my dear, here in London we ladies of the *ton* are conscious that the eyes of the world are upon us. It is up to us to take the lead in matters of fashion. What we wear today, the ladies of Harrogate will be wearing next year. And one thing we simply cannot afford to do is allow ourselves to be seen in last year's colors. Now take my word for it. That lovely turquoise, and that fresh green are going to be the talk of the town. Wear them, and you will immediately establish a reputation as a woman of great style."

Not for a second was Antoinette taken in by this dissertation. If I permitted myself to be clad in that hideous lime green silk, she thought, I'd resemble a third-rate actress impersonating Maid Marion.

Antoinette was in no mood to tolerate any further argument. Turning to the bewildered mercer, she instructed sweetly, "Kindly send to the modiste the gentian blue muslin, and *eau de nil* silk and also some sage green wool for my riding habit."

Lady Anne's mouth tightened. "Really, Miss Aston! This is too vexing of you. I distinctly recall that the Duke gave me full authority to choose your new wardrobe. He will not be at all pleased when he learns that you have displayed an ungrateful disregard for my taste and judgment."

"The Duke, Lady Anne, expects me to dress with the style and dignity befitting a future Duchess," retorted Antoinette hotly. "I would remind you that I am not a young woman who needs to dress in gaudy, eye-catching clothes in order to snare a husband. I am betrothed to the Duke of Lyveden and I intend to dress in a manner which is proper to my status."

"Bravo! Well spoken indeed!" exclaimed a tall, well-upholstered lady as she swept into the shop.

Antoinette regarded the newcomer curiously. Although no longer young, the woman was still extremely attractive with a full, generous mouth and challenging dark eyes which were directed now at the Lady Anne.

"Not often I hear you put firmly in your place, Lady Anne! And by such a beautiful girl too. I do admire people who speak their minds."

Lady Anne's gloved hands were tightly clenched. But she replied smoothly, "May I introduce Miss Antoinette Aston, Lady Melbourne." Lady Anne went on guilelessly, "Unfortunately, Lady Melbourne's passion for free speech does not appear to have influenced her husband. In all his umpteen years in Parliament her husband has been known to open his mouth only once."

Lady Melbourne ignored the taunt. Smiling at Antoinette, she declared, "But you must be the Duke of Lyveden's future bride! My dear, I am delighted to make your acquaintance. All London is talking about you!"

Antoinette said in surprise, "So soon? But I only arrived in the capital last night."

"Word travels fast in London," Lady Melbourne assured her, "especially when the news concerns something as unexpected and eventful as the Duke of Lyveden's engagement. In fact, I was speaking to the Duke just a few minutes ago. I told him he cannot be allowed to keep you all to himself. Everyone is agog to meet you. Is there to be an engagement ball?"

"Indeed not," said Lady Anne, putting a protective arm around Antoinette. "Miss Aston has led an extremely sheltered life and such an occasion would send her into the most fearful panic. We must all do our outmost, Lady Melbourne, to introduce her most gently into the rigors of the London social scene."

Antoinette blushed. How she loathed this elegant, poised woman who seemed intent on making her feel like a gauche, untutored country girl.

Lady Anne guided Antoinette toward the door. "Pray excuse us, Lady Melbourne. This has been Miss Aston's first visit to Bond Street and I'm sure the experience must have bewildered and exhausted her. No doubt she is anxious to return home now, and rest."

Lady Melbourne smiled warmly at Antoinette. "I hope you will call on me soon, Miss Aston. I should like us to be friends. I can assure you, not all London society resembles a viper's nest." And to the auburn-haired woman she murmured, "Take care, Lady Anne. *Do* take care."

Antoinette left the mercers feeling comforted by her encounter with Lady Melbourne. She knew instinctively that in this handsome older woman she had found an ally. And the knowledge was confirmed by the fact that on the drive back to Curzon Street, Lady Anne Monteith said not a word but stared out of the window with icy, unseeing eyes.

Several days passed before the opportunity arose for Antoinette to question the Duke about Lady Melbourne. Since her encounter with the lady at the mercers, Antoinette had been plunged into a whirl of activity. Morning and afternoon boxes and parcels containing her new gowns, bonnets, gloves, shoes and lingerie were delivered from Bond Street. Lady Emma was beside herself with excitement, rushing down from the schoolroom and tearing open the boxes to exclaim delightedly over each new gown.

And then, of course there was London to explore. Lady Anne Monteith had very kindly offered to accompany the Duke and Antoinette as he showed London to his future bride.

"You see it all with a man's eye, Alexander," Lady Anne informed him with a coquettish laugh. "Whereas I shall be able to point out to Antoinette the lovely gardens . . . and that clever little milliner hidden behind St. Paul's . . . lots of little, feminine things too trivial for you to notice, Alexander, but to endless fascination to Miss Aston and myself."

"That is most handsome of you to offer to accompany us," declared the Duke. "We shall be delighted to have the pleasure of your company, won't we, Antoinette?"

"Yes, of course," smiled Antoinette with a sinking heart. "Although I must confess to a dreadful pang of guilt that we are imposing so much on Lady Anne's time and generous nature."

"Not at all," demurred Lady Anne, adding with a sideways glance at the Duke. "It is I who am honored to be seen in the company of a couple who are the talk of the town."

Antoinette was burning to know what was the Duke's true opinion of the Lady Anne. She appeared, when in his company, to be so sweet, so helpful, such a dear true friend. Yet Antoinette knew her to possess a spiteful streak and a venomous tongue. Was the Duke truly deceived? Antoinette studied him carefully. But his impassive face revealed nothing to her.

Despite the presence of Lady Anne, Antoinette was thoroughly impressed by her tour of London. She shivered as she regarded the sinister portals of the Tower of London through which so many had gone never to return . . . yet how her spirits lifted as she stood on Westminster Bridge and surveyed the sparkling waters of the Thames, and listened to the cheerful calls of the watermen. She was awestruck by the grandeur of St. Paul's, and to her delight as they passed by magnificent Carlton House, the Prince Regent himself came riding out in his impressive yellow carriage. In the evenings, there were visits to Drury Lane where the area outside the celebrated theatres was thronged with carriages and merry-makers, the air filled with laughter, music and perfume.

Antoinette adored every moment of it. Yet happy as she was, after a few days she could not repress a slight feeling of claustrophobia. The tall buildings and the noise and bustle of London were beginning to make her feel hemmed in. Increasingly, she found herself thinking with longing of the open moors of Yorkshire with the fresh wind scudding the clouds across the sky and the sweet spring grass soft underfoot.

To her surprise, the Duke seemed instinctively to understand. For without her uttering a word about her feelings, he said one morning, "I think that if I were in your situation, Antoinette, I should by now be beginning to feel a little homesick for my own native landscape."

"I do love London," Antoinette assured him. "City life is hectic, yes, but exciting too! Yet I must confess, I do sometimes long for a breath of country air."

He motioned her toward his carriage. "I cannot promise you anything as grand as your Yorkshire Dales. But let me show you that London is not all brick, slate, and endless congestion."

He took her then on the most enchanting drive through the pastoral outskirts of the city. To the hamlet of Brompton, near Kensington, lush with flowering orchards and market gardens. They went to Paddington and enjoyed a short stroll across the open, green fields, and then drove through Chelsea where Antoinette admired the pretty gardens bright with spring flowers.

At Whitehall gate at noon, Antoinette was amazed to see milk being served to eager Londoners, at a cost of a penny a mug. And even in St. James's Park, so near to the Palace, cows and deer grazed contentedly in the meadow.

It was here, as they walked by a canal overhung by graceful willows, that the Duke politely inquired of Antoinette if she found London society agreeable.

Antoinette chose her words carefully. "Lady Anne, of course, has been most generous in devoting so much time to me. And when we were shopping the other day, I was introduced to Lady Melbourne who was extremely civil to me."

The Duke laughed. "Ah yes, Lady Melbourne. A noble woman. She was married very young, I believe, to the dull, insipid Melbourne."

"Oh dear. She has such a cheerful countenance, I had no notion she was bored with her marriage," said Antoinette.

"Save your sympathy," smiled the Duke. "Lady Melbourne is more than content—she has a whole clutch of wealthy, handsome lovers. But she is admirably discreet and never flaunts them in public. I am glad to hear that she was kind to you. She was most disappointed when I informed her that I would not be holding an engagement ball."

Antoinette said nothing. This particular topic had become a thorn in her flesh since Lady Anne had displayed such malicious amusement over Antoinette's lack of experience at such events.

The Duke went on thoughtfully. "Stupidly, I had not realized that so much interest would be aroused by my announcement of our engagement. But talking to Lady Anne, I have come to accept that it would only be right and proper to introduce my fiancée formally into society. Otherwise people might begin to suspect that all is not as it should be. Since I have embarked on this charade of presenting you as my betrothed, it seems only fitting that I should carry off the affair with *elan*!"

Antoinette's mouth felt dry. He had been talking to Lady Anne. What new fiendish scheme had she put into his head? "What . . . what do you mean, present me formally into society? How would that come about?" she asked nervously.

"I propose to hold a reception," he informed her. "Nothing too grand or frightening. I shall invite between fifty and a hundred people to Curzon Street to make your acquaintance." He smiled. "Don't look so alarmed! I shall be at your side. And I am sure Lady Anne will give you every support and assistance."

That is exactly what I am afraid of, thought Antoinette wryly. Boldly, she inquired, "You mentioned some time ago that there were three London ladies whom you were considering as your future Duchess. Will the other two be present at this reception?"

Briskly, he replied, "I shall most certainly send an invitation to Miss Susannah Clegg. She is a dear, uncomplicated girl. But as for the third young lady, the Honorable Cecilia Lowe, well, I hear that you have frightened her away. She departed yesterday for France."

"But I have not made the acquaintance of Miss Lowe," protested Antoinette. "How could I have frightened her away?"

"I gather she heard of the engagement, and that you are an exceedingly beautiful girl," said the Duke. "She learnt that Lady Oxford is already in France giving soirees for the elite of Parisian society, so she has gone to join her there."

Antoinette sighed. "Paris! Now those hateful wars with the French are finally over, everyone seems to be flocking over the channel. Lady Emma was telling me that the most popular song at the moment is *All the World's in Paris*."

"I regret to surmise that its popularity will be short lived," said the Duke grimly. "Napoleon is a wily old fox. It won't be long before he's marshalling his forces against us once more."

He glanced up, surprised to find that Antoinette was not listening to him. She had moved off the path and with an intent expression on her lovely face, was moving from spot to spot on the grass.

"Whatever are you doing?" he called.

Antoinette smiled. "We have a saying in Yorkshire. When you can cover five daisies with one foot, then you know Spring has truly arrived. There! Look! One, two, three, four, five daisies all under my boot. So it is truly Spring at last!" She whirled around, flinging her arms in the air, the blue ribbons on her bonnet flying in the breeze.

The Duke stood watching her, and for a moment a wistful expression crossed his handsome face. "How wonderful to be so young, so carefree," he murmured.

Antoinette caught his words and ran across to him. "You do not understand," she said. "I am young, yes. But hardly carefree. It is a strain for me masquerading twenty-four hours a day as your fiancée. Watching every word, every gesture, every move. And because of my youth, I feel so hopelessly immature at times. I do so want to be a credit to you. I am terrified that at this forthcoming reception I shall make a fatal slip and cause you the most dreadful embarrassment by revealing our engagement as a fraud."

Antoinette bit her lip, horrified at herself for so impulsively pouring out her feelings in this way. Why, had it not been for the Duke, she would still be in the clutches of the evil Eleanor LeStrange. He had rescued her from an unmentionable fate, brought her to London and provided her with a new identity, a new life of luxury and ease. How ungrateful he must think me, Antoinette berated herself. That I should stand here bleating at the difficulty of my situation!

Hastily, fearing his wrath, she began to blurt an apology. "I beg your pardon. I did not mean—"

He raised a hand to still her words. A smile touched his lips. "No, no. I appreciate that I have placed you in an extremely difficult position, but I assure you, you have no cause for concern. Your bearing, your demeanor, your manner are all exquisite. I am proud of you, Antoinette."

Antoinette flushed at the unexpected compliment. "My main concern is not to let you down," she murmured.

"If you do make a slip," he said, his gray eyes glimmering with laughter, "promise me you'll do it in style. I am reminded of Colonel Mackinnon, a renowned swell celebrated for his practical jokes. I happened to be in Spain when he took it upon himself to impersonate the Duke of York."

Antoinette gasped. "The Duke of York? Oh, what effrontery!"

"I assure you, he was extremely convincing. He was invited to a splendid mayoral banquet and with the willing assistance of his regiment he carried off the impersonation brilliantly. Then when a huge bowl of punch was served he quite literally lost his head. To the horror of his hosts, the 'Duke of York' suddenly dived head first into the bowl and threw his heels into the air!"

Antoinette laughed and felt a surge of gratitude to the Duke. She knew that he had recounted this tale of Colonel Mackinnon's daring impersonation to reassure her that her own masquerade was insignificant in comparison.

That night, Antoinette lay awake well past midnight, thinking about the Duke. She had never before met a man who possessed such a complex personality. He can be so kind, so understanding, she mused. Without my saying a word, he realized that I was yearning for a glimpse of the countryside. He fully appreciates my anxieties in posing successfully as his fiancée and he does everything possible to make me feel at ease.

And yet . . . this considerate, sensitive, intelligent man was cold-bloodedly setting about selecting a wife. Not once, Antoinette realized with contempt, has he expressed an iota of affection for Lady Anne Monteith, Lady Susannah Clegg, or the Honorable Cecilia Lowe who has defected to Paris. It seems not to occur to him that one might just possibly want to love one's wife!

Antoinette's hand reached out and touched the gold locket resting safely on the bedside table. Love. Did my mother love my father? Or was she forced into an unhappy, arranged marriage? Who gave her this locket? And why did she take such trouble to leave it with me as a baby?

Questions, questions. And no glimmer of an answer to any of them. When the ordeal of the Duke's reception is over, resolved Antoinette, I shall pay a visit to the lawyer, Mr. Tomkins. It may be that since we last spoke, he has received further news on my identity. Oh, she sighed restlessly, how I wish I knew who I really am! I am longing to call on Mr. Tomkins and begin my private quest into my past.

But first there is the reception to be endured. All London will be there! How interesting, that the Honorable Cecilia learnt of the Duke's engagement and turned tail for Paris. Clearly, Lady Anne and Lady Susannah are made of sterner stuff. I shall be intrigued to meet Lady Susannah and observe her attitude toward the Duke. But at the moment, it has to be admitted that Lady Anne Monteith looks like the front runner for the Duke's hand. Regrettably, there is no question of *her* beating a retreat to Paris!

I do believe she is convinced by our fabricated tale of how the Duke and I met and fell in love. But she has not yet abandoned her own hopes of becoming the Duchess of Lyveden. From the determined gleam in those frosty blue eyes, I opine that she will fight with every weapon at her command for the right to wear the fabulous Lyveden tiara!

Nine

"Lord and Lady Portchester . . . Sir Gerald de Lisle . . .
Lady Holland . . ."

The *ton* of London were crowding into the Grand
Saloon, curious to make the acquaintance of the Duke of
Lyveden's new fiancée. The Duke, dashingly handsome in a
wine-colored velvet evening coat and white breeches, stood
by the great double doors of the Saloon, and presented Antoinette to his guests.

The strain on Antoinette was enormous. As each distinguished personage made their entrance, Antoinette was
conscious of being under severe scrutiny. Naturally, the *haute
monde* were eager to inspect this new addition to their ranks.
But as their eyes raked over her, Antoinette felt increasingly
akin to an exotic variety of hothouse bloom, freshly imported
from a strange, faraway land.

Not that all the guests regarded her unkindly. Lord
Portchester gave her a friendly wink. Lady Melbourne smiled
warmly and the Compte de Tessigne made a great show of
kissing her hand.

But the imperious Lady Holland was distinctly brusque.
Lord Alvanley positively undressed her with his impertinent
cool gaze, and several guests were unable to resist barbed,
mocking remarks about her Yorkshire background.

"Yorkshire!" exclaimed the simpering Lady Lucinda
Clare. "That is a place hundreds of miles away, is it not? Do

they speak English, there, Miss Aston, or do you have your own quaint, foreign language?"

Antoinette simmered with rage but the Duke cut in curtly. "Unlike young ladies in London, Lady Lucinda, all Yorkshire girls are taught to keep a civil tongue in their pretty heads."

Then came Lady Caroline Spencer, who gave Antoinette a brilliant smile and declared guilelessly, "I have heard, Miss Aston, that in Yorkshire you have a fancy for eating the most unexpected foods in concert, like cheese with apple pie. Thank heavens I am never required to travel so far north. I fear my delicate constitution would rebel at such a distasteful diet."

"Not at all, Lady Caroline," replied Antoinette pleasantly. "I am convinced you would find the juxtaposition of sweet apple and sharp cheese a poignant reminder of certain social conversations here in London."

The Duke laughed as Lady Caroline turned away, clearly unable to make up her mind if Miss Aston had been teasing her.

"Bravo!" he murmured. "The guests are all assembled now and you have withstood the ordeal magnificently. And do not look so anxious, Antoinette. I assure you, their bark is worse than their bite."

Antoinette smiled tremulously. "I just wish they would stop staring at me so!"

"What do you expect when you look so breathtakingly beautiful?" he demanded. "Every woman in the room is envying your beauty. And every man is envying me!"

The Duke spoke the truth. As the guests mingled under the blazing chandeliers, they were loud in their admiration of the golden-haired girl so exquisitely dressed in a gown of palest violet, scattered with pearls and amethysts.

"She is, of course, quite lovely," Lady Anne Monteith commented to Lady Holland. The auburn-haired girl fingered the emeralds at her white throat. "My one fear is that she may be too fragile to withstand the rigors of London life, not to mention the strain of becoming a leading society hostess."

Lady Holland tapped her fan against the crimson silk

149

damask curtains, "Your concern for the girl is most touching, Lady Anne. But you would do well to remember that Miss Aston was robust enough to put your nose severely out of joint."

"And what, pray, is the meaning of that remark?" glared Lady Anne.

The older woman snorted with laughter. "Don't get on your high horse with me, my dear. I'm too long in the tooth to be fooled. Ever since you came *Out* you've had designs on the Lyveden tiara. And now you're hopping mad that an unknown beauty from Yorkshire has snatched it away from you."

"She may be betrothed to the Duke but she hasn't yet maneuvered him to the altar," replied Lady Anne coolly. "The wedding, I would remind you, is not for six months. Much can come to pass in that time."

Lady Holland motioned a liveried footman and took a glass of chilled white wine from the silver salver. "Well I must confess, I always thought you had a greater chance of success with the Duke than Lady Susannah Clegg. Oh see! The Duke is taking Miss Aston across to the very lady herself. Let us draw closer so we can observe the confrontation! I would not miss it for worlds."

But if Lady Holland had expected sparks to fly between Lady Susannah and Antoinette, she was doomed to disappointment. To her surprise, Antoinette found it impossible to dislike the dark-haired Lady Susannah. She was a pretty, plump girl with a pale, oval face and round brown eyes.

She clasped Antoinette's hands in hers and declared warmly, "I am so glad to make your acquaintance, Miss Aston. I understand this is your first visit to the capital and you have brought the sunshine with you! Oh, it has been the most unendurably cold winter!"

The Duke smiled down at Lady Susannah, and observing the tenderness in his gaze, Antoinette experienced a sharp stab of jealousy. With her, he was unfailingly polite, scrupulously courteous. His gray eyes as he regarded her were often laughing, mocking, or grave. But never tender.

Swiftly, Antoinette took a grip on herself. What was she

thinking of? Of course the Duke retained not a jot of affection for her. She was to him no more than an employee, a servant to be treated with gallant respect, and honorably pensioned off when her use to him was at an end.

Beware, Antoinette! she warned herself. Do not fling yourself so thoroughly into the role of his fiancée that you begin to believe it is all for real. You are play-acting. It is a charade, a masquerade, nothing more. If you delude yourself with foolish fancies you will only have yourself to blame at the bitterness you will feel when the Duke takes either Lady Anne or Lady Susannah as his bride.

Yet what woman could in all honesty deny her innermost desires when she was in the company of this oh so masculine man? It is not merely his title, his wealth, his rugged good looks which set my blood afire, thought Antoinette. There is more, much more. His complex personality. So charming one minute, so cruelly ruthless the next. There is the manner in which he moves . . . that quietly confident stride, the commanding set of those broad shoulders. He is at all times a man in possession of himself. And yet, at times there is a fire in his eyes, an urgency in his voice which arouses in me an irresistible urge to goad him beyond the point of endurance. To make that self-control crack and release wild, dark passions . . .

She was conscious of a cool hand on her arm. "Miss Aston, are you feeling unwell? Is the heat in the Saloon affecting you? Why, you are trembling!"

Recovering her poise, Antoinette murmured to the anxious Lady Susannah, "Forgive me, I was momentarily affected by the bright light from the chandeliers. But it has passed. I am perfectly myself again now, I assure you."

Concerned, the Duke pressed a glass of cold wine into her hand. She could not meet his eyes. How dreadful that her girlish imaginings of a moment ago had manifested themselves in such a marked, physical manner! I must be careful, Antoinette realized. I must keep a rigid watch on my capricious, fevered mind.

The Duke was regarding her strangely. For one appalling moment she believed him to be reading her very thoughts.

Then he said calmly, "Pray continue, Lady Susannah. You were telling us how you diverted yourself during the inclement winter months. Tell me, did you go down to skate on the frozen Thames?"

"Well, we set off one day, one Tuesday as I recall." Lady Susannah smiled. "Or was it a Wednesday? How silly of me. I really cannot remember. No, I think it must have been Wednesday after all because Mama is always at home on Wednesdays and it was important that I should be back at the house in time to assist her in receiving the guests. Dear Mama gets in such a pother, you know, about whether the lace on her dress is curling from the heat of the fire or whether shawls are being worn knotted high or low this season. Dearest Mama —I said to her only last week . . . or was it the week previous? No, it was last week because she had just bought some fine new French lace from the new haberdasher's in Piccadilly. Such a commotion outside the shop because I slipped on the ice scuffing my new boots most terribly . . ."

As Lady Susannah chattered on, Antoinette was amused to notice the Duke's face set in a glazed expression. Was he, perhaps, contemplating a lifetime of sitting opposite Lady Susannah at the dinner table listening to interminable conversation about shawls and lace and what the haberdasher had said last Tuesday . . . or was it Wednesday?

And yet, mused Antoinette, it had to be admitted that the Lady Susannah would make some man a fine wife. She was pretty, and good-natured. She was the type of girl who would make a devoted mother. Inevitably, the Duke would bear this strongly in mind, as it was clear that he needed healthy sons to secure his line.

But does Lady Susannah possess enough *savoir faire*, poise and self-assurance to assume the ermine mantle of a duchess? Antoinette thought not. She would do well, Antoinette decided, married to a wealthy country squire. A man so immersed in his pursuits of shooting, hunting and fishing that he would regard with tolerant amusement his pretty wife's prattles about the minutia of her day.

The Duke of Lyveden was hardly such a man. Although he spent much of the year at his vast country estate in Hampshire, he was a person of cultivated tastes. Both rugged country sports and the civilized conversation of the dinner table gave him equal pleasure. And the woman who wed him, Antoinette realized, would be required to feel mistress of each situation. No, the homely Lady Susannah would not do at all.

Lady Anne Monteith appeared to be of the same opinion. With a rustle of emerald green silk she moved to the Duke's side, and murmured playfully, "Now Alexander! It is unforgiveable of you to monopolize Lady Susannah in this manner. Are you unaware that the Compte de Tessigne is pining to make her acquaintance?"

Antoinette looked on helplessly as a swift, meaningful glance was exchanged between the auburn-haired woman and the Duke.

Thank you for rescuing me, signalled the Duke. *I confess I was finding Lady Susannah a trifle tedious!*

Remember we have been friends for many years and I understand you very well, was the message returned by Lady Anne.

The Duke turned to Antoinette. "Would you excuse me for a moment while I introduce Lady Susannah to the Compte."

"Have no fear, Alexander," Lady Anne responded. "I will keep a watchful eye on Miss Aston while you are from her side."

As Lady Anne drew Antoinette toward a group of guests standing near the large panel of chinoiserie wall hanging, the golden-haired girl was only too well aware that Lady Anne would indeed be watching—and waiting. Waiting for Antoinette to say the wrong thing to the wrong person, to make a crashing conversational blunder which would mark her out as a simple country girl from Yorkshire. Someone to be pitied and gossiped about: *Can you imagine such a girl as Duchess of Lyveden? My, Alexander must be out of his mind choosing such a dimwit . . .*

But Antoinette had not come to this reception unprepared. Realizing that she would need all her wits and facts at her command, she had spent long hours closeted with the

Duke's sister. Although Lady Emma was not yet *Out* (and indeed was only permitted to attend this reception for one hour) she nevertheless possessed a mine of information on the private lives of all the distinguished guests.

So it was that Antoinette was careful not to refer to the French wars to Lady Caroline Spencer for her brother was recently killed at Rouen. She remembered that Lady Holland was a Whig hostess to whom the very whisper of the word Tory was anathema. With Lord Portchester, she was careful to make no mention of the theatre as his son and heir had recently scandalized the family by running off with an actress.

Instead, she made a conscious effort to guide each conversation along smooth, uncontroversial lines. With tact and charm, she encouraged each guest to talk about themselves, their interests, diversions and amusements. But of herself she said little. Whenever anyone tried to probe too deeply into her past, Antoinette lightly turned the conversation back to themselves, with such a becoming modesty that for the most part they had no notion what she was about.

But at last, Lady Lucinda Clare declared dryly, "My, Miss Aston. I was always given to understand that you Yorkshire girls were uncommonly forthright. Yet you are so reticent about yourself! Surely you do not consider yourself such a dull creature that you have nothing at all of interest to tell us about your life?"

As Antoinette stood stunned by this outrageous incivility, Lady Melbourne came galloping to the rescue. Rounding on the smirking Lady Lucinda, she remarked tartly, "It appears to me, Lucinda, that Miss Aston is displaying singular good sense. For just as no man is safe with another's secrets, so no woman is safe with her own."

Lady Anne Monteith's pale blue eyes gleamed. "Why, Lady Melbourne! Surely you are not implying that Miss Aston has a dark, intriguing past which she desires to conceal!"

Antoinette held her breath. Had the dreadful moment of exposure arrived? She had imagined Lady Melbourne to be her friend. But was the older woman playing her false? Could she have stumbled on the truth about her engagement to the Duke?

Then to her relief, she observed Lady Melbourne wagging a warning finger at Lady Anne Monteith. "If your tongue gets much sharper, my dear, you'll cut yourself on it. Of course I was implying no such thing about Miss Aston! I meant merely that nothing is so tedious as a woman who chatters incessantly about herself. A sense of private dignity is most becoming in a woman and in this Miss Aston is an example to us all."

Hastily, Lady Holland changed the subject. The dangerous moment was over. But as Antoinette's eyes met those of Lady Melbourne, she thought with sudden intuitive certainty: *she knows!* Lady Melbourne has discovered the truth about me. How these facts have come into her possession I cannot possibly tell. But having found me out, this wise, dear lady is clearly determined to keep the knowledge to herself. I recall the Duke remarking on her admirable sense of discretion. My secret is safe with her.

By eleven o'clock, the reception was over. The Duke escorted Antoinette back to the adjoining house on Curzon Street and stood with her for a moment in the hall.

"It was a success." He smiled. "Everyone was enchanted with you, Antoinette. You played your part to perfection. I assure you, you are now the toast of all London."

As Antoinette bade him goodnight, and climbed the stairs to her splendid bed chamber, her fatigue lifted at the kind sincerity of his words. He had understood what a strain the evening had been for her. He had appreciated that she would be anxious to know if she had been a credit to him. And he had given her in full measure the reassurance she sought.

But what a contrast, she thought, was this gracious, courteous man with the Duke I saw revealed earlier this evening when Lady Emma had requested to be allowed to stay longer at the reception. She had drawn her brother into the seclusion of a window arbor the better to plead with him.

Antoinette passing by, heard the Duke say firmly, "No, Emma. You must learn not to argue with me in this manner. I said you may stay for an hour and that time is now up."

"But I am not a child, Alexander!" protested the dark-haired girl, her hands clutching at the folds of her white silk dress. "What harm can come to me here in your house, in the company of your chosen friends and acquaintances? Please do not send me home to bed so soon. I shall be miserable lying in my bed chamber listening to the laughter and merriment issuing from next door!"

"Emma, I will not tolerate this disobedience!" snapped the Duke. "You are fifteen-years-old, a schoolgirl, and not yet *Out*. I am responsible for you. And I will not have my sister parading herself in public at such a tender age."

"Oh don't be so stuffy, Alexander! Really, sometimes I wonder how you ever managed to make such a charming girl as Antoinette fall in love with you. If you treat her in the same pompous manner that you treat me, then she is due for an extremely miserable time when you two are wed!"

The Duke's tone was Arctic. "You will return home this instant, Emma. I will call for Mrs. Reynolds to escort you. And tomorrow afternoon I shall call on you in the school-room to inspect the lesson I set you on European climates. It is finished, I trust?"

Emma replied tearfully, "Don't be such a beastly bully, Alexander! No it isn't finished! You know I find learning about temperature variations insufferably boring." She stamped her foot and glared defiantly up at her brother.

"And I find it equally boring dealing with the tantrums of a frivolous fifteen-year-old girl. Now remove yourself from my sight, Emma, or I'll throw you over my shoulder and carry you home!"

Furious, but having no choice but to admit defeat, the girl turned and pushed her way through the crowd toward the door. Antoinette's heart went out to her. Impulsively, she stepped into the arbor and murmured, "Your Grace, forgive me, but I could not help overhearing. May I say a word on Lady Emma's behalf?"

"No you may not," said the Duke coldly.

"But it does seem so harsh to send her home early from what is supposed to be your very own engagement reception. Lady Emma was enjoying herself so much! What harm—"

"Miss Aston!" cut in the Duke, his voice curling like a whiplash. "I fear you are forgetting yourself. The occasion of this reception has clearly gone to your head. May I remind you that we are not, in fact, engaged, and for you therefore to presume to criticize or even comment on my family affairs is an outrageous intrusion which I will not tolerate!"

Stung, Antoinette had turned away and removed herself as far as possible from him at the other end of the Grand Saloon. He had not said, *you are a servant—kindly remember your place,* but the message had been writ clear in his steely gray eyes.

Shall I ever understand him, wondered Antoinette, slipping on her filmy night robe. Why is he like this—kind one moment, then cutting the next? Yes, it would be better if I learned to hold my tongue and not provoke him to anger, but there are times when I am in his presence, when I am possessed by a reckless boldness of spirit which I find impossible to repress.

She held up a candle to her reflection in the glass and asked herself in bewilderment, "Why do I allow him to affect me so deeply, so passionately. Why?"

The following morning, Antoinette made her way up to the third storey of the Curzon Street house to an airy room overlooking the garden. As she pushed open the door, Lady Emma stared guiltily and banged shut the lid of her desk.

"Oh!" she said in relief as Antoinette entered. "I thought it was Alexander." Smiling, she drew from her desk a novel by Mrs. Mary Meake. "I brought it home from the circulating library. Alexander would be furious if he knew! But you won't tell him, will you, Antoinette?"

"Of course not," Antoinette reassured her, wandering around the room which smelled of ink and beeswax. The walls were lined with reference books of every description while on the governess's desk sat a large round atlas. Antoinette gave it a whirl and remarked, "I take it, then, that your brother hasn't yet engaged another governess for you?"

"No, and I am glad for that," replied the dark-haired girl. "Alexander has been setting my lessons himself. But he has been so preoccupied with other things of late that all he ever sets me to do is geography. And it is all so dreary. What interest have I in whether it is hotter in June in Paris or Florence? Why should I care about rock structures in the Alps?"

Antoinette wandered across to the window and gazed down on the garden where the paths were bordered by drifts of blue forget-me-nots. She felt so much in sympathy with the vibrant fifteen-year-old sitting forlornly at her desk. She understood the girl's longing to be out in the fresh air, wearing a pretty dress instead of a childish smock. Naturally, Lady Emma was yearning to take her place in society, to laugh and dance with all the carefree abandon of youth.

But her brother was adamant that until she reached her sixteenth birthday, she must attend to her lessons. Sorry for Lady Emma though she was, Antoinette realized it was her duty to support the Duke's attitude toward his sister.

"You must not feel anger against your brother," she advised Lady Emma. "It is only natural that he should wish you to complete your education."

"Oh yes," sighed Lady Emma. "I know he has a loathing of pretty, empty-headed girls with nothing more on their minds than the ribbons for their new bonnet. If only he would set me some more interesting work to do. It is so numbingly boring sitting here day after day by myself writing essays on temperature variations!"

"You say such a subject has no relevance to your own life," said Antoinette. "But what if you were embarking on a tour of Europe. I imagine that when you marry, your new husband will take you across the channel on a wonderful Wedding Tour. But how will you know which clothes to choose to take with you if you have no notion what the weather is going to be like in all the different countries you will visit?"

Lady Emma's gray eyes sparkled. "Why yes . . . I had not thought of it in those terms." She clasped her hands, thinking hard. "Well, first there would be the sea crossing. I confess I have not the first notion what I should wear on a boat."

"Neither have I," replied Antoinette, "for I have never

been to sea. I imagine it would be quite windy, don't you? But how can we find out for sure?"

Lady Emma jumped to her feet and ran to the bookshelves. "Let us look in one of Admiral Nelson's books. That will be sure to tell us what conditions to expect as we cross the channel!"

Antoinette smiled as she watched the girl eagerly riffling through the leather bound volume which detailed Admiral Nelson's voyages. The next two hours passed swiftly. Together, Antoinette and Lady Emma planned an extensive wardrobe which would take the girl through Paris, Versailles, and into Italy.

"Heavens, is it really that hot in Venice in July?" exclaimed Lady Emma. "I shall require parasols, then, and bonnets with shady brims."

She stood up and paraded in a grand manner across the schoolroom. "My, I confess I am quite fatigued with this heat," she declared in a devastating imitation of Lady Anne Monteith's distinctive drawl. "Perhaps I should recline awhile in that enchanting gondola!" She collapsed onto the floor, laughing helplessly.

Behind her the door flew open, and the Duke of Lyveden strode into the room. "Just what is going on in here?" he demanded furiously. "Emma, did I not warn you that if you continue wilfully to refuse to attend to your lessons then I shall treat you to a lesson which will leave you unable to sit down for a week!"

As he advanced, grim faced, on the terrified Lady Emma, Antoinette flung herself between them. "Your Gra—Alexander! Please do not be angry with Lady Emma. I assure you, she has been attending most assiduously to her studies."

The Duke raised a sardonic eyebrow and said bitingly, "I seem to recall, Antoinette, instructing you last night never, under any circumstances, to interfere in my family affairs!"

"But Alexander, Antoinette has been helping me with my lessons," protested Lady Emma, scrambling to her feet. She rushed across to her desk and held out to him a sheaf of closely written papers.

"Look, I have been on a grand tour of Europe! I know

that even in summer it can be extremely cold at night on a ship, so I must take warm clothes. Paris is hot, and dry and dusty but when I cross the Alps I must be careful not to take a chill. Then in Florence, the nights are balmy so I shall wear dresses of fine cool muslin and my prettiest slippers for dancing under the stars!"

The Duke was gazing at Antoinette in amazement. "But you have never travelled, Antoinette. How do you know so much about Europe?"

Antoinette waved a hand at the book lined shelves. "We have volumes here to assist us with the basic information. As for the details, the music, the scented nights, the ladies in Florence enjoying iced fruits, why, you told me all that yourself."

He smiled then, remembering how they had sat together at an inn on the way down from Harrogate and he had recounted his adventures on the Grand Tour of his youth.

He regarded his shining-eyed sister, and remarked, "I apologize for my hasty remarks, Emma. It is good to see you so filled with enthusiasm for your lessons."

"But the time just flies by when Antoinette is here helping me," cried Lady Emma. "Please may she come every day, just for an hour or so, to teach me?"

The Duke frowned. "I fear you are asking too much of Antoinette, Emma. You must remember that she now has many social engagements to fulfill."

"But it would give me great pleasure to assist Lady Emma in her studies," Antoinette assured him. "As a child I had many lonely hours to fill, but I was allowed free access to my uncle's library. I would never profess to be a learned academic but there is much I could usefully pass on to your sister."

"Your uncle?" queried Lady Emma. "But I understood you were brought up by your grandmother, Antoinette?"

Antoinette bit her lip at the slip. "There . . . there was an elderly gentleman living nearby whom I regarded as an honorary uncle . . ."

The Duke said hastily, "Yes, indeed, well, Emma, if Antoinette is content to devote some of her time to you then I think we should accept with gratitude."

The dark-haired girl flung her arms around his neck. "Oh thank you Alexander! You know, you can be awfully frightening at times. But deep down I know you to be the most wonderful man in all the world!"

The Duke hurriedly cleared his throat and Antoinette was amused to witness his discomposure at this spontaneous rush of affection from his sister. He stroked her hair and said gruffly, "I will leave you then. Oh, and don't forget to take a fan to Florence, Emma. The nights are still and airless, and you will be glad to be able to create a small breeze to refresh you after all that dancing under the stars."

As the door closed behind him Lady Emma said impulsively to Antoinette, "There! Is that not typical of my brother? He never does or says the things you expect him to."

My sentiments exactly, thought Antoinette wryly. She sat down at the governess's desk and closed the myriad of books which were lying there. "Well, I think we have had sufficient serious learning for today, Lady Emma."

"May we continue this afternoon?" inquired the girl eagerly. Then her face clouded. "Oh no. I forgot. I have an engagement to ride in the park with Lady Lucinda Clare this afternoon."

Antoinette was pleased at this news for she had urgent and private business of her own to attend to after mid-day. "I am sure you and Lady Lucinda will enjoy a most entertaining ride." She smiled. "You will be able to discuss everything that happened at last night's reception."

"Oh I did enjoy it," laughed Lady Emma. "Did you see Lady Holland arguing with Lord Portchester? My, she was waving her arms around like one conducting an orchestra!"

In Lincoln's Inn, the lime trees were just coming into fresh green leaf. Several pale-faced young law students walking through the courtyard glanced with appreciative interest at the golden-haired girl in the pretty pink sprigged muslin dress. They watched the bright late April sunshine glinting on her hair and felt a reluctance to return to their lonely studies in musty, attic chambers.

Antoinette was unaware of their admiring glances. She

walked purposefully past the brass plate which declared this to be the chambers of Messrs. Locke, Hawe and Tomkins, and once inside asked the graying clerk if he would announce her arrival to Mr. Tomkins.

Nervously, she fingered the locket at her throat. Suppose he does not remember me, she thought anxiously. He was extremely kind to me that day at Beck Lodge when he came to tell me the astounding news about Dr. Aston's Will. But he must be a busy man with many important legal affairs to attend to for a score of influential clients. Will he snort with annoyance at the suggestion of spending a few minutes with me?

By way of an answer, Mr. Tomkins himself appeared in the doorway. "My dear Miss Aston, what a pleasure to see you again!"

He ushered her into his chambers and offered her a chair on the opposite side of his handsome walnut desk. With relief she gazed into his bespectacled eyes. What a calm, reassuring presence he was in her life!

He smiled. "I understand that since we last met, your fortunes have changed in the most dramatic fashion. I read the notice of your engagement to the Duke of Lyveden in *The Times*. May I offer you my most sincere good wishes for your future happiness."

Antoinette lowered her eyes, feeling suddenly ashamed of perpetrating such an outrageous fraud on this sincere, kindly man. For the umpteenth time, she wished with all her heart that circumstances were different. If only she could be sitting with Mr. Tomkins secure in the knowledge that she was truly the intended of the Duke of Lyveden. How proudly, then, she would meet the lawyer's gaze!

He was regarding her expectantly. "Mr. Tomkins, I have not called to see you with respect to the matter of my engagement to the Duke of Lyveden. It is merely that I am still no further toward solving the mystery of my parentage. I wondered if any fresh information had come to light in the past couple of months?"

He arose and lifted a small locked box onto the desk. "In truth, I was hoping you would call, Miss Aston. For only a few days ago I received a package from Mrs. Cedric Aston of Beck Lodge." With slow deliberation, the attorney unlocked the box and continued. "It appears that on the lady's arrival at Beck Lodge, she instigated a thorough spring clean of the house, and in one of the attics, among some insignificant private effects of Mrs. Edith Aston, she found this."

He handed Antoinette what at first sight appeared to be a simple piece of folded blue velvet. Curiously Antoinette opened it out. She gasped and her heart began beating wildly.

Lying on the blue velvet was a miniature portrait of an exceedingly beautiful young woman. Antoinette gazed down at the familiar golden hair, the brilliant cornflower blue eyes and breathed, "It is my mother, I know it."

Mr. Tomkins' dry tones cut through Antoinette's surge of elation. "Now, Miss Aston, I do feel it would be advisable to keep to the known facts and not embark into the realms of surmise. We have no proof whatsoever that the woman in the portrait is your mother. Though I must confess, there is a striking resemblance to yourself."

Antoinette smiled at him, her lovely eyes shining. "Your caution is understandable. But I assure you, this lady is my mother. Every instinct tells me it is so." She turned the portrait over and cried with delight. "Oh see! There on the back is written the letter N." Swiftly, she unclasped her locket, and laid it on the portrait. "Yes, it fits exactly! And the letter N on the portrait marries with the same letter engraved on the locket."

Mr. Tomkins leaned forward and examined the jagged edges of the miniature. "There seems no doubt at all that this was forcibly removed from your locket, Miss Aston."

"By Dr. Aston's wife, Edith!" declared Antoinette with a flash of inspiration. "Don't you see? She believed the woman in the portrait to be her husband's mistress. In a fit of rage and jealousy she tore the painting from the locket and hid it—"

The attorney held up a hand. "Not so fast, Miss Aston! What a fertile imagination you possess. You forget that Dr. Aston's mistress was in fact Miss Eleanor LeStrange. He believed wrongly that she was the mother of the child he found on the doorstep. When he and his wife gazed for the first time on the portrait in the locket, he would have told her in all truth and with every conviction that this woman was not his mistress." The attorney paused, a frown creasing his brow. "And yet . . . because the locket and portrait were found with you, it would be natural to assume that the painting was of the mother. Why, then, should Dr. Aston have denied this evidence and assumed that the mother was in fact Eleanor LeStrange?"

"Because he never saw that portrait!" declared Antoinette with conviction. "Consider, Mr. Tomkins. A footman goes to the door and finds a child lying abandoned in a basket on the doorstep. What would he do? Why, his first instinct would be to call for the mistress of the house. He would know that the first need of a hungry, crying baby is the maternal presence of a woman. Edith Aston was no fool. She probably suspected that her husband had been unfaithful to her. When she went to the baby—me—and found the note saying *please take care of baby Antoinette*—she put two and two together and spat with rage at the result."

Mr. Tomkins gazed at her over steepled fingers. "Masterly, Miss Aston!"

"What I do not understand," said Antoinette slowly, "is why Cedric Aston's wife should have taken the trouble to send the portrait to you. After all, her husband turned me out of the house. How did she know that the portrait she found with Edith's things in the attic had any relevance to me? And in view of her husband's treatment of me, why did she not simply throw the portrait into the fire?"

"I believe she felt remorse at Cedric Aston's treatment of you," said Mr. Tomkins. "He had told her as much as he knew about you and the locket, and he probably mentioned the engraved letter N. When Mrs. Aston found the painting with the same letter written on the back, I believe she sent it to me in the hope that it would in some small measure compensate you for the misery you suffered at the hands of her husband."

Antoinette sighed. "Oh, I am so happy to have the portrait! Words cannot express how much it means to me. But it has still not solved the question of who I truly am. If only I knew more about this lady with the same color hair and eyes as mine!"

"Perhaps it would help if you could determine who painted the portrait," suggested the attorney practically. "I'm afraid I possess not a jot of artistic knowledge myself. But if you could show the painting to someone with an insight into the subject, he might possibly recognize the artist's style."

Antoinette leaped to her feet. The Duke of Lyveden, she thought triumphantly. His house on Curzon Street contained some of the most celebrated portraits in all England, and he was renowned for his taste and judgment in his collection of oil paintings.

Bidding a swift farewell to Mr. Tomkins, Antoinette left Lincoln's Inn and hurried back to the Duke's residence. On being admitted, she made her way toward his library. She had no doubt that she would find there some pamphlets which discussed the merits of the prominent portrait painters of the day. How wonderful it will be, she thought, if I can study them and determine for myself who it was who painted my mother's portrait.

She rushed into the beautiful green and gold library, then halted in dismay as she realized that the Duke himself was seated in one of the big leather armchairs.

"I—I beg your pardon—I did not mean to intrude," she stammered.

"Come in, Antoinette." He smiled, laying down his book. "Was there a particular book you wished to borrow?"

Observing that he was in a mellow mood, Antoinette took out the portrait from her reticule. "I am anxious to discover the name of the artist who is responsible for this work," she said. "I wondered if his style was familiar to you."

The Duke took the miniature across to his writing table and examined it carefully with a magnifying glass. Then he smiled, and regarded Antoinette with interest. "My, but the likeness is remarkable, Antoinette. Is this beautiful woman your mother?"

But Antoinette's secret was still too precious to her to be shared. And she could not forget the Duke's cold, disinterested tone way back in Harrogate when he had declared,

I do believe it would be best if we kept this arrangement on a purely business level. I have no urge to pry into your private life or your past.

Accordingly, she replied with wary vagueness, "I believe her to be an ancestor, yes. But tell me, is it possible for you to name the artist?"

He was silent for a while as he held the portrait to the lamp and scrutinized it minutely. "Yes," he said slowly. "Look at the delicate brush strokes on the hair, Antoinette. I know of only one artist capable of producing such delicate work in miniatures such as this. His name is George Howland. He has a studio in Chelsea opposite Lord Alvanley's stables."

Antoinette felt dizzy with elation. At last she was making progress! Tomorrow after her session in the schoolroom with Lady Emma, she would set forth for Chelsea and talk to George Howland about the mysterious N, the golden-haired beauty in the portrait. By this time tomorrow, thought Antoinette tremulously, I shall know the name of my mother. I shall know who I really am!

Ten

"He has a studio in Chelsea, opposite Lord Alvanley's stables," the Duke had said. "Dashed impudent fellow was forever hanging out of his window waiting for Alvanley's sister to return from her ride in the park. He kept inviting her to sit for him. Alvanley was obliged finally to go around and remonstrate with the rogue."

"Heavens, was there a fearful ruck?" Antoinette had inquired.

The Duke had smiled. "Oddly enough, to Alvanley's surprise he rather hit it off with Howland. The chap possessed enormous charm and a fund of amusing stories. They finished off a few bottles of claret together and Alvanley became quite a patron of the fellow."

This conversation was uppermost in Antoinette's mind as she hesitantly banged the brass knocker of the narrow Chelsea house. She had no doubt that she had come to the right address. Across the cobbled mews, the stableboys and grooms shouted to one another as they mucked out the stables which bore Lord Alvanley's distinctive crest.

Antoinette was not surprised to observe that Mr. Howland's house showed sad signs of neglect. The window shutters were broken, hanging from their hinges. The brass doorknocker had not been cleaned for months and much of the brickwork was crumbling away. But Antoinette assumed that a man of artistic temperament had little inclination for domestic running repairs. His mind would be on his work, transferring on to canvas the singular beauty of his current sitter. And at night, when his day's labors were over, he would no doubt stroll by the moonlit river before meeting other artists, sculptors and musicians in one of the taverns along the embankment.

There was no sign of life in the house. Anxiously, Antoinette banged the knocker again. Suddenly the door was wrenched open by a sullen-looking girl with dull, matted red hair.

"Will you kindly stop banging on the door in that boisterous manner!" she snapped. "I've got quite enough to do clearing up this wreck of a house without you giving me a headache into the bargain. What do you want?"

Taken aback, Antoinette clutched her pretty primrose parasol in both hands and murmured, "I am so sorry to disturb you. I wonder if you could tell me if Mr. Howland is at home?"

The girl laughed. "From what I've heard of George Howland, he's probably at this minute standing before the golden gates attempting to bribe St. Peter with a case of best claret and a scandalous story of his encounter with the Devil." She leaned against the doorpost and went on flatly, "George Howland is dead, my dear. Passed away three months ago."

Antoinette stood in the bright sunshine feeling numb with despair. Oh, what monstrous ill fortune! If only, she thought, I had come here just a few months ago Mr. Howland would still have been alive. He was my only hope of discovering more about my mother. Now there is no one to turn to. No one who can help me.

Courteously, remembering her manners, she murmured to the red-haired girl, "I am so very sorry to hear of Mr. Howland's death. It must have been a very great shock to you."

"Oh, save your sympathy," said the girl. "He was no kin of mine. My husband's a confectioner and we've only just moved in to this house. I haven't even had time to engage any servants. God knows, I need some help. The place is in the most fearful state. Old wine bottles, discarded canvases, endless boxes of papers. It'll take me months . . ."

As the girl gave vent to her complaints, Antoinette saw a ray of hope. "You say Mr. Howland left some papers," she remarked. "I wonder, would there have been any receipts for payment he received for his portraits."

Someone must have commissioned that portrait of my mother, Antoinette realized. If George Howland had kept a copy of the receipt or a note of the sitter's address . . . her spirits soared as the girl nodded.

"Yes, there was a box full of somesuch rubbish. I burnt it all yesterday. Took me hours, it did, because the kitchen range is all clogged up. Shouldn't think the thing's been properly cleaned for years."

With her hopes again dashed, Antoinette prepared to thank the girl and bid her farewell. There was clearly nothing more to be learned here for she had come on a totally fruitless errand.

But by now the red-haired girl had recovered from her initial bad humor and seemed inclined to talk. "I expect you were hoping he'd paint your portrait," she said conversationally, eyeing Antoinette's pale primrose muslin dress admiringly. "I understand he had quite an eye for a pretty girl."

"He was not married, then?" inquired Antoinette politely, longing only to terminate this conversation and return to Curzon Street where she would lock herself in her chamber and weep the bitter tears of disappointment.

The girl shook her head. "The story goes that he only loved once in his life. A beautiful, fair-haired girl she was. Such a tragedy. She bore him a child but before he could set eyes on it she disappeared from London and killed herself."

Antoinette was now all attention. "And the child?" she whispered. "What happened to the baby?"

The girl shrugged. "Lord knows. The mother probably killed it as well. She was mad, you see. Incredibly beautiful, but quite, quite mad."

Stunned, Antoinette turned away. She began to run down the mews, as if to escape from the terrible implications of what she had discovered. It was all too much of a coincidence not to be true, she thought wildly, turning onto the path which led by the river. My mother's portrait was painted by George

Howland. The woman he loved and who bore his child was a golden-haired beauty. The description fits my mother exactly. And she abandoned the baby and killed herself because she was deranged. Does that mean then, that if I am that abandoned child, then I too carry the seeds of madness?

Breathless, with her heart hammering with fright, Antoinette sat down on a yew seat overlooking the water. Blankly, she regarded the gliding barges, the ducks squabbling over a piece of bread, the birds hovering overhead waiting to swoop at the merest glint of a fish under the water.

How can everything look so calm, so ordinary, she wondered wretchedly, when my life has been turned so violently upside down. Oh, how I wish I had not come to Chelsea! I should have let well alone. Far better to have lived with the mystery of my parentage than to have discovered today such appalling facts about it.

She leaned forward on the seat, mesmerized by the smoothly flowing river. With the sun sparkling on it, the water looked so cool, so inviting.

"Miss Aston!" A man's authoritative voice cut through her fevered contemplations. Turning, she observed a distinguished looking, silver-haired man waving to her from his carriage. "Miss Aston! It is imperative that I talk to you for a moment!"

Antoinette gazed at him in horror as the chill of recognition swept over her. This was a face from her past . . . from Harrogate and her hateful liaison with Eleanor LeStrange. It was none other than the Earl of Rothsey, the man whom Miss LeStrange had encouraged to be the first to deflower her in that hateful house of shame. Thanks to the Duke of Lyveden, she had escaped, by the skin of her teeth, from the unwelcome embraces of this elderly earl. But now, here he was in London! To her dismay, she saw that he was descending from his carriage and was striding purposefully toward her.

Antoinette waited no longer. Leaping up from the seat, she turned her back on the earl and ran for her life along the river path. Behind her, she heard the earl call, "Miss

Aston! Pray do not run away. There is an urgent matter which I must discuss with you!"

The golden-haired girl paid him no heed. Like a hunted animal she dodged and weaved through the narrow mews, the winding lanes of Chelsea, choosing a cunning route which he would find it impossible to follow by cumbersome carriage. And there was no question, she knew, of a man of his advanced years being able to pursue her on foot.

As she sped along the lane which led beside the Chelsea Hospital, Antoinette was overcome with disgust at the persistence and lust of the Earl of Rothsey. Why, from all outward appearances he was an extremely respectable, distinguished gentleman. He had a kind face, upright bearing and an unmistakeable air of breeding and gallantry. Oh, how the eye was deceived! For she knew for sure that the earl's elegant bearing and cultured manner concealed a lecherous spirit, a dastardly urge to take advantage of young, innocent girls.

She found herself suddenly in Sloane Square which today was crammed with flowersellers. Cherry blossom, lilac and May overflowed from the ruch baskets strewn around the square, and the air was filled with the flowersellers' cries as they vied with one another for customers.

"Sweet violets! Lovely fresh primroses! You'll see none better in all London!"

"Take home some cherry blossom, miss? It'll bring you good luck, I promise you!"

Antoinette smiled wryly, feeling suddenly exhausted. She was miles away from Curzon Street and her legs felt as if they would carry her no further. Yet she dare not hire a carriage to take her home, for had she not that very morning refused the convenience of the Duke's own carriage?

"There is no necessity for you to walk to Bond Street," the Duke had said, happening to chance upon her as she emerged from the house. "Perkins and the carriage are at your disposal at all times."

But Antoinette, naturally, had not wished the sharp-eyed Perkins to know that her destination was Chelsea, not the frivolous environs of Bond Street.

"Thank you, but it is such a lovely day. After my session with Lady Emma in the schoolroom I would welcome a breath of fresh air," Antoinette had replied smoothly.

Yet how she wished now that Perkins would magically appear with the comfortable velvet-lined carriage! Wearily, she began the long walk up Sloane Street. And then, as if in answer to her prayer, a carriage drew to a halt beside her. Antoinette glanced at it fearfully, in case it should be the Earl of Rothsey but to her relief she noticed the crest of Lady Melbourne painted on the dark brown door.

Thankfully, Antoinette accepted Lady Melbourne's invitation to enter the carriage. It was only as she sank down onto the leather seat that Antoinette realized what a curious sight she must present to Lady Melbourne. Her dress was splattered with mud from her dash along the river path. Her bonnet was askew with the ribbons untied. She was flushed, dishevelled and, she realized, somehow during her flight from the Earl of Rothsey she had lost her pretty primrose parasol.

But the wise Lady Melbourne appeared not to notice Antoinette's state of disarray. "Have you been to the Sloane Square flower market?" she inquired pleasantly. "It is quite charming there at this time of year. May is quite my favorite month in London. The weather is clement and every garden is filled with blossom. I shall be so sorry to take my leave of it all."

"You are quitting London?" inquired Antoinette, deeply relieved that Lady Melbourne had avoided any mention of her windswept appearance.

"Just for a week or so," replied the older lady. "In fact I shall be going to your native homeland, Yorkshire. Lord Hebdon is holding a May ball and as I am godmother to his obnoxious son I feel obliged to attend."

Antoinette's spirits lifted at this news. She recalled that Lord Hebdon was cousin to Lady Anne Monteith. It seemed probable then, that Lady Anne would also shortly be journeying north for the ball. How delightful London will be, mused Antoinette, without the threat of Lady Anne's supercilious drawl sounding in my ears!

Lady Melbourne went on; "And how are you enjoying

172

London life, my dear? You are not finding us all too overwhelming, I hope?"

Antoinette smiled. "No, not at all. It is all the most wonderful experience. Each day brings fresh excitements and diversions—there is never a moment to be bored."

"Tell me, have you visited Almack's yet?" inquired the dark-haired woman, amiably.

Antoinette was aware that Almack's was one of the most exclusive clubs in the capital. "No," she said, "The Duke has never suggested that we patronize Almack's."

Lady Melbourne laughed. "That does not surprise me in the least! The Duke of Lyveden will have no truck with the place. Oh!" she held up a hand at Antoinette's worried expression. "Do not be alarmed. I assure you, it has the utmost respectability. I insist that you accompany me there tonight. I will send my carriage for you. Yes," she murmured thoughtfully, "I think you will find it quite an education, Miss Aston!"

Lady Emma, when she heard of Lady Melbourne's invitation, was beside herself with excitement. "Why Antoinette, this is a sign that you are truly accepted into the highest echelons of society! Lady Lucinda Clare was so upset at not being on the invitation list, she threw a fearful tantrum and tore her best riding habit to shreds."

Antoinette was reclining on the drawing room sofa with her aching feet propped up on a velvet stool. "I had not realized there was so much cachet involved in being admitted to Almack's," she said. "But tell me, who is in charge of the club? Who issues these coveted invitations?"

Lady Emma bent to stroke her sleeping kitten who was curled up by the hearth. "Almack's is controlled by certain patronesses. The most important are the Ladies Castlereagh, Hersey and Cowper. They hold a ball and a supper there during each week of the Season and any lady who is denied an invitation hastily invents an out of town engagement rather than admit to the shame of being barred from the club."

Laughing, she continued, "Mr. Henry Luttrell composed such an amusing verse about it. At least, I thought it was amusing, but poor Lady Lucinda was not at all entertained:

All on that magic LIST depends;
Fame, fortune, fashion, lovers, friends;
'Tis that which gratifies or vexes
All ranks, all ages, and both sexes.
If once to Almack's you belong,
Like monarchs, you can do no wrong;
But banished thence on Wednesday night,
By Jove, you can do nothing right."

"Heavens!" admitted Antoinette. "I must hasten upstairs and choose my most elegant dress for the occasion."

Lady Emma knelt on the floor with her kitten, her face wistful. "I do wish I were anticipating an evening's merry-making at Almack's. But all I have to look forward to is an interview with my brother. He left a message saying he has some important reading matter for me to peruse."

"Take heart, Lady Emma," Antoinette consoled her. "It is only another five months until you come *Out*. And then you will be able to dance the night away to your heart's content."

The girl's face lit up at the prospect. "Oh yes! And by then you will be married to Alexander. We shall have balls, and parties, and routs! And I shall be so proud to have you as my sister, Antoinette!" She ran across the drawing room and embraced the girl in the primrose yellow dress.

Antoinette stood with tears stinging her eyes. What a sham this all is, she thought wretchedly. Oh how I hate this deception. Lady Emma is such a sweet, honest girl. I value her friendship highly. Yet I know when she learns that I have played her false, she will have nothing but contempt for me.

Oh, dear, she thought as she ascended the stairs to change her dress, if only I had known when I agreed to embark on this charade, what a conflict of emotions and loyalties it would arouse in me!

King Street, in fashionable St. James's, was thronged with carriages. As Lady Melbourne swept Antoinette through the elegant portals of Almack's she kept up a running stream of information.

"Almack's was built around 1765 by a man called William Macall. With typical Scot's canniness he inverted his name and called the building Almack's so as to divert any criticism of the design from himself."

As they entered the gilded main Assembly Room, Lady Holland hastened to greet them. "My dear Miss Aston, what a pleasure to welcome you to our little gathering. And how enchanting you look. That dress is quite the most divine shade of blue."

"In all modesty, I feel I must claim a small measure of the credit for the delightful appearance of my little protégée," said Lady Anne Monteith sweetly, insinuating herself into the group. "The Duke placed her entirely in my care, you know. I was quite touched at his confidence in my good taste."

By now, Antoinette was unsurprised at the barefaced effrontery of Lady Anne's remarks. But had I truly relied on you, Lady Anne, she thought, I should be standing here now dressed as gaudily as a gypsy at a hiring fair.

They were joined by Madame de Lieven, the delicately-boned wife of the Russian ambassador. She too expressed her pleasure at Antoinette's presence, and then went on airily, "Such a disappointment that your fiancé did not find time to accompany you!"

The burst of laughter which followed this remark quite mystified Antoinette. Lady Melbourne took her arm and explained: "I'm afraid the Duke is resolute in turning his back on Almack's. He maintains that our balls are unexciting and our refreshments of lemonade, tea, bread and butter and cake are only fit for the nursery."

"And yet I am given to understand that most people regard an invitation to Almack's as a most welcome event," Antoinette said. "Surely the *haute monde* of London were not clamoring merely for a drop of lemonade and some stale cake?"

"It is, of course, our charming company and witty conversation which make us so prized," laughed Lady Anne. "Reputations are made and broken at Almack's, Miss Aston. I do hope you manage to stay the course!"

Antoinette had learned by now to ignore the auburn-haired lady's taunts. She gazed around the room. On the dais, an orchestra was playing and beyond in a smaller chamber, the green baize tables were set out ready for whist and loo. "Such an elegant scene," she murmured politely, "and how finely dressed the gentlemen are. All in knee-breeches and white cravats."

"It is one of our little rules that the gentlemen be attired thus," murmured the Countess of Lieven. "Why, I recall once that even the Duke of Wellington himself was turned away from the doors when he dared to present himself here wearing trousers!"

Antoinette was beginning to understand the Duke of Lyveden's aversion to Almack's. She could not imagine one such as he taking kindly to a parcel of society hostesses dictating his mode of dress!

Lady Holland waved her fan and inquired languidly, "Is the Duke of Wellington still smitten with Harriette Wilson? One hears such fascinating tales, one hardly knows what to believe."

"It appears that half the men in London are to be seen visiting the pert Miss Wilson," said Lady Anne tartly. "Goodness knows, she has had enough years of practice in accommodating them. She and her sister were being kept by certain gentlemen of rank when they were barely fourteen-years-old, you know."

Madame de Lieven lowered her voice and with sparkling eyes informed the group, "These young girls are found, you know, at female academies. I have heard that there are certain married women who infiltrate these schools on the pretext of purchasing cast-off clothes for their servants. They seize on any girls whose parents can no longer afford the fees and offer them a home. But of course the sweet innocents are soon made to work for their living!"

"My, how scandalous!" exclaimed Lady Anne delightedly.

"It is quite the most wicked thing I ever heard," declared Lady Holland, her face alight with vicarious pleasure.

Lady Melbourne said nothing but Antoinette was aware of her brown eyes regarding her quizzically.

Lady Anne fingered the pearls at her throat, and declared, "My, Madame de Lieven, you always manage to entertain us with the most scurrilous stories! But tonight I have one for you. Tell me, have you heard about Colonel Mackinnon's latest exploit?"

The women crowded around, eager to hear more.

Happy to be the center of attention, Lady Anne reminded them of Colonel Mackinnon's notorious liaison with a certain married lady of their acquaintance. "Finally, as always happens, he grew tired of her and stopped calling at her house. She was beside herself with rage and wrote to him demanding the return of a lock of hair she had given him. But the Colonel did not reply. Instead," Lady Anne laughed, "he sent his valet to her, bearing a large packet of locks of hair of all differing shades along with a message inviting her to pick out her own property!"

While the ladies exclaimed delightedly over this tale, Antoinette recalled that the Duke of Lyveden had himself mentioned Colonel Mackinnon to her. But the anecdote he related, although amusingly outrageous, had held no hint of immodesty. How considerate of the Duke to spare my blushes, mused Antoinette, a wry smile touching her lips.

Before long, Lady Melbourne was prised away by the elegant Lady Jersey to make up a table for whist. No sooner was Lady Melbourne out of hearing than the other ladies in the party began to tear her reputation to shreds.

"I hear she is much taken with young Lord Westburgh," murmured the Countess of Lieven. "They were seen riding in the park after dusk the other evening!"

"No, no," cut in Lady Anne Monteith eagerly, "that was just a passing dalliance. "It is Lord Egremont who holds the key to her heart at present. I noticed them at the opera last night. They were in different parties but from the significant glances passing between them, it was plain what was afoot."

"I don't know how she manages to attract so many men at her age," said the Countess waspishly.

"Oh, she is careful not to be seen too often in daylight," Lady Holland put in. "Soft lamps and candlelight are so much more flattering to a woman of her years. It must be so fatiguing, however, for the poor soul, encasing herself in those rigid corsets from dawn to dusk."

Madame de Lieven patted her tiny waist. "Thank heavens I have no need to resort to such measures."

She drifted away to the supper table and Lady Anne Monteith declared with a knowing laugh, "No wonder the Countess is able to eat like a horse yet retain her girlish figure. She requires a mountain of food to provide the energy to sustain her for the effort of running around London and causing scenes with all her husband's mistresses!"

Antoinette sipped a glass of lemonade. Yet even the sweetened drink could not remove the sour taste from her mouth. How ironic it all is, she thought. This is such a glittering occasion with the orchestra playing so melodiously, the handsome men laughing with beautiful women by the blazing light of the chandeliers.

And yet the civilized splendor of the scene is all a sham. Beneath the docile smiles, the professions of friendship and good will, there is nothing but malice and venom. Is there anyone here tonight whose reputation has not been demolished and who, in turn, has not taken a deft pair of scissors to the good name of another?

To her horror, Antoinette realized that the perfumed society ladies were now rounding on her. "You must be so looking forward to your wedding, my dear," murmured the Countess of Lieven. "Have you chosen your wedding ring yet? And you must tell me where you are planning to go for your Wedding Tour."

"I believe the Duke plans to surprise me with the exact route of our Wedding Tour," replied Antoinette with a calmness she did not feel. Of course such a tour had never been discussed between them. And naturally, no ring had been purchased. For instead of sweeping through Europe on the arm of my handsome new husband, I shall be consigned to a small cottage in the depths of the country and given an allowance in return for the promise of my silence.

Meanwhile, Lady Anne Monteith had been carefully scrutinizing the other guests at Almack's. "How strange. I can see no sight of Lady Susannah Clegg. Surely she received an invitation?"

It was plain that the Lady Anne hoped no such thing. Her pale blue eyes gleamed with pleasure at the prospect of the Lady Susannah having been dropped from the all important Almack's list.

Lady Holland shook her head. "Oh were you unaware, my dear? She and her parents are entertaining the Duke of Lyveden tonight for dinner."

Lady Anne looked as if she had been slapped in the face. Antoinette, too, was confused. Surely the Duke had not decided to ask the tedious Lady Susannah to become his bride?

Lady Anne rallied. "But my dear Miss Aston, why are you not at your fiancé's side this evening? Naturally, we are delighted that you chose to honor us here with your presence, but was the Duke not sorely disappointed that you could not accompany him?"

"Unfortunately," Antoinette said, thinking quickly, "I had a slight headache this afternoon and told the Duke I would be unable to accompany him to the Cleggs. However, shortly after seven my head cleared, and as I found myself so unexpectedly without an engagement for the evening, I decided it would be pleasant to visit Almack's."

It was a graceful and convincing reply. Observing that she had momentarily silenced the ladies, Antoinette decided that it would be wise for her to leave now while she was in a winning position.

Although Lady Melbourne had placed her carriage at her disposal, Antoinette elected to walk home from St. James's. It was a beautiful balmy May night with a gentle breeze wafting the fragrance of lilac and May blossom from the nearby gardens. Antoinette breathed deeply of the scented air, glad to be ridding herself of the polluted atmosphere of Almack's.

How glad I am, she decided, that I did not grow up in such a society. I may not have been born into a wealthy family, and in many ways my upbringing was austere. Nevertheless, I was taught the things which are true, honest and right. Unlike the painted, perfumed ladies I was with tonight, I at least possess a sense of true values, and to me that is worth far more than all the titles, all the wealth in the world.

At that moment, Antoinette longed for a magic carpet to spirit her back to the beloved Dales of Yorkshire. She yearned to walk in the clean fresh air and watch the young lambs frisking on the hillsides.

But here were the lights of Curzon Street beckoning her back to the sophisticated world of the capital . . . and, she discovered to her horror, to the sinister implications of her sojourn in Harrogate with Miss LeStrange.

As she entered the house, Mrs. Reynolds, the housekeeper, thrust a long package into her hands. "This was delivered earlier this evening, Miss Aston. And there is a note for you as well."

Intrigued, Antoinette took the package into the drawing room and lit the lamp in the window seat. She tore off the wrapper and was amazed to discover that the package contained her primrose yellow parasol which she had mislaid on her flight from the relentless Earl of Rothsey.

The accompanying note confirmed her worst fears.

Dear Miss Aston, she read,
> *I have the honor to return your parasol which you dropped by the river in Chelsea this afternoon. I fear my unexpected approach must have alarmed you. But it is most important that I talk to you on a subject of mutual interest. Since the nature of the matter is somewhat delicate, I should appreciate a private interview with you at a place and time to suit your convenience. I remain, yours most respectfully, Rothsey.*

Angrily, Antoinette crammed the note into her reticule. How dare the man pursue her in such a flagrant fashion! He must have seen the notice in *The Times* of my engagement to the Duke, and thus ascertained my address in London. But what barefaced effrontery to continue to attempt to seduce a girl who he now imagines to be betrothed to one of the most influential men in the land! Has he no shame? No doubt he believes that the Duke has no notion of my past association with Miss LeStrange. He is convinced that I would never put myself to the blush by taking his note to the Duke and insisting that he call the Earl out!

Antoinette leaned back against the silk cushions on the window seat. Her head was throbbing in the most alarming fashion. Oh, she thought wretchedly, is there no escape from the taint of Eleanor LeStrange. Is my misfortune in becoming involved with her to haunt me for ever? Is it not bad enough that I suspect myself to be the unfortunate love child of a charming, if dissolute artist and a poor, crazed golden-haired beauty?

Outside, the rumble of a carriage heralded the arrival home of the Duke of Lyveden. Antoinette drew aside the curtain and watched as he descended from his carriage. His face was in shadow, and revealed nothing to Antoinette of the outcome of his dinner engagement with Lady Susannah and her family.

"Thank you, Perkins," said the Duke. "I shall not require you again tonight."

"Very good, Your Grace."

So, mused Antoinette, the Duke will not be whiling away the night over the card tables at Whites or Boodles. But then he has more urgent matters on his mind. No doubt he will pour himself a glass of brandy, and give himself up to the earnest contemplation of to whom he shall accord the accolade of Duchess of Lyveden. The sophisticated Lady Anne . . . or sweet-natured, dull Lady Susannah?

Feeling suddenly irritated at the thought of these two ladies, Antoinette crossed to the sidetable where lay a pile of books. Perhaps there is something here to distract me from my unsatisfactory evening and lull me to sleep, she told herself.

Lying on top of the pile of books was a printed tract and a message in the Duke's hand.

My dear Emma, Antoinette read,
> *Please forgive me for not keeping our appointment this evening. I had quite forgot a long standing (and oh so boring) engagement to dine with the Cleggs on the occasion of their silver wedding.*

> *However, I came across this today, which I should
> like you to peruse most earnestly. I remain your
> affectionate brother, Alexander.*

Antoinette's first reaction was one of relief. So he had not, then, finally decided on the Lady Susannah! He had merely dined with the Cleggs out of obligation, not choice.

Feeling considerably cheered, Antoinette examined the tract which the Duke was so eager for his sister to read. It was headed *Advice to a Daughter* and had been written over a century ago by the Marquis of Halifax.

> *It is one of the disadvantages of your Sex that young
> Women are seldom permitted to make their own
> Choice . . . There is Inequality in the Sexes and . . . for
> the better Economy of the World, the Men, who were the
> Lawgivers, had the larger share of Reason bestowed upon
> them . . . you have more strength in your Looks, than we
> have in our Laws, and more power by your Tears than
> we have by our Arguments.*

Stunned, Antoinette read through the tract again. Then she flung it down and paced around the drawing room. Her heart was hammering, her blood racing . . . she was so angry she felt consumed with a passionate, pent up rage.

Suddenly, she knew what she must do. She ran upstairs and hurried into her dressing room. From the rack of beautiful evening gowns, she chose a particular style which had been selected for her by Lady Anne Monteith. Antoinette had known she would never wear the dress. She had agreed to it only because she had endured three hours of Lady Anne's company and yearned only to escape from the dressmakers and seek the seclusion of her bed chamber.

As the cool, wine-red silk slipped over her shoulders, Antoinette shivered with excitement. Yes, she thought defiantly, this dress is perfect for my purpose tonight! The neckline was cut daringly low, revealing an immodest expanse of her high, youthful bosom. Her creamy shoulders were bare and the nipped-in waist was so tight she could scarcely breathe.

Antoinette twirled before the long mirror, debating whether to apply a little artifice to her complexion. She decided against it for her cheeks were already flushed with anger, and her eyes were sparkling with a wild excitement that far outclassed any false lustre belladona would lend them.

Satisfied at last with her appearance, Antoinette ran downstairs and out into the street. She had not far to travel. Within a few moments she was being admitted to the house next door by the Duke of Lyveden's butler. Concealing his amazement at her startling appearance, the butler informed Miss Aston that his master was in the library.

"Shall I announce you, Miss Aston?"

"No thank you," answered Antoinette, her blue eyes glinting dangerously. "I should like to surprise my fiancé!"

She marched boldly down the hall and blazed into the library, slamming the door behind her.

Eleven

The Duke leaped to his feet as the sound of the slamming door shattered the silence of his library. "What the deuce!" he exclaimed, his gray eyes staring in disbelief at the apparition in glowing red silk.

Antoinette raised a languid eyebrow, smiling at his consternation. He had changed into a dark blue velvet smoking jacket. A half-finished cigar and a glass of brandy lay on the mahogany table beside his brass-studded leather chair.

"Are you not pleased to see me, Alexander?" she drawled, moving across and boldly pouring herself a measure of brandy. She raised the glass to her rosy lips and drank the amber liquid down in one gulp, welcoming the fire it caused to rage within her. But the burning liquid was as nothing compared to the scorching fury pulsing through every inch of her body.

The Duke stood hands on hips, his face grim. "What is the meaning of this intrusion?" he demanded. "And why are you dressed in such a flagrant manner? Surely you did not venture out to Almacks in such vulgar attire?"

"Oh, but indeed it would have been most suitable!" cried Antoinette, running her hands down the flimsy silk. She noticed the Duke's eyes darken as they followed the movement of her fingers over the rounded curves of her figure.

To tantalize him further, she pirouetted around the room, declaring lightly, "To be sure, I have had the most entertaining evening. I have been consorting with the cream of London society. And shall I tell you what was the basis of my conversations with the *haute monde?* Why, which married lady was having an affair with whom, and which unmarried lady had been seen entering a certain peer's room at midnight, and how although Lady X is shortly to marry Lord Y, the child she will bear him in seven months time will most certainly not be his. Do you know, my lord Duke, as I stood and listened to it all, I realized that I could just as well be back in Harrogate, sitting in Miss LeStrange's parlor hearing her relate her exploits with her courtesan ally Lauretta Kaye."

The Duke had clearly decided that it was time to assert his authority. "What nonsense is this!" he snapped. "Are you deranged, Antoinette?"

"No, I am not deranged. I am sickened!" she retorted hotly. "I am appalled by the corrupt, malicious society in which you live! A society where it is considered smart to invent witty lies, where to tell the truth is regarded as naive, where an act of kindness is looked on with suspicion, where—"

"One moment!" the Duke cut in curtly. "Did you not tell me yourself that Lady Melbourne, for one, has shown great kindness and civility toward you?"

"Oh yes!" cried Antoinette bitterly. "I would not deny that. But even she, a lady who has extended to me the hand of friendship, even she is like the rest—unfaithful to her husband with a string of lovers! Admittedly, she is discreet, but is it not sickening to you that no one in this entire rancid city appears ever to marry for love? Do none of them possess a shred of genuine affection and respect for their husbands?"

The Duke turned away. "You are young, Antoinette. You do not understand London ways."

"On the contrary, I now understand very well!" protested Antoinette. "I am a diligent pupil, Your Grace. The most important lesson I have learned is that the ladies of high society are in essence no different from the Eleanor LeStrange's and the Lauretta Kaye's of this world. Oh, they have fine silk dresses and matchless jewellery. Their accents are refined, their manner cultivated to a rare degree. But underneath their perfumed finery, they are libertines at heart."

"Antoinette, I warn you, you are skating on very thin ice," said the Duke bitingly.

As if he had not spoken, Antoinette continued challengingly. "Are you not taken with the fine gown you bought me, Your Grace? You see, since it is my role to pose as a fine London lady, I decided to take the lead and dress in a manner fitting to what is truly expected of me. We all are courtesans here, so why not robe oneself as one?"

The Duke gripped the arm of his chair, his knuckles white. "Have you quite taken leave of your senses?" he demanded, his mouth set in a hard line.

Antoinette smiled, and replied in a soft, mocking tone, "Oh, you need no longer pretend with me! Indeed, I am surprised that you have for so long treated me with such respect. But now I have grown up. I am wise in the ways of the London world into which you have whirled me. Come now. Admit it. You are longing to take me in your arms and make love to me. Surely you have not forgotten my hours of instruction at the hands of Miss LeStrange? She taught me well, you know, in the likes and needs of gentlemen like yourself—"

The mahogany table fell to the floor as the Duke kicked it aside. Steely eyed, he strode across the room, seized Antoinette by the arm and slapped her hard across the face with such stinging force that she was sent flying across the room.

As she knelt on the carpet, gasping with the impact of the blow, the Duke said icily, "I apologize for striking you, Antoinette, but you must admit, I was sorely provoked. Now kindly return to your room and we shall say no more about the incident."

Antoinette scrambled to her feet, her anger numbing the burning of her cheek which still bore the imprint of his furious hand. "No!" she cried, surprising him with her defiance. "I am not your fifteen-year-old sister, to be spanked and then sent to bed by her arrogant older brother! Why can't you admit that the reason you struck me was that I had struck at you—and too near the bone for comfort!"

His face livid with anger, the Duke took two paces toward her. But Antoinette faced him boldly. "You will have to beat me senseless, my lord Duke, before you will stop me saying what I came to say! For the truth is that you too are as corrupt as everyone else in the capital. You too are planning a cold-blooded, loveless marriage. And I have no doubt that as soon as you return from your splendid Wedding Tour, you will be inviting the romantic attentions of one or others of the many willing society hostesses in London."

"You stupid girl!" shouted the Duke. "You have not the first idea what it is like to be a man in my position. Don't you understand that for someone like me, marrying for love is a luxury, an indulgence I have not the time to permit myself? Yes, I must wed soon. I am in my thirty-first year and it is essential that I have heirs to secure the line. But most important of all is the need to provide my sister with a secure background for her first Season."

Observing Antoinette's scornful glance, he went on urgently: "Let me explain, Antoinette. You were contemptuous earlier of Lady Melbourne's lovers. But the reason she is unhappy with her husband is that she married the dull clod when she was sixteen, and knew no better. I have no wish for Emma to make the same mistake. I want her to enjoy several Seasons playing the field, attending a ball with one beau, riding in the park with another, escorted to the opera by a third. I want her to learn about the ways and wiles of young men so that when she does marry, it will be for the right reasons. For despite your cynical assumptions, Antoinette, there are some of us who still believe in the value of married love."

Such was the sincerity of his tone that Antoinette was silenced for a moment. Then she laughed scornfully. "My, what a noble speech! How ironic that it should fall from the lips of one who is preparing to embark on a loveless marriage. What a fine example you are setting to your sister, my lord Duke!"

The Duke's voice was distant with rigid self-control. "You have no understanding of these matters, Antoinette. Of course I should prefer to marry a woman with whom I was in love but one cannot fall in love to order, you know. The plain fact is that it is timely that I should marry, and I must take my choice from the ladies in society who are available to me."

Antoinette shuddered with distaste. Her gesture clearly

irritated him more than any words could have done when he exclaimed, "Can't you see that life as a Duke is not all one round of privilege and pleasure? I have immense responsibilities. A vast estate in the country with hundreds of tenants dependent on me for employment. They will be looking to me to marry and have sons who will be trained to manage the estate properly. Then there is Emma. I am adamant that when she comes *Out* she shall have the benefit of a wiser, married sister who will guide her toward womanhood."

"Indeed," replied Antoinette acidly, moving toward the fireplace. "I am surprised you entrust such an important task to a mere female. From the tract you gave your sister to read this evening, I gather that you believe us to be singularly lacking in common sense." She quoted, with her voice laced with acid:

"The men . . . had the larger share of Reason bestowed on them."

Observing the Duke's sardonic smile, Antoinette went on hotly, her blue eyes blazing: "You claim to have your sister's best interests at heart, yet you yourself are encouraging her to grow up into an empty-headed doll, with no spirit, no sense of adventure, no initiative. If she listens to you all she will care about will be her appearance in the mirror, and pouting, and simpering and learning how to make her eyes dew with tears to win favor and affection from her beaux."

The Duke's mood appeared to have changed. He indicated a chair. "Will you not be seated, Antoinette? Anger is an extremely taxing emotion in my experience."

Suspecting that he was being patronizing, Antoinette said coolly, "Thank you, but I prefer to stand."

The Duke seated himself in his leather armchair and slowly sipped his brandy. "Did it not occur to you, Antoinette, that by presenting Emma with that *Advice to a Daughter* I was merely indulging my somewhat eccentric sense of humor? I thought Emma would find the lines amusing and see the irony of the situation."

"I see," said Antoinette thoughtfully. "But that is a dangerous game to play, my lord Duke. For you are clearly unaware that your sister admires you beyond all others. Your every word is law to her. I should have thought if you desired to introduce her to a world of irony, you should have encouraged her to read the works of Miss Jane Austen."

The Duke stroked his chin, his gold signet ring glinting in the lamplight. "Oddly enough, only the other day Lady Melbourne remarked that the Prince Regent had commended Miss Austen's works to her. Perhaps I should buy Emma a specially bound edition of all Miss Austen's books."

"No, no!" laughed Antoinette, "that would overwhelm her and make the exercise seem too much like a school lesson. I'm sure she would be much better pleased if you quite casually gave her one book—as a little Whitsun gift—perhaps *Pride and Prejudice* would be an excellent choice. Why the very first line is delicious in its irony!"

The Duke sat back in his chair and regarded the beautiful girl standing by the mantel. His gray eyes glimmered with amusement. "Well," he declared, "is life not strange? Fifteen minutes ago you scorched into this library and aroused me to such a rage that I was on the point of hurling you through the window. Yet here we are now, engaged in a discussion about English literature!"

Antoinette laughed, unable to deny the humor of the situation. Confused, she lowered her eyes and murmured helplessly. "Oh, why is it that you always do the unexpected thing and throw me into a turmoil of conflicting emotions?"

"I protest!" he cried mockingly. "It is you, my dear, who has a gift for the unexpected action. One minute you are standing on a deserted Yorkshire road with snowflakes in your hair, a picture of delightful, country innocence. Then I find you consorting with Harrogate's most notorious courtesan. I bring you to London and you charm the *haute monde* with your elegant air, your refined demeanor. And then you whirl in here, dressed as brazenly as an actress, and proceed to harangue me for my alleged misdeeds!" He smiled and said softly, "Shall I ever know the real you, Antoinette?"

Antoinette could feel herself melting, seduced by the Duke's low, caressing tones and his overwhelming physical charm. She turned away, wrestling with herself, quite forgetting that her inner conflict was mirrored in her face in the glass over the mantel.

Antoinette struggled to keep control of her capricious emotions. No, she thought furiously, I shall not allow him to manipulate me. He is a man of the world, experienced in the handling of rebellious fillies. He may have every woman in London setting their caps at him, and swooning with delight if he so much as glances in their direction—but I have no intention of joining their ranks. I dare not. When my role as his fiancée is finished, I want to be able to walk from this house with my head held high, unsoured by regret or self-pity. How pitiful I should look if I allowed myself to be beguiled by the Duke's lethal charm.

Maintaining an icy edge to her voice, she remarked, "It is interesting, my lord Duke, how often Lady Melbourne's name creeps into the conversation. Tell me, is she by any chance a party to the truth about our engagement?"

"How astute of you to realize that," the Duke complimented her. "I have known Lady Melbourne since I was a boy. I find it impossible to conceal anything from her."

"And does she approve of your wilful deception of London society?" inquired Antoinette.

The Duke laughed. "She is most amused by the whole affair. Whenever we encounter one another, at the theatre or the opera, she gazes at me over the top of her fan and directs such an arch look in my direction—I have great difficulty keeping my face straight!"

"My, how fearfully entertaining!" exclaimed Antoinette sarcastically. "How delightful for you and Lady Melbourne to be sharing such an amusing secret joke. But why did you not tell me that she was a party to the deception? Have you any notion how foolish I feel thinking back over my conversations with the lady and realizing how she must have laughed at me?"

The Duke waved a dismissive hand. "You are reacting in an over-sensitive manner, Antoinette. The point is that when you were newly arrived in London I decided that you had quite enough to occupy you without burdening you with the task of remembering who knew of our deception and who didn't. I thought it would be easier for you if we simply assumed that no one apart from us two was aware of the true relationship between us."

Antoinette tossed her golden curls and whispered in a mocking, simpering tone, "Ah, yes. I had forgot. We females are blessed with such bird brains and are quite incapable of remembering anything besides the name of the clever little milliner near St. Paul's."

The Duke's eyes darkened. "Take care, Antoinette," he warned. "Do not provoke me further."

"On the contrary!" she flared. "It is you who provoke me!"

Although the Duke was a large man, he was athletically built and fighting fit. The speed with which he moved from his chair astonished Antoinette. As he bore down on her, she backed nervously toward the door.

"Damn it, you have tried my patience too far!" he exclaimed. "I am not accustomed to having beautiful young women invade the peace of my library and then proceed to engage me in a maddening and quite pointless argument!"

"Pointless is it?" Antoinette retorted boldly. "How typical of your arrogance. For the person most under discussion has been you—but of course, you consider yourself to be so perfect that any criticism of your splendid self is brushed aside as irrelevant."

She had gone too far. His mouth was set in a firm, hard line. His eyes were the color of slate after rain. His hand, as he seized her bare shoulder, was trembling with rage.

"Be silent, you little minx," he muttered furiously, "for now I'm going to give you what you deserve."

Instinctively, Antoinette raised her hand to shield her face from the stinging blow she knew he was about to inflict on her. Roughly, he pulled her to him, his long fingers twined in her hair, pulling her face up toward him. He knocked aside her protective hand and bent over her, crushing her lips to his.

For a moment, Antoinette stood stunned in his embrace. She had expected him to beat her. But instead he was kissing her . . . oh, how he was kissing her! His mouth on hers was warm, firm and savagely demanding. Against her will, Antoinette found herself whirled into a new world where nothing mattered except this man, his kiss, his hands in her hair. She yielded, kissing him in return with a rapture so great that a low moan escaped from him. In a frenzy of passion, he covered her face, her throat, her bosom with burning kisses, his hands tearing the thin silk around her neck. Utterly abandoned, with her golden hair streaming loose around her bare shoulders, Antoinette clung to him, her blood like liquid fire. He lifted her up, then, and carried her across to the sofa. Antoinette gazed up at him, and saw that he, like her, was consumed with desire.

He crossed to the window to ensure that the curtains were tightly drawn. As he did so, Antoinette's eye fell on a book he had been reading before her dramatic entrance into the library. It was a short appreciation of the works of the artist George Howland.

Antoinette felt as if she had been doused with cold spring water. Suddenly, the mists of passion cleared. She remembered who she was, where she was, and what she was on the point of doing.

As the Duke turned around from the window, he found the girl in the red dress on her feet and unable to meet his eye. Terrified that he would throw her back on the sofa and ravish her, Antoinette gathered up her skirts and ran for the door.

"Antoinette, wait!" commanded the Duke.

She paid no heed. She fled down the hall, ignoring the astonished gaze of the footmen. Once inside the house next door, she sped up to her apartment and flung herself face down on the bed.

What have I done, she thought frantically. Oh dear, *what* have I done?

But she knew the answer. However painful, however embarrassing, the truth had to be faced.

I have fallen in love with the Duke of Lyveden, she whispered miserably. Oh, how could I be such a fool as to allow such a thing? To fall in love with a man so far out of reach, a man who is after all, my employer and who will have no use for me in a few months' time.

But it is not my fault! I had no notion that he would suddenly seize me and kiss me in that . . . that most ruthless fashion. And how was I to know that once in his arms, I would behave like a wanton, craving his kisses, surrendering to his most intimate embrace, yearning for his touch with every fibre of my being. Who could not love a man who aroused such a response in her? I would never have believed myself capable of acting in such a wild, unbridled manner. Yet when his lips were on mine, there was no sense, no reason in the world at all. I wanted only him. And yes, it must be admitted: had it not been for my eye happening on that book about George Howland, then in all probability I would have yielded to the Duke, there on his sofa.

Antoinette's cheeks burned as she considered what he must think of her. Oh, it is most unfair, she realized with an inward wail of despair. With his passion, his strength, his fiery kisses, he has made me fall in love with him. Yet clearly, in his eyes, I am just another conquest. It is probably commonplace for him to provoke such a heated response in a woman. No doubt half the society ladies in London have experienced untold rapture at his practiced hands.

Yet it is different for me. For looking back, I see now that my love for him has been growing, slowly but surely, ever since that first day we met on the road to Harrogate. I have found him by turns aggravating, kind, ruthless, courteous, arrogant, considerate, cold-blooded and scorchingly passionate. He has confused, bewildered and perplexed me. But I have never been bored in his company. Indeed, when he enters a room, it is always as if the colors glow more brightly and the air is charged with a strange, exciting current.

Slowly, Antoinette slid off the bed and crossed to her toilette table. Her face in the glass confirmed her worst fears. Her blue eyes were luminous with love. Her face was rounded and flushed while her lips were red and luscious, looking almost bruised from the violence of the Duke's kisses.

Aghast, she gazed at the tightly waisted red silk dress. It was not the ripped bodice which appalled her. She had, it must be admitted, invited that by wearing the dress in the first place.

But what possessed me to do such a thing, wondered Antoinette. I recall returning from Almack's in the most fearful temper, loathing what I had seen and heard there. Then I read the tract the Duke had set Lady Emma to read, on *Advice to a Daughter,* and from that moment on it was as if a demon possessed me. I was not myself. I raged into this dressing room, selected this most revealing dress . . . and then to think that I had the impertinence to storm into the Duke's library and goad him into treating me so savagely.

Hastily, Antoinette stripped off the red dress unable to bear the sight of it any longer. Yes, she thought, it was all my fault. Until now, the Duke has behaved toward me with the utmost respect. There have been many occasions when he could, if he wished, have taken advantage of me. Why, on the journey down from Harrogate, it would have been a simple matter for him to have pretended that the inn was full, and it would be necessary for us to share a room. . . .

But he has never stooped to such cheap devices. It was I who provoked him into treating me roughly. Like a madwoman, I refused to heed the warning signs. I drove him to the edge, forcing him finally to lose his self-control and attack me. Except, of course, that then everything rebounded on me and it was I who melted under the fire of his kisses. I who would willingly throw myself into his arms and beg him to do as he wished with me.

It was as if, she thought, I found myself in the grip of a wild, untameable emotion . . . a madness. *Madness.* The word seared through her mind. Horror stricken she remembered the painter, George Howland. He had been in love with a golden-haired beauty who had borne him a child and then disappeared. *She was incredibly beautiful . . . but quite, quite mad.*

Antoinette subsided onto the velvet stool, the color draining from her cheeks. Since that fateful hour when she had visited George Howland's house, she had contrived to push to the back of her mind the knowledge that the woman she believed to be her mother had almost certainly been insane. But now the facts had to be faced.

Have I, too, the demon madness within me, whispered

Antoinette, aghast. Along with my mother's English good looks, did I also inherit her insanity?

What else could it be, she mused, that caused me to act in such a tempestuous manner with the Duke this evening. Why, I was so bold, so familiar, so impertinent. And above all, I was inviting. Yes, let it be said, deep down I wanted him to take me in his arms and ravish me.

Antoinette buried her head in her hands and gave way to a storm of weeping. Oh, this is terrible, she sobbed. I have acted disgracefully! What must he think of me? By my inflammatory behavior this evening I have lost all dignity in his eyes. He will never again hold me in respect. But it is not my fault! I was possessed. Truly possessed by something evil within me which I never before knew existed and which I do not understand!

How can I face the Duke again? How can I continue with this charade of our engagement, when the very sight of him, the sound of his voice, the very mention of his name is enough to set me atremble with desire. And worse, how can I meet his gaze when I know his gray eyes will hold nothing but contempt for me?

Limp with fatigue, Antoinette fell at last into bed. She fell asleep immediately but her dreams were troubled. The next morning she slept late. It was as if her mind preferred the comfort of the unconscious state and was reluctant to face the reality of the harsh morning light.

On awakening Antoinette resolutely refused to allow herself to lie and mope over last night's traumatic events with the Duke. I must not think of him, she decided. If I once allow myself to dwell on my feelings for him, I shall sink into a morass of self-pity and shame.

My longing for him will make me pale and languid, and I shall be unable to concentrate on anything else in the world but my love for him. No, I must not permit myself to give way to my emotions. It is bad enough that I have fallen in love with him, but I must not compound the agony by revealing to him that he has made another conquest.

Fortunately, Antoinette had another urgent matter to

attend to, to divert her attention from the Duke. She sat at her writing table and composed a formal few lines to the Earl of Rothsey.

Dear Sir, I am most grateful to you for your courtesy in returning my yellow parasol. However, I must make it plain that I have no desire for any further social intercourse with you and I should be glad if you would desist in insisting on paying me such unwelcome attention. I remain, yours cordially, Antoinette Aston.

She sealed the letter and handed it to Perkins for delivery.

"Shall I wait for a reply, Miss Aston?" inquired the driver.

"Thank you, no, Perkins," replied Antoinette coolly. "There will be no reply."

Lady Emma was engaged in dancing and music classes that day, so Antoinette was not required in the schoolroom. Anxious to avoid the Duke, she took the carriage to Bond Street, and engaged in a little window shopping. There she encountered Lord and Lady Portchester, who prevailed upon her to ride with them in the Park. So the day passed and it was not until five o'clock that Antoinette returned to Curzon Street.

To her surprise, as she entered the house, the housekeeper came rushing down the stairs, her cap askew, her gray hair in disarray.

"Oh Miss Aston, thank heavens you are returned! I am quite at my wits end!"

"What has happened?" demanded Antoinette. "Is it Lady Emma? Has she fallen ill? Has there been an accident?"

Mrs. Reynolds wrung her hands. "She has gone, Miss Aston! Gone to the May revels with the rogue brother of her ex-governess!"

"But this is dreadful!" Stunned with shock, Antoinette began firing questions at the harrassed housekeeper. "How did this happen, Mrs. Reynolds? Are you sure? Where is the Duke? Has he been informed?"

Swiftly, the housekeeper explained. "Miss Welch, the ex-governess, called at the house and inquired if Lady Emma would care to accompany her to the revels. I distinctly heard Lady Emma refuse, and then Miss Welch left."

"She refused to go with Miss Welch?" queried Antoinette. "Then—"

Mrs. Reynolds held up a trembling hand. "Then everything became confused. Miss Welch went off in her carriage. Next thing I knew, there was Lady Emma, standing in the street talking to that dreadful Ralph Welch. She seemed upset but he was laughing. Then I heard him say, "Come on, Lady Emma, we'll catch up with my sister at the May revels." And they both jumped into his gig and disappeared down Curzon Street. Oh my," wailed the gray haired woman, "the Duke will never forgive me! He's been at his club all day. Oh dear, what am I to say to him when he returns?"

Fleetingly, Antoinette registered the fact that while she had spent the day making strenuous efforts to avoid the Duke, he in turn had ensconced himself at the club, thereby avoiding her! But this was not the time nor place to dwell on the implications of his actions. The essential thing now was to find Lady Emma and bring her back to the house before the Duke was aware of her absence.

Swiftly she ordered the carriage to be brought to the door. As Perkins held open the door, she inquired, "The May revels, Perkins, where are they held?"

"In the garden of Lord Alvanley's house, Miss Aston. He has a rather large garden, I understand, backing onto the river at Chelsea. But if I may say so, Miss, it is not the sort of gathering which a lady like yourself should grace."

"That is just as I feared," murmured Antoinette to herself. Aloud she instructed pleasantly, "To Chelsea, if you please, Perkins. As fast as you can!"

Eager to show his prowess with the horses, Perkins cracked his whip and they set off at a brisk pace. As the carriage bowled down Park Lane, Antoinette mused on Lady Emma's sudden decision to run off with Ralph Welch. He was the man, Antoinette recalled, who had taken her (unchaperoned) to the Frost Fair last winter. The Duke had been livid with his sister over that incident, and it was this which had precipitated his decision to take a wife and thus provide a stable background for the girl.

But apart from telling me about the Frost Fair, Lady Emma has never again mentioned Ralph Welch, thought Antoinette, bewildered. Surely she has not been harboring a secret crush on him for all this time? She felt suddenly sick as she realized that it was just possible that Lady Emma had been meeting Ralph Welch secretly. It was not unheard of for an unscrupulous dancing teacher or music tutor to agree to turn a blind eye to the tryst of a pair of lovers . . .

As for Ralph Welch, it was plain to see what his intentions were. No doubt at this very moment he was persuading Lady Emma what a great diversion it would be if they eloped to Gretna Green. And Lady Emma, desperate for excitement, tired of her schoolroom and her dowdy smocks, would be all too ready to agree!

Frantically, Antoinette tapped on the carriage wall. "Faster, Perkins! Faster!"

She clung to the leather strap as the carriage careered down Sloane Street and then stopped. "Can't get no nearer, Miss," Perkins informed her. "There's such a crush of carriages 'round Lord Alvanley's house."

Antoinette waited no longer, but jumped down and ran along the road, following the sound of laughter and music. Her head was throbbing and her hands were sticky with heat. The air was heavy and oppressive.

But in Lord Alvanley's splendid garden, lights blazed, fountains flowed and an orchestra played vigorously. Pride of place was taken by a tall Maypole around which a dozen young maidens were dancing. Antoinette raised her eyebrows at the scanty nature of the girls' dresses, but then her attention was caught by a beautiful circular bower of orange trees. Each tree was lit by lamps and festooned with strings of flowers. There were booths for tea and wine, with gaming tables laid out and an area cleared for dancing.

Over two hundred people were present. Most of them, Antoinette realized, were in dangerously merry mood. The women were garishly dressed and overpainted, while the men roved in packs, their hands reaching out in the lamplight to squeeze a willing waist here, and steal a kiss there.

But there was no sign of Lady Emma. Anxiously Antoinette made her way down the garden, nimbly avoiding a young buck who attempted to whirl her into the frenzy around the Maypole. Down by the river, a number of tents had been set up, all garlanded with flags and fresh flowers. It was cooler here near the water, and as Antoinette lifted her head she felt the first drops of rain fall upon her cheek.

Then came the scream. It issued, she realized, from the tent furthest away, down by a clump of silver birch trees in the corner. Another scream—high pitched, female, the cry of a terrified girl.

Blindly, Antoinette ran toward the tent. She wrenched aside the flap and found a dark-haired girl tussling with a tall, fair-haired young man. A plain, sharp featured woman lounged on a garden chair, laughing at the girl's frantic struggles.

"Let her be!" shouted Antoinette, making a dive for the young man's hair. "Lady Emma, are you all right?"

Lady Emma's gray eyes lit with relief as she recognized Antoinette, "He dragged me in here," she spluttered, writhing in Ralph Welch's drunken grasp. "He says he will not let me go until I kiss him."

Antoinette disliked Ralph Welch on sight. His weak chin, cruel mouth and cold blue eyes repelled her. Seizing his fair hair, she yanked, with all her might. He yelled in protest, released Lady Emma and with a vicious blow knocked Antoinette sideways.

"Interefere with my little bit of fun, would you?" he glared at Antoinette. "Well I fancy it will be even more enjoyable with two lovely ladies to play with!"

Miss Welch giggled. "I'll guard the tent entrance, Ralph. I'd like to see you tame two wildcats!"

Goaded on by his sister, Ralph Welch pounced on Antoinette and crooked his arm around her neck. His other hand closed on the terrified Lady Emma. "Down!" he ordered. "Lie down on the grass, both of you."

Lady Emma opened her mouth to scream but the ex-governess leaped across and pinched her hard on the cheek. "Do as he says!" she hissed. "Or it'll be the worse for you!"

But her last words were drowned by a sudden, insistent drumming on the roof of the tent. There was a crack, followed by a loud boom.

"Just a passing summer storm," announced Ralph Welch, his lascivious eye boldly exploring Antoinette's rounded bosom.

Miss Welch screamed. "Ralph! Look out!"

Whirling around, Antoinette realized that the crack they had heard had not been lightning after all. Instead, the tent pole had broken. The tent, sodden and heavy now with the insistent rain, was in imminent danger of collapse.

Wasting no more time, Antoinette took advantage of the confusion. While the shrieking Miss Welch and her brother flailed among falling lengths of wet canvas, Antoinette seized Lady Emma's hand and dragged her out into the open. The storm was at its height now, with dancing lightning reflected in the waters of the Thames.

"Quick, let us shelter under those trees," cried Lady Emma, as the deluge of rain poured down upon them.

"No! Trees are dangerous cover in a storm," instructed Antoinette. "We had best go up to the house."

"I don't want to leave the garden!" insisted Lady Emma, her drenched hair sending streams of water over her shoulders. "I must stay here."

"Don't be absurd!" protested Antoinette, beginning to lose patience with the girl. She pulled her by the arm. "Come, we must take shelter!"

"No! I will not!"

A burst of laughter interrupted them, swiftly followed by a large dark blue cloak which enveloped both girls. For one dreadful moment, Antoinette imagined that Ralph Welch had captured them again. But as she and Lady Emma were firmly guided along the lower garden path, she was amazed and relieved to hear the Duke of Lyveden's sardonic tones:

". . . the most ridiculous sight I have ever seen. A torrent of rain falling from the skies and two totally unprotected ladies standing drenched to the skin arguing about whether or not they should take shelter! How bizarre!"

A door creaked. Then, blessedly, the ground was dry underfoot. Emerging from the voluminous cloak, Antoinette saw they were standing in a small summer house, overlooking the river.

Lady Emma was glaring at her brother. "How dare you make me out to be a mindless ragdoll, Alexander! I had good reason for not wanting to leave the garden!"

The amusement had gone from the Duke's voice as he retorted harshly. "I am more interested, Emma, in hearing your reason for being in this garden in the first place! And in the company of that blackguard Welch!"

Such was the fury in the Duke's gray eyes that even Antoinette trembled with fright. Oh dear, she thought, however is poor Lady Emma to explain herself?

But Lady Emma was staunchly standing her ground. Boldly she lifted her glistening face to her brother and said, "I came here to look for Tabitha. My kitten."

"Your kitten?" echoed the Duke, bewildered.

Lady Emma nodded. "You see, Miss Welch called on me and asked me if I would care to accompany her to the May revels. I refused. But while we were talking, Tabitha jumped out of the window and began to explore Miss Welch's carriage. When Miss Welch drove away, I realized to my horror that she had taken poor Tabitha away with her!"

"And then Ralph Welch arrived?" inquired Antoinette.

"He had been there all the time, sitting preening himself in his new gig," replied Lady Emma, tossing back her damp hair. "When I saw what had happened to Tabitha, I was so distraught I ran and asked him for help."

"He, of course, was delighted to oblige," said the Duke dryly.

Lady Emma gazed up at her brother, her gray eyes huge with anguish. "Oh Alexander, he is the most evil man! He dragged me into a tent and . . . well, if Antoinette had not arrived when she did . . . oh, I dread to think what would have happened to me!"

It was at this point that Antoinette realized that the Duke

had not yet addressed a single remark to her. Nor had he met her eyes. In the darkness of the summer house, her cheeks burned with shame. *After my behavior last night, he has clearly decided that I am quite beneath his notice. I do believe his aim now will be to see as little of me as possible.*

As if to bear out these painful thoughts, the Duke said, "Emma, you and Antoinette will proceed home directly. I understand from Mrs. Reynolds that Perkins drove Antoinette here in the carriage, so he will take you home."

"But Tabitha!" cried Lady Emma. "I cannot leave her here. The last time I saw her she was sitting high up in a silver birch tree. It was while I was trying to entice her down that Ralph Welch—"

"I shall bring home the kitten for you," promised the Duke. He added grimly, "And I shall also make my mark most severely on Ralph Welch."

Antoinette shivered. She held no brief for Ralph Welch. Nevertheless such was the controlled fury in the Duke's voice as he spoke his name, that Antoinette felt a pang of sympathy for the young man who was shortly to receive the milling of his life.

Observing that Lady Emma's teeth were beginning to chatter with cold, Antoinette took the Duke's cloak and wrapped it around the girl. "Come now. Let us return home. Your brother will bring Tabitha later. But meanwhile we'll ask the cook to heat up some milk for her."

By the time the two girls reached Curzon Street, Lady Emma had started to sneeze. The following morning, Mrs. Reynolds confirmed that the young lady had indeed taken a chill and would be confined to bed for a few days. Antoinette spent most of the morning in Lady Emma's room, reading to her and playing with the little black kitten who seemed none the worse for her adventure at the May revels.

Lady Emma slept after luncheon. Outside, the rain still teemed down, making it impossible for Antoinette to venture out. She wandered into the small blue drawing room overlooking the garden and took up some embroidery. But after half an hour, she examined her work and threw it down in disgust. It was not merely that the stitches were disgracefully uneven, but whatever had possessed her to embroider a corn-flower a vivid shade of orange?

Restlessly, she crossed to the sidetable and picked up a copy of *La Belle Assemblée*. It contained a drawing of the delightful ensemble the Honorable Cecilia Lowe had worn to Lady Oxford's salon in Paris.

Lady Susannah Clegg, Lady Anne Monteith, the Honorable Cecilia Lowe. Originally they had been the three leading contenders for the Duke's hand. But now Cecilia had fled to Paris, and little had been heard recently of the worthy, but tedious Lady Susannah.

Was the Duke, then, intending to propose to Lady Anne? Antoinette felt a dull ache in her heart at the thought. Yet from his point of view, she realized, Lady Anne has clearly triumphed over the other two. His aim, presenting me as his fiancée, was to determine the true character of the ladies concerned. The Honorable Cecilia took the huff and turned her back on him for Paris. Lady Susannah has been amiable enough to me whenever we have met . . . but she appears to have ensured that we have not encountered one another that often. Yet Lady Anne Monteith, in contrast, has endeavored positively to seek my company. Indeed, rare and bright has been the day in which she did not loom large in my life, drawling, "Dearest Antoinette, how delightful to see you again!"

In the Duke's eyes, it must have appeared that she was sweetly and considerately offering me the hand of friendship. Oh yes, Lady Anne, you have surely passed the test with flying colors. Before the year is out, you will be the proud possessor of the glittering Lyveden tiara!

"Good afternoon. I trust I am not disturbing you?"

Antoinette gasped. The Duke's low even tone, his commanding presence in the doorway just when she least expected it, startled her into the naive blush of a young untutored girl.

She found it impossible to look at him. Impossible not to remember the ardor of their kisses, the savage intensity of their embraces just two nights previously. Every inch of her body prompted her to throw herself into his arms and surrender to her desires. Yet her conscience flooded with guilt and shame, counselled caution, urged restraint.

To her surprise, the Duke seemed equally ill at ease. He, the master of self-control, stood before the mantel, his fingers drumming on the marble top.

Antoinette put aside her magazine, and sat in the window seat, her hands clasped firmly together to prevent them trembling. Why had he come? Was he preparing to initiate an embarrassing postmortem on her extraordinary conduct in his library two nights ago?

As the Duke began to speak Antoinette's heart sank. "Since . . . since what occurred between us in the library the other night," he said gravely, "I have been engaged in some hard thinking."

Antoinette turned to gaze from the window, to conceal the blush staining her cheeks. Was he expecting her to apologize for her outlandish behavior? Well I shan't, she thought defiantly. That would only lead to more discussion, explanations, accusations.

Antoinette said quietly, "Your Grace, can we not consider the episode closed?"

"No!" he exclaimed, pacing the room. "I was angry with you the other night, Antoinette. I admit it, and I apologize. On reflection, I realize you were right about so many things. Especially about this whole question of our sham engagement. We must put an end to this charade, Antoinette, here and now!"

So, thought Antoinette wretchedly, he has come to tell me that my time in Curzon Street has ended. I am to be pensioned off and despatched forthwith from his life. And I have no one to blame but myself. By my wild, undisciplined behavior I have made myself an embarrassment to him. It is only natural that he should wish to be rid of me without delay.

Pale faced, she rose to her feet and said unsteadily, "I quite understand. There is no more that needs to be said. If you will excuse me, I will make arrangements to leave immediately."

"Leave?" he rounded on her, his handsome face full of alarm. "What do you mean? There is no question of you leaving me now, Antoinette. Not when I have fallen so deeply in love with you!"

Antoinette stared at him, unable to believe her ears.

He strode across the room and took her hands in his. "My dearest girl," he murmured, his voice low, his eyes full of tenderness. "You have made me realize that love between a man and a woman is the highest emotion we can attain. Sadly, it is not the lot of all of us to find it. But when it does exist between two people, one should not deny it. One should rejoice in one's good fortune and thank God for the wonderful gift of love. When I came here yesterday evening and found you gone I thought I had driven you to run away. I was in despair . . ."

"I do not understand," whispered Antoinette, her heart beating wildly. "You . . . you talk of denying love as if you have felt this affection for me for some time?"

He laughed softly. "I fell in love with you the first moment I saw you. When you stood on that Yorkshire road with snow spangling your hair. After the perfumed, sophisticated women I had known in London, you were like a breath of pure fresh air entering my life. You were so natural, so honest, so full of life. But then," he sighed, "the events of the next few weeks threw me into confusion. After Emma's escapade at the Frost Fair with that rogue Welch, I realized that I must marry. And then I returned to Harrogate and found my pure, springtime girl in the company of a lady of loose morals . . ."

Antoinette lowered her eyes. Oh yes, she could well imagine what the Duke must have thought of her!

He went on: "I thought of my duty, to my heirs, my line, my estate. As a Duke, it is expected of me that I marry an equal, a lady well versed in social procedure, who will not only bear me sons but who will grace my country mansion and play to perfection the exacting role of society hostess."

Yes, thought Antoinette, the Honorable Cecilia, Lady Susannah and Lady Anne. Any one of them would have been eminently suitable for such a task.

"But I could not let you go from my life," continued

the Duke in an agitated tone. "Hence I hit on the solution of bringing you to London as my fiancée, yet the next moment I'd find you dancing girlishly across the daisies in St. James's Park. How I longed to sweep you into my arms and make love to you! But then I remembered that I was not free to marry as I wished. I believed that as a Duke I had these dreary responsibilities and duties to my line. It was only when you whirled into my library the other evening and goaded me to a pitch of fury, that I saw sense at last. You broke down the barriers, Antoinette. I felt in such a fever for you that I could not restrain myself—"

Blue eyes met gray across the room and they both relived the glorious passion of that tempestuous kiss. He advanced toward her, murmuring, "From the manner in which you returned my ardor, Antoinette, I know my love for you is not in vain. Come, kiss me again, and tell me that you will be my bride. Let us abandon this masquerade of an engagement and face the world in all honesty as a truly betrothed couple!"

Tears stung Antoinette's eyes as she felt his strong arms embrace her. The moment she had prayed for, but never in her wildest dreams had imagined could ever happen, had come true. The man she loved with all her heart and soul had asked her to marry him. Somehow, by some sweet magic, he had fallen as passionately in love with her as she was with him.

Hopelessly, against a rising flood of tears, she struggled for words. She knew this to be the most agonizing moment of her life. With a great effort of will, she composed herself long enough to murmur brokenly, "Your Grace . . . you do me great honor. But I am sorry, I can never, ever be your wife!"

Twelve

The Duke looked as if he had been stabbed. With anguish in his eyes he declared, "Antoinette, have I done something to offend you? Oh, I freely confess I shall not be the easiest man in the world to be wed to. I have a fearful temper—as you well know. And I do not suffer fools gladly. But I love you with all my heart and I give you my word that I shall do my utmost to make you happy."

Shaking, Antoinette turned away and buried her golden head in her hands. Oh how she loved him! How she longed to hurl herself into his arms and declare herself his and only his forever!

But at the forefront of her mind was the haunting spectre of another. They say she was mad, thought Antoinette wretchedly. And it is likely, then, that I too carry the same seeds of madness. The Duke needs heirs. How can I, then, in all conscience agree to marry him knowing that I may pass on this fearful insanity to his children? I cannot run that risk.

"Antoinette what is it? What is wrong?" demanded the Duke. "Are you concerned that your origins are too humble for you to take your place in society as my duchess? If so, then your fears are quite unfounded. For you possess a natural grace and dignity, my dear, that far outclasses many ladies bred to wealth and privilege. Believe me, I shall be the proudest man in England if you will agree to be my bride!"

Antoinette felt as if she had been flung into the most

terrible nightmare from which she would never wake up. She knew she should take her courage in both hands and explain her fears to the Duke. She should tell him, honestly and boldly, why she could not marry him.

But how can I place him in such a dreadful dilemma, she pondered miserably. He has declared his love for me. Yet when I reveal that I believe there to be madness in my family, he will be forced to consider the health of his future heirs. His line must be continued. I shall then be placing him in the terrible situation of having to retract, to make gallantly courteous excuses for not marrying me after all. I shall have to stand here and watch his eyes veil with embarrassment. Oh, it would be too shaming!

I am not brave enough to do it, she realized. I, who believe in honesty and mutual trust, would rather take a more convenient evasive attitude than give voice to the truth.

The Duke took her gently by the shoulders and turned her to face him. His hand was in her hair. "Kiss me," he commanded softly. "Then no words will be needed between us."

Antoinette knew that at the first sweet touch of his lips she would be lost. He would sweep her away on a tide of desire which would completely destroy all sense of logic, reason and duty. Violently, she flung herself away from him and placed herself out of reach on the other side of the pale blue sofa.

Steeling herself, she said with a coldness denied by the fire in her blood, "Your Grace, I fear you are taking advantage of my situation. I agreed in all good faith to accompany you to London to pose as your fiancée. I believe I have kept my part of the bargain. I should be glad if you would keep yours."

Amazed, his gray eyes bored into her. "But . . . but the other night—in the library. Do you now deny the ecstasy you shared with me?"

Antoinette affected an amused laugh. "Did I not warn you that Miss LeStrange had trained me well? Naturally, I was taught how to simulate passion, desire, ardor! I am surprised that a man of your experience in the world was deceived by my playacting." She moved languidly to the window and continued coolly: "However, I must assure you that marriage plays no part in my plans, my Lord Duke. When my role as your fiancée is finished, I propose returning to Harrogate and setting up a rival house in opposition to Miss LeStrange."

"I do not believe it," he said flatly.

Antoinette shrugged. "I assure you, it is the truth." She smiled mockingly. "Indeed, from the success of my, er, performance with you the other night, I do believe I shall soon be running a very successful little business!"

For what seemed an age he stared at her, his expression unreadable. Antoinette gazed back, her blue eyes hard, her hands behind her back gripping the window ledge to prevent herself rushing forward and spilling out the truth to him.

Then it was over. Without another word he turned on his heel and left the room, slamming the door behind him.

Ashen-faced, Antoinette stood by the window, listening to his receding footsteps in the hall. I love him, she thought, dizzy with longing, but I had no choice but to drive him away. And now I have lost him forever. She threw herself down on the window seat and waited for the bitter tears to fall. But such was her anguish that she felt numb with grief. Dry-eyed, she curled up against the soft silk cushions and rested her throbbing head against the cool glass, wondering what on earth was to become of her now.

At six o'clock Mrs. Reynolds tapped on the drawing room door.

"Excuse me, Miss Aston. But Lady Emma is most insistent that you take supper with her up in her chamber."

Antoinette rose to her feet, her limbs feeling stiff after so many hours curled up on the window seat. She managed a smile as she said, "Of course I'll go up and keep Lady Emma company. I'll take her supper tray to her myself."

Lady Emma was propped up on three lace pillows. Her cheeks were flushed, her eyes brightly feverish. It would be another few days yet, Antoinette realized, before the chill passed and Lady Emma was allowed downstairs again. However, her appetite was hearty and she attacked with relish the delicious roast chicken which Cook had basted in butter. Antoinette was not at all hungry, and fed most of her supper to a delighted Tabitha.

When she was finished, Lady Emma pushed aside her tray and pulled out a book from underneath her pillow. "Look, Antoinette! See what Alexander gave me this afternoon."

It was, Antoinette saw, a beautifully bound copy of *Pride and Prejudice*. So he had taken her advice and bought the book for his sister!

"The Duke has excellent taste," said Antoinette quietly. "I am sure you will be most entertained by Miss Austen's astringent style, Lady Emma."

The dark-haired girl laughed. "My, Antoinette, how formal you are! You always refer to me as *Lady* Emma, which makes me feel as ancient as Lady Holland. And you even call your own fiancé *the Duke,* as if he is a person with whom you are barely on nodding terms!"

The girl's laughter and her innocent remarks were the last straw for Antoinette. Something broke inside her, and the tears she had held back for so long began to fall, streaming down her face and dewing Lady Emma's silk coverlet.

Distraught, Lady Emma threw her arms around the weeping girl. "Antoinette! What have I said? What is wrong? Oh dear, please do not cry so! I cannot bear to see you so upset. Will you not tell me what is troubling you?"

Suddenly, Antoinette found herself pouring out the whole story to Lady Emma. She told her everything, right from the moment she learned the truth about Dr. Aston's Will to the events of this afternoon, when she had lied to the Duke and driven him away.

The relief of shedding the burden of pretence was enormous. Antoinette felt as if a great weight had been lifted from her shoulders now that Lady Emma knew the truth about her. Lady Emma sat up in bed, hugging her knees, an incredulous expression on her face as she assimilated what Antoinette had told her.

"You must not be angry with your brother for deceiving you over the engagement," whispered Antoinette. "You know he only has your best interests at heart."

"Angry!" cried Lady Emma. "Oh, I am not at all furious with him! I think it is the most romantic tale I ever heard!" She clasped Antoinette's hands. "And you do love him, don't you? I can see it in your eyes!"

"Yes, I love him with all my heart," said Antoinette softly. "But you do understand, don't you, why I had to send him away. I could not run the risk of being responsible for bringing madness into your family."

"No," said Lady Emma firmly, "I think you should have told Alexander the truth, instead of leaving him with a false impression of you." As her gray eyes filled with tears, she gasped in a choked voice. "Oh, Antoinette! I have just realized! He gave me that copy of *Pride and Prejudice* as a going away present. He left this afternoon for Yorkshire, to attend Lord Hebdon's ball."

Antoinette nodded. The cream of London society were travelling up for the ball—including Lady Anne Monteith, cousin of the host.

Lady Emma said frantically, "But Antoinette! If my brother is in a rage because you have refused to marry him, he'll most like go straight up to Yorkshire and propose to Lady Anne Monteith. You know he's determined to marry before I come *Out*. And Lady Anne will accept him like a shot!"

"I should imagine so," said Antoinette wearily, stroking the sleeping kitten who lay curled up at the bottom of the bed.

Lady Emma screamed, "Antoinette, I can't bear Lady Anne! I should die if I were forced to accept her as my sister! She's supercilious, arrogant and when Alexander's not looking she can be downright spiteful."

"I'm sure you are exaggerating," murmured Antoinette. "And you must admit, that in many respects she will make a most splendid duchess."

"I won't have that cat as my sister!" shouted Lady Emma. "I won't—*I won't!* If Alexander marries her, I shall run away. I shall marry the first man who asks me!" She seized Antoinette by the shoulders. "Antoinette, you have got to stop him proposing to her!"

"How could I do such a thing?" demanded Antoinette, alarmed by the girl's feverish expression.

"You must go up to Yorkshire and tell Alexander that I beg him not to marry Lady Anne. Tell him that if he does, I shall throw myself in the Thames. If, as you say, he has my best interests at heart, he is bound to pay attention to my views on his choice of a wife."

Antoinette sighed. "Really, Lady Emma, you can't reasonably expect me to go—"

"If you won't go then I will," blazed Lady Emma, scrambling out of bed. "I mean it! I'll hire a carriage and travel night and day to Yorkshire!"

Antoinette caught hold of the girl's nightgown and pushed her back into bed. "You are staying right where you are!" she said firmly.

"Then you will go?" cried Lady Emma eagerly.

"Well . . . I . . ."

"Promise! *Promise* me you will go!"

The girl was in such an agitated state that Antoinette realized that she had no choice. "Very well, I give you my word. I will speak to your brother on your behalf. But I can give no guarantee that he will listen to me."

Lady Emma sank back on the pillows, a peaceful smile on her face. As her eyelids drooped, she whispered, "Thank you, my *sister.*"

Antoinette ordered the Duke's second carriage to be made ready for her at dawn the following morning. Already, her heart was heavy at the prospect of the task ahead of her. She wished she had not agreed to Lady Emma's preposterous and impertinent scheme. Antoinette could well imagine the Duke's reaction on receiving instructions as to whom he may and may not marry! He will throw the house from the windows, thought Antoinette wretchedly—and me after it!

However, she had given Lady Emma her word, and there was no going back on that. Had she refused to go to Yorkshire, Lady Emma would most likely have worked herself into a thoroughly deranged state, and Antoinette would have felt responsible. And deep down, she could well understand the girl's distress. To be sure, thought Antoinette, as the carriage left London, the last person I should desire as a sister is Lady Anne Monteith.

Although it was a long journey through the heart of the English countryside, it passed all too quickly for Antoinette, so greatly was she dreading what lay before her at Hebdon Hall. Ironically, it was impossible to drag her thoughts away from love and marriage, for even the countryside itself was in full bridal array, with May blossoms brocading the trees and delicate white ladies' lace clouding the roadside. As they crossed the first broad lonely sweep of Yorkshire moor, Antoinette's heart leaped as she observed the brilliant splashes of yellow gorse which made the moors look emblazoned with perpetual sunshine.

She arrived in the village of Hebdon at six o'clock on what she knew was the evening of the ball. Obviously, she could not saunter into the Grand Saloon of Hebdon Hall clad in her muslin travelling dress. Accordingly, she directed the carriage driver to the dower house on the estate, where she knew Lady Melbourne to be residing during her stay in Yorkshire.

The butler at the dower house informed her that Lady Melbourne had already left for the ball. Lady Melbourne's maid, however, recognized Antoinette and showed her to a bed chamber where she might change and refresh herself after her journey.

An hour later, Antoinette was ready. She was wearing a stunningly beautiful dress of white silk, in Grecian style, embroidered at the hem with a deep panel of gold marguerites. Her hair was caught up into a knot of curls by a white embroidered ribbon, and around her throat gleamed her exquisite gold locket.

She examined her reflection in the long glass, and confessed herself satisfied. She had never before in her life attended a ball. She was also sure that this would be the last time she would ever set eyes on the Duke of Lyveden. It promised to be a momentous and traumatic occasion. Antoinette knew that however terrified she may be inwardly, her outward appearance must exude confidence and style.

When I look back on this night, she thought, throwing on a light wool cloak, I don't want to remember myself as some cringing idiot, so overwhelmed by the occasion that she fell at the first post, and muffed her interview with the Duke. No, I must take care to keep my dignity and my wits about me. My heart may be broken, but my head must be held high.

Hebdon Hall was a sprawling seventeenth-century mansion built of magnificent York stone. Already, on this balmy night, the terraces were thronged with guests, their priceless jewellery glittering in the lamplight, their perfume vying with the scent wafting up from the nearby rose garden. Three orchestras played in the house itself, while a fourth was situated on a far lawn, tempting the young and bold to kick off their slippers and dance barefoot on the Spring grass.

It was an enchanted night. One made for romance, thought Antoinette, gazing up at the full moon which cast a silvery light over the hundred windows of the house.

Along with a tide of arriving guests, Antoinette was swept into an elegant anteroom alongside the enormous Grand Saloon. The double doors to the Grand Saloon were thrown open, and gradually the guests were passing through from the anteroom, to be announced in stentorian tones by the bewigged footman.

As she drew near the double doors, Antoinette's arm was taken by Lady Melbourne. She was looking very stately in lavender silk, with mauve ostrich plumes in her hair.

"Ah, Antoinette, I am so glad you were able to come after all," she smiled. "The Duke told me that you had kindly offered to stay in London and take care of Lady Emma. I take it she is fully restored to health now?"

"Oh . . . er, yes. She is certainly making her presence felt!" laughed Antoinette, noting with relief that the Duke had taken the trouble to make this social excuse for her absence. He had not, then, been in such a towering rage that he declared to the world that their engagement was at an end.

The two ladies had reached the entrance of the Grand Saloon.

"Lady Melbourne and Miss Antoinette Aston!" blared the footman.

They glided forward, Lady Melbourne bowing to her acquaintances and Antoinette's eyes shining in delight as she observed the sumptuous silk wallhangings, and the garlands of early roses twined along the orchestra's dais. How wonderful it would be, she thought wistfully, if I were genuinely here as the fianceé of the Duke of Lyveden, with the delightful prospect before me of hours of dancing and merrymaking.

But alas, that is not my lot tonight. I have a task to perform. And the sooner I get it over and done with, the better.

As with all women in love, she knew, the instant she entered the Grand Saloon, where the Duke was standing in the room. Had she entered any strange room in the world blindfolded, she could unfailingly have made her way to the Duke's side.

He was standing now near the tall doors which led out onto the terrace. Antoinette's heart sank as she saw that he was deep in conversation with Lady Anne Monteith. The auburn-haired girl was looking exceptionally attractive this evening, in an emerald green gown encrusted with diamonds. She had the patina and self-assurance of one who was born rich, and intended, through marriage, to be even more wealthy and influential.

Taking a deep breath, Antoinette made her way toward the couple. Lady Anne was gazing up at the Duke, a coquettish expression in her pale blue eyes. The Duke had his back to Antoinette. But as she grew near, it was as if he sensed her presence. He turned, and for a split second his gray eyes lit up as he regarded the lovely golden-haired girl in the white silk dress. Then the mask of self-control slipped back into place and he said courteously,

"Antoinette, how delightful to see you, my dear. I take it that my sister is well?"

Antoinette smiled wanly, blessing the Duke for his tact. He could not but be surprised at her unexpected arrival at the ball. Especially after their shattering last encounter in the blue drawing room in the house in Curzon Street. But gallantly, he was greeting her with all the true warmth and poise that a man would normally display toward his genuine betrothed.

"I . . . I wonder if I might have a private word with you?" murmured Antoinette. "I bring an urgent message from your sister."

The Duke turned to Lady Anne and said politely, "I wonder if you would excuse us, Lady Anne, while I converse alone with my fiancée?"

Lady Anne did not move. Her eyes were wintry, her voice loaded with malice. "Your fiancée!" she spat. "My dear Alexander, I fear you have been sadly misled about this girl. I arrived here in Yorkshire a few days ago, and spent a profitable morning making inquiries about Miss Aston."

"Indeed? How diligent of you, Lady Anne," said the Duke cuttingly.

The auburn-haired girl ignored the note of warning in his voice. She pointed an accusing finger at Antoinette, and declared shrilly, "She is an imposter. She is not the orphaned daughter of a wealthy squire as she led you to suppose. And what's more, I have it on good authority that she resided for some time at the house of Harrogate's most notorious courtesan, a Miss Eleanor LeStrange! I'm sorry, my lord Duke, but you will have to accept that your fiancée is nothing more than a woman of loose morals, a cheap—"

"Be silent!" commanded the Duke. He took Antoinette's trembling hand, and declared, "You are speaking of the woman I love. I know her to be a person of integrity, honesty, warmth and loyalty. Her origins mean nothing to me. Be she

216

peasant or princess, it is she I intend to make my bride." He gazed deep into Antoinette's eyes. "If she will have me?"

"Oh!" murmured Antoinette, quite overcome with emotion. "I . . . you do not understand . . . there is much I have not revealed to you . . ."

"There! At last she is speaking the truth!" exclaimed Lady Anne viciously. "The whole situation is absurd, Alexander! You are a peer of the realm. You cannot possibly marry a common doctor's niece!"

"There is no question of him marrying a doctor's niece," cut in another authoritative voice. To her amazement, Antoinette observed the distinguished Earl of Rothsey striding toward them. The sight of the silver-haired earl drained the color from her face. Oh, what shameful revelations was he about to let slip about her sojourn with Eleanor LeStrange?

The Earl of Rothsey glared at the girl in the emerald green dress. "It is you who have been misled, Lady Anne. Miss Aston is, in fact, no relative of the late Dr. Aston. I, too, have been making inquiries around the village of Linton-on-Craven."

"Yes, yes, I was coming to that," said Lady Anne impatiently. "She was disinherited from the doctor's Will, although she was brought up as his niece—no one in fact knows who her true parents are."

"There you are quite wrong," announced the Earl, his blue eyes regarding Antoinette affectionately. "I am delighted to tell you that the young lady is, in fact, my granddaughter."

In the stunned silence that followed, Antoinette was aware of all their eyes upon her: the Duke's loving; the Earl's, faintly amused; and Lady Anne's, lethal with horrified disbelief.

That was the last Antoinette remembered before the room suddenly tilted and she fainted into the Duke's arms.

When she regained consciousness she found she was lying on a rug outside on the cool terrace. The guests, quite understandably, were abuzz with excitement, but Lady Melbourne was efficiently keeping them at bay.

"Away with you, Lady Lucinda! Heavens, have you never seen a girl faint before?"

"Lady Anne, your face will crack right in two if you continue to scowl like that. I suggest you find Lord Hebdon and tell him to start the dancing."

Gradually, the revellers drifted away, and Antoinette was left alone on the terrace with the Duke and the Earl of Rothsey. They assisted her to her feet, and took her to sit on the terrace wall, overlooking the illuminated rose garden.

"Sorry to give you such a shock, my dear," apologized the elderly Earl, with a twinkle in his eye. "I've been trying to speak to you for months now. But every time I got close to you, you turned tail and ran away from me!"

"I . . . I fear I misunderstood your intentions," smiled Antoinette shakily, reassured by the warmth of the Duke's strong hand in hers.

The Duke said, "Will you tell us what you know about Antoinette, sir?"

The Earl sighed. "I blame myself entirely for having placed Antoinette in this confusing situation. You see, it all began when my son Mark married a very beautiful French girl by the name of Natalia."

Antoinette gasped. "Natalia! Why the letter N engraved on the back of my lovely gold locket . . ."

"It was my wedding gift to her," nodded the Earl with a smile. "She looked so like you, my dear. Breath-takingly beautiful, with the same brilliant blue eyes. She and Mark were divinely happy. But then, stubborn creature that I was, I quarrelled with Mark and in the heat of the moment I cut him out of my Will. He and Natalia took themselves off to Yorkshire, and before the breach could be healed between us, Mark was killed in a hunting accident. I had heard that Natalia had borne him a child but to my dismay and distress I could not trace her."

Antoinette's eyes misted with tears. "I know what happened," she said softly, "she was destitute—and proud. She laid me on the steps of Dr. Aston's house with the gold locket and a note begging him to take care of me."

The Earl said brokenly, "She died soon after, probably of a broken heart. I found her grave just the other day, a few miles away in Grassington. There is just a simple inscription giving her name and the date of her death."

The Duke added slowly, "So months ago, when we were all in Harrogate, you first set eyes on Antoinette, and recognized her as your granddaughter?"

"Naturally, I couldn't be a hundred percent sure," said the Earl. "But her resemblance to Natalia was so striking—and then there was that distinctive gold locket around her neck. I was positive it was my wedding gift to Natalia. But I did not want to alarm Antoinette by discussing the matter with her publicly. I felt deeply ashamed of my treatment of my son, and I desired to speak with Antoinette privately on the matter. But that, I fear, proved impossible!"

Antoinette laughed. "Oh, how simple, how obvious it all seems now! And to think that for all these months I have been desperately worried about the mystery of my birth. I still cannot believe that I am really your granddaughter, and that my name is not Aston but . . ." she gazed, perplexed at the Earl. "What *is* my name?"

"Our family name is Leigh," the Earl told her. "So your correct title is the Lady Antoinette Leigh."

"Not for long it's not," laughed the Duke. "For I intend to waste no time in giving you my name, Antoinette! I take it," he went on softly, "that there is to be no more nonsense about you refusing to marry me?"

Her starlit eyes gave him her answer. The Earl of Rothsey cleared his throat. "Well, I can see you two young people have much to discuss. And I am promised to Lady Melbourne for the first minuet. But I shall insist on claiming the supper dance with my lovely new granddaughter."

"It will be my pleasure, grandfather," said Antoinette shyly.

He bent and kissed her hand. "I am so glad to have found you, my dear, and although I know I am soon to lose you again to Lyveden here, it comforts me to know that you

219

could not have chosen a finer man as your husband. God bless you both."

When the Earl had departed to find Lady Melbourne, the Duke slipped an arm around Antoinette's slender shoulders, and said quietly, "Now, Antoinette, I do believe, you owe me an explanation. Have you any idea how tormented I felt when you told me you would not marry me? My God, I thought I would go mad. I did not for a moment believe your absurd suggestion that you had been playacting in your affection for me. So why, then, why did you refuse me?"

Haltingly, Antoinette replied, "You said you thought you would go mad . . . there indeed lies the whole key to the matter. For it was I who believed I was the daughter of the artist George Howland and his beautiful, insane mistress . . ."

When she had told him her story, the Duke gathered her into his arms and held her close. "My dearest, Sweet Antoinette! What courage, what fortitude you have displayed. But now these last troubled, confused months are behind us. I love you so much, my angel girl."

"Oh and I love you!" she breathed, raising her face for his kiss.

Tenderly, his mouth closed on hers, and they stood for a long time in the moonlight, all sense of time abandoned in the rapture of their passion. Then he put her from him, and they listened to the music of the violins issuing from the house.

"We must return to the ball." He smiled. "And I warn you, I shall allow no other man but your grandfather to partner you tonight."

Antoinette gave him her hand, and swept into her first ball on the arm of the man who was the first, last and only love of her life.

ABOUT THE AUTHOR

Caroline Courtney

Caroline Courtney was born in India, the youngest daughter of a British Army Colonel stationed there in the troubled years after the First World War. Her first husband, a Royal Air Force pilot, was tragically killed in the closing stages of the Second World War. She later remarried and now lives with her second husband, a retired barrister, in a beautiful 17th century house in Cornwall. They have three children, two sons and a daughter, all of whom are now married, and four grandchildren.

On the rare occasions that Caroline Courtney takes time off from her writing, she enjoys gardening and listening to music, particularly opera. She is also an avid reader of romantic poetry and has an ever-growing collection of poems she has composed herself.

Caroline Courtney is destined to be one of this country's leading romantic novelists. She has written an enormous number of novels over the years—purely for pleasure—and has never before been interested in seeing them reach publication. However, at her family's insistence she has now relented, and Warner Books is proud to be issuing a selection in this uniform edition.

ROMANCE...ADVENTURE...DANGER

DUCHESS IN DISGUISE
by Caroline Courtney
(94-050, $1.75)

The Duke of Westhampton had a wife in the country and a mistress in town which suited the Duke but not his wife. So, being as audacious as she was innocent, she undertook to win his attention by masquerading as a lady he did not know—herself.

WAGER FOR LOVE
by Caroline Courtney
(94-051, $1.75)

The Earl of Saltaire had a reputation as a rakehell, a dandy and a demon on horseback. What lady of means would consider marrying him if she knew the reason for the match was to win a bet? When he won the wager he never gambled on loosing his heart!

LOVE UNMASKED
by Caroline Courtney
(94-054, $1.75)

Charles Somerford intended to be the Duke of Lexburgh and Lady Lucinda, his bride. But Lucinda was in love with a man whose face she had never seen, who always wore a mask on those fateful occasions when he had come to Lucinda's aid. Could he now save Lucinda from marriage to a man she despised?

GUARDIAN OF THE HEART
by Caroline Courtney
(94-053, $1.75)

The Marquis of Rossington was a libertine whom the ladies of the London ton loved too well for their own good for they learned too late that he loved no one. To this man, Sir John Lawley had assigned the guardianship of his beautiful daughter. Any man would have seen that he would soon need a GUARDIAN OF THE HEART.

DANGEROUS ENGAGEMENT
by Caroline Courtney
(94-052, $1.75)

The Earl of Templecombe had dared to kiss Miranda Melbury at their first meeting. Now it was rumored that the earl was looking for a new source of funds. Was he planning an offer to Miranda because she had become an heiress or did he plan to finance his future by more criminal means?

THE FORTUNES OF LOVE
by Caroline Courtney
(94-055, $1.75)

To marry the man she loved Davinia Sinclair must solve a riddle and find a treasure—but not the riddle she pondered nor the treasure she expected.

YOUR WARNER LIBRARY OF CAROLINE COURTNEY ROMANCE

YOUR WARNER LIBRARY OF CAROLINE COURTNEY